W9-BDW-146

Ask your bookseller for the Spectra Special Editions you have missed:

Out on Blue Six by Ian McDonald
The Nexus by Mike McQuay
Phases of Gravity by Dan Simmons

STRANGE TOYS

Patricia Geary

BANTAM BOOKS
NEW YORK · TORONTO · LONDON · SYDNEY · AUCKLAND

To my Tramp Family

STRANGE TOYS

A Bantam Spectra Book / July 1987

2 printings through June 1989

ISBN 0-553-26872-4

Published simultaneously in the United States and Canada

Bantam Books are published by Bantam Books, a division of
Bantam Doubleday Dell Publishing Group, Inc. Its trademark,
consisting of the words "Bantam Books" and the portrayal of a
rooster, is Registered in U.S. Patent and Trademark Office and in
other countries. Marca Registrada. Bantam Books, 666 Fifth
Avenue, New York, New York 10103.

PRINTED IN THE UNITED STATES OF AMERICA

O   11 10 9 8 7 6 5 4 3 2

ACKNOWLEDGMENTS

Thanks to the Bunting Institute for my Carnegie-Mellon Fellowship. And thanks to the LSU Research Program for my Summer Stipend.

I would like people to simply blank
their minds and not to see with their
eyes only, but with their whole being.
Unfortunately, people like only what
they fully understand. But once you
understand something, it becomes
a thing of the mind only.
It no longer touches the heart.

—Ushio Amagatsu

PART I

*

CHAPTER ONE

June and I were lashing together poodle tepees, assembled from dried anise stalks, when we saw the saddle-oxford sheriff's car cruise up the hill, past the lemon grove we were sitting in, and down the sweep of our driveway.

"I bet they got her." June barely looked up from her tepee, which was considerably better constructed than mine. The tip of her tongue protruded crossways; she was concentrating like she did at the piano. Pale blue pointy glasses slid down the nose of her round face.

"I bet they didn't." But that was because I couldn't imagine Deane in jail. Would they let her bring her Elvis pictures? Once she had made paper dolls of the whole family. Once she had said my hair smelled sweet as a kitten's. Last time the police brought her back, she'd screamed at me and June: *Fuck those goody-goodies.* June had cried, huge mouth wailing open, but then she'd never liked Deane to begin with. Four years older than June, Deane had gotten the first horse. At nine, I was three years younger than June, seven years younger than Deane, and I hated horses. They bit your hair off.

She put the finished tepee down in its lot. This one belonged to Mimi, one of the original blue poodles. Cherie, who was mine, was not getting as elegant a domicile. Worse, I'd dropped her in the mud. Small plush dogs didn't make the best outside toys, but we felt the poodles needed autumn homes. They were tired of being cooped up in our bedroom.

"Looks good," I said.

It did. June had read three books on Indian design, and her composite of anise stalks, twine, and peacock

2

feathers was elegant. Further, she'd made a little crazy-paving path from Mimi's front door to the creek. The creek flowed regularly every afternoon: we hauled a garden hose down into the grove and ran the water for our rivers, lakes, and dams. With all the trouble over Deane, neither Stan nor Linwood had noticed.

"We better go see what happened." June stood up, pulling down her shapeless sweater. It looked like Stan's.

We started gathering up our stuff. If we waited until they told us what was going on, we'd never know anything. We were supposed to think, for instance, that Deane was still happily attending that grisly Catholic girls' school they'd put her in last year—from which she habitually escaped—and we weren't supposed to notice her furious outbursts on the weekends she visited home. We certainly weren't supposed to know that they'd put her there because some of the people she hung around with were serious bad news, making mysterious trips down to Mexico. There was also some story around town about Deane and the football team, but even June hadn't a clue what that meant.

Standing up, I tried to brush some of the mud off my red pedal pushers. Hopeless. My Keds were deeply crusted and so were my socks, but since we had to sneak up through the avocado grove and across the stable in order to enter the back door unseen, the dirt hardly mattered.

We gathered up the poodles, not improved from their outing, and piled them into my sweater. I tied the sleeves together and the bundle was a neat package.

The living room, I could sense as we lay bellies-down in the hallway, was heavy with concern. The sheriff was sitting closest. All you could see were a big black boot and a pair of manicured hands.

"—until she's eighteen," he said.

"Then what?" Stan was angry.

"You keep her. Or," he spread his hands, "she could go to prison."

I tried to imagine Deane, her beehive hairdo and thick eyeliner, in black-and-white-striped PJs.

"Prison!" Linwood shrieked. "You can't send your own daughter to prison!"

Stan sighed, like Eeyore. "Nobody's sending anybody to prison. She's more your daughter than mine, anyway."

"She might go," the sheriff said. He was a big help.

Linwood started sobbing. My arms tingled, I wanted to comfort her.

"Unless she wants to talk," he added.

"June!" Stan bellowed suddenly, appearing around the corner of the hall. His head floated above us like a furious balloon. "Take Pet and get the hell out of here! Go to your rooms and stay there!"

Two hours later and we were still sitting in June's room. It was seven already and we usually ate around six-thirty.

"Do you think she'll squeal?" I asked.

June shrugged. She was beading poodle bags. Each poodle had his own drawstring bag with matching pillow. Inside were their toys, whistles or miniature decks of cards, or other stuff we got from nickel vending machines. They got tons of presents on their birthdays.

I was trying to bead Pierre's collar; beading was June's latest discovery, but it was hard to get your fingers to sew the letters so you could read them.

"Think we'll ever see her again?"

"If we don't, I get Ace."

Ace was the stallion who'd thrown Deane, when she'd gotten two broken arms and a double concussion. Her foot had gotten caught in the stirrup, and she'd been dragged a mile or so. Linwood said she hadn't been the same person afterward.

"As if they'd let you ride him."

"They would." June squinted at her collar and pushed her glasses up her nose. "They don't care what I do."

Actually, she did pretty much as she pleased. I was more closely watched, being the youngest and all, or at least I had been until all this police business started. Now, they ignored me too.

I got up from the floor and strolled over to the felt board propped against the poodle pavilion. HAPPY HAL-LOWEEN, POODLES! it said, in orange and black and green. A month early, but so what? I'd made some pumpkins and ghosts and a smiling witch on a broom-stick, the regular stuff but whimsical. The felt board was *my* specialty.

"We're missing Dobie Gillis," June pointed out.

I crossed over and clicked on the black-and-white portable. Stan had given it to us last Christmas. The year before was the aquarium, now residing in the garage. All the fish had died from ick in three weeks, and I didn't have the heart to carry on. This year we were expecting our own telephone, not that June would let me use it.

I sat back on the floor and watched Maynard G. Crebbs playing the bongo drums. He was so silly, face too goofy, yet there was something about him, with that little goatee and those ragged sweatshirts. He could sit around San Francisco, reading poetry in one of those coffeehouses with the candles on the tables. Deane had told me all about beatniks. Perhaps when I grew up, I'd live in New Orleans—that's where we'd vacationed last summer—and dance in one of those sequined G-strings. If I had breasts.

There was a loud knock on the door and Stan walked in. He looked sorry for himself. "Your mother wants to see you in the living room," he said.

I looked at June.

"When I finish this collar," she said.

Linwood was sitting on the gold couch, smoking a thin cigar in a long rhinestone holder. Her face was puffy. Usually I adored her, was the perfect slave, but now something about both of them irritated me. I sat cross-legged in front of the fireplace. June and Stan sat on the couch.

"Your mother has something to say to you girls," Stan heralded, palace guard before queen.

"Deane," Linwood began, "was picked up by the police last night."

Automatically, I felt guilty.

"She ran away from school." Stan took over.

"Again," June said.

Stan and Linwood exchanged glances. He got up, paced a minute, and sat down in the green chair, lighting a cigarette with a show of despair. He looked like a movie star. So did Linwood, of course. "She ran away three days ago. They finally found her last night."

"What did the nuns do to her?" *Jane Eyre* had made a great impression on me.

Everyone looked at me like I was a dope.

"When they found her, she had her hair cut short and dyed black." You could tell this part was one of the worst for Linwood; her voice was especially regal.

"An improvement, no doubt." June was mumbling into her fingernails, which she was biting.

Linwood started to cry.

I felt guilty again, but what could I do?

"We thought you girls were old enough. We thought you should know what's going on," Stan said in his best adult voice. Then, to Linwood, "Oh, hell!"

"What else did she do?" June looked up. "We know she did more than run away."

"That isn't any of your business." Stan stubbed out his cigarette and stood up. "I'm going to put some TV dinners in the oven. There's one beef and one fried chicken."

I thought about Deane's long golden hair. I liked it best right after she washed it, before she pinned it into the beehive. "Beef," I said, knowing June preferred the chicken.

At bedtime, while I was waiting for Linwood to come kiss me good-night, I opened up my cigar box, the one that my friend Gaylin had gotten from her father for me. Linwood's cigars came in regular packages, and they were really cigarillos, anyway. All my special stuff was stored in the box. When I opened the lid, the world was made of delicious, endless possibility. Item by item, what I had wasn't so thrilling: a silver dollar from Las Vegas, a crisp five-dollar bill, and three freshly minted quarters; some hand-pulled taffy left over from Bible School (but wrapped in wax paper and still fairly tasty); my unopened copy of Jesus's life—it began with a black sheet of paper. You were supposed to show this to someone and tell them, "This was the color of my heart before I found Jesus." You kept flipping the pages, all solid colors, through the blue of the sky and the green of the grass and the red of His Blood until you ended up with a pure white page, the color of your redeemed heart. I loved the whole thing—it was so simple yet effective!—and I had shown my first copy to everyone in the family many times, until Linwood took it away from me. I was saving this untouched copy for the future. Also in the box was a mysterious piece of brick with the single letter *P.* I'd found it one recess on the playground, as if it had been left for me. And my first-place certificate, neatly folded, along with the blue ribbon, for the Vista Junior Talent Contest. And the silver badge Gaylin had sent me from Carlsbad Caverns that said HI PET LOVE GAYLIN. And my tiny mammy doll from New Orleans, made out of a clothespin. There was some other stuff, but that was the best.

Sitting there with those things, I had the strangest feeling... I almost wanted to pray to them, but *pray* wasn't exactly right. Contained in their box, faint aroma of cigar, they exuded energy, real energy.

And that energy was only for me.

But the weirdest part was, I had this sudden, intense feeling that somehow, someway these objects were with me for life. It was as if they had *attached* themselves to whatever it was that made me *me*. Plus, there was something that could be done with them—what?—as if they could be made into a kind of machine, a generator to manufacture... what?

Linwood walked in as I was contemplating my cigar box.

The expression on her face was as remote as the Snow Queen's. But her flamingo-colored lounging pants, decidedly not Snow Queen garb, matched her lipstick exactly.

Her absentminded kiss on my forehead didn't connect: no splotch for me, no smear for her.

"Good night, dear." She turned to leave.

"What about the three good deeds?" I was one of those overly conscientious children who would never screw up if she found herself ensnared by a magic toad or stranded in the woods with only the enchanted ax for company.

"Oh, yes." Resigned, conscientious too, Linwood sat down on the edge of my bed.

"June tripped me in the hall this morning and called me lard bucket. Later, I put the fancy Ginny doll nightgown under her pillow."

Linwood nodded. Obviously, she was thinking about other things.

"Then, I gave a beggar woman a hundred gold coins."

"That's nice, dear."

"And when I traveled to the planet of Xtbay, I declared a fortnight of feasting and rejoicing."

She patted me on the arm, mumbled something about doing unto others, and out she went, Emeraude wafting in her passage.

Then the magnitude of it all struck: for the first time in my entire life, I had *lied*.

Interesting, I thought, cross-legged on the bed, *I lied. I'm still alive, nobody cared, and it was fun!*

Was this my first entry into the world of crime? Was this how Deane got involved in the shadowy world she seemed to inhabit? First you lied, then you cheated, then you snuck around. . . .

As if contained in a spinning pink globe before me, I saw the planet of Xtbay that my lie had created: bright purple fields, shining orange water, men and women dressed in silver suits like astronauts, their faces the faces of unknown animals. Already they'd begun to celebrate; I could smell the unfamiliar, intoxicating odors. A whole fortnight—lucky them!

Then I felt crummy. A lie was a lie and the Bible told you that was no good. Deane was in some cold dark jail, and Linwood was sick with worry, but I was exulting in deceit and its own accompanying power.

Perhaps there was something I could do to get God's attention?

I could stay up all night, praying and fasting, though the fasting bit was moot since who ate at night anyway. Or . . . a brainstorm! I could do like they did in the Old Testament: I could make a sacrifice.

Remembering Cain and Abel and what God had to say about that, I considered Rose and Pansy, my two small green turtles, who fretted out their miserable existence in a kidney-shaped plastic pool, complete with green plastic palm. As consolation or company, their contribution was minimal. And real blood was a more-appreciated sacrifice than, say, flowers or ears of corn.

I watched them sleeping on their plastic island.

No way. I couldn't do it. I hated to step on an ant or squash a sowbug. Perhaps one day I would move to India.

I scanned the shelves where my dolls lived. I had thirty-three of them, ranging in size from my Teri Lee doll to Roberta, my favorite with her glossy cap of dark curls, to the six Ginny dolls grouped at the far end. But I had qualms there, too. Year after year of *The Nutcracker Suite* had convinced me that those hard bodies really lived, if only you knew when to look, or what to look for. Even as I slept, they danced around my bed, the night progressing in increasingly frenzied circles.

The poodles (unthinkable; June would kill me) and my stuffed polar bears (forget it), my dolls, a pair of dim-witted turtles: except for my box, that was the sum of my possessions.

And as much as I loved Deane and Linwood, the box was out of the question.

I stared out the window, wondering what to do. Deane's room was dark and lonely on the far side of the backyard. If you had nothing to sacrifice, or were unwilling, like Cain I suppose, to sacrifice what you did have, what was second best?

You could sacrifice yourself... you could make yourself do something that you were afraid to do.

I didn't have to think long before I knew what I had to do: go out to Deane's room. Even in broad daylight, even when she was in there, her room was totally scary.

My stomach lurched. I sat back down on the bed. Maybe God would admire my bravery and make things okay again with our family. Though what *okay* might consist of seemed pretty hazy.

Actually, this room of Deane's that I was about to go out to was one of Linwood's explanations for why she had "gone bad." At first, having part of the garage turned into a teenage apartment had seemed like a good idea. For instance, Deane could play her rock and roll music as loud as she liked without bothering anyone. She could have her friends over and they could all shriek and enjoy the din while the normal people in the big house slept on. After a fair amount of pleading and whining, Stan and Linwood had the room refinished for her, and it was nice—a big bedroom with a window seat, her own bathroom, and even a tiny hotplate and a miniature fridge. They decorated it in a pink flower print set off with candy-stripe accents, and the effect was a fantasy set out of *Seventeen*, the ideal bobby-soxer smacking her gum as she lolls across her bed, Princess telephone propped at her ear, flipping through movie magazines and doing her nails as she gossips with girlfriends about the school hop.

The idea was that this would be Deane's room and then when she moved away June's room and then finally mine. Except that what seemed to happen was that Deane didn't stay there so much as she did disappear. Since you couldn't hear the rock and roll music, you sure couldn't hear her creep out at night past the stable, nor could you hear any of her unsavory friends sneaking in. And besides, Deane had done a bit of redecorating. I'd only made two visits there this year, the last one being the time Deane had put the hex on Stan to make him break his arm.

Going out there at night... why, this was the kind of thing Nancy Drew did!

I could do it too.

I rose from the bed in search of my go-aheads, and then I sat back down. Should I include June?

The negatives: I was sick of her for the day. She was always pinching me and telling me I was fat and trying to bully or trick me into playing Monopoly or Risk, both of which I loathed. If I told her the plan, then suddenly it would become her idea, and she'd decide how we'd do it, and there I'd be, once again playing dull old Watson to her brilliant Holmes.

The positives: as the older sister, she would be responsible. If anything went wrong, they would blame her. And, I never got hurt when June was around—I mean, unless she was the cause of pain. No matter how much she despised me, she always watched out for the sharp branch or the odd gopher hole.

This was a stumper. Already I was going for second best by not murdering Rose and Pansy. What good was a sacrifice without some feeble show of courage?

I would go alone.

Rising from the bed with conviction, I flicked off the reading light and on the carousel night-light, with its bobbing, glowing horses, and waited for my eyes to adjust to the dark, already spooky. I slipped on my go-aheads and checked out my flannel PJs: fortunately, they were a size too small, so the legs wouldn't catch on anything. I crept to the window and raised it; the sheers blew ghostly in the breeze. Unlatching the screen, I eased my bottom onto the sill, legs dangling down into the dark.

Frozen for the moment, not quite summoning the nerve to jump, I thought about how alone I was.

The moon twirling out over the silent green prairie of the lawn.

Then Ace nickered from his stable, and one of our twenty cats screeched as if at that instant being gutted with a machete, and I slid down the windowsill to plop damply on the grass below. Exactly how was I going to get back up?

Too late now. Don't farewell: fare *forward*.

The entrance to Deane's room was around the corner

from the pepper tree, and first I tripped over the big metal cat dish, which was glowing like a beacon in the moonlight, no one else could possibly have missed seeing it, and then the sprinkler, pop right on the shin, and then a missing croquet wicket, the one we'd been trying to find for several weeks.

Toes smarting, I approached her door, fearful, watching the snails glide across the concrete and leave their slimy coded messages. But you have to push inside.

The strangeness of the interior odor apprehended me like a large, splayed hand. Sandalwood incense, I knew that smell, and gardenia cologne, and cigarettes (Deane had started smoking when she was ten), but there was also a weird, herby smell, burnt and sweet, and another bad one—tar? sulfur?—and another one, the worst, like the bird the cats killed that day and didn't eat, the one with the maggots.

Anyway, I wanted to turn right around. Instead, I flicked on the light switch.

Well, what can I tell you? Even my Chinese fairy tale books never prepared me for this.

Things! Clusters and clusters of bright things: ceramic statues, to begin with, three feet tall of Jesus and the Virgin Mary, and dozens of candle holders, skinny ones like snakes and short fat ones, with stubs of wicks and long, shimmering rivulets of wax, and tiny carved dolls, Japanese and African and some that looked familiar, and strings of black and yellow and red glass beads, and crucifixes, there must have been more than a hundred crucifixes, and countless bowls of what looked like rotting fruit and dead flowers, teeming with ants. Decay: that was one of the bad smells.

Deane's room had always been strange, but not this strange.

There were lots of bright scarves, too, Mexican scarves tacked up on the walls, sequins and cacti and señors reposing sombreros-downward next to their beasts of burden. I tried to see some kind of pattern in all the chaos, and then I saw that all the jumble was stacked on a series of orange crates, which wound around the room like a crazy, sloppy worm carrying its baggage of decoration to the masterpiece: a stepladdered series of crates in the far, dim corner.

Gingerly, I picked my way through the unpleasant rubble until I was directly facing the grand tower. In homage, piles and patterns of colored sand were carefully arranged around.

Well, I knew what that sand was all about. It had been here before, the last time I'd visited; Deane had made hex signs with the sand last spring, when she got Stan to break his arm. She'd made interlocking circles with that Nazi sign in the center. But these patterns looked more complicated than those. These looked like Egyptian hieroglyphs, which June and I had studied last year when we were making up our codes. We started out to create a common language, but June wanted to make all the rules, so, for once, I said no, and we went our own ways, her with Junese and me with Pettish, which was a big waste of time because nobody had anyone to write to. Still.

These symbols were even more elaborate than hieroglyphs, and stranger. Who was Deane casting a hex on now? I looked more closely, even though my stomach went cold. In the center of the floor-mural was a large red configuration, a woman wearing a wild headdress with green, yellow, and blue spiraling points, a cross between an Indian chief and an angel. Except her face had only one eye, cyclops, and she had four hands, each one holding a tiny doll with a miniature headdress of green, yellow, and blue spiraling points, only one eye, and four hands holding etc. Whatever it meant, I didn't like it.

Little shivers raced up and down my forearms.

Get the hell out.

I straightened up from my kneeling posture, examining the sand drawings. And then I was eye to eye with my whole reason for being out in Deane's room: a stuffed cat.

Not any old stuffed cat. This was my lost kitten, Marmalade.

Not even for an instant did I believe she was still alive, that's how poor the taxidermy job was. But it was definitely Marmalade. Stuffed in a sausage-casingesque way unlike any shape she had ever assumed in real life, she was positioned upright, her blue glass eyes wide, wider than ever a living creature, as if she could see things in a beyond-the-grave panorama that was beyond the limit of my imagination. A red and green Christmas bow was grisly around the stiff fur of her neck.

Oh, Marmalade! My first kitten, all my own. And I thought she'd run away.

This was adult anger, my first, and it ran hot and cold flashes the length of my spine. Fury. Hurt. Deane was a fiend, and not my sister. I despised my pity for her; I had come out here to help, but now I wanted to destroy.

That sweet kitty, her life wasted; I felt sick. There she sat in that nasty pack-rat den of cheap debris. I wanted to burn the whole thing down, preferably with Deane in it. But I wasn't convinced that would hurt Deane as much as it would Stan and Linwood.

Revenge. How could I get revenge?

Well, it was weird. As if I were a Geiger counter, and the object uranium, I automatically walked into the bathroom, opened the cabinet beneath the sink, and rifled through a large box of Kotex. (I wasn't exactly sure what they were, except that they somehow made the difference between being a kid and being taken seriously.) Anyway, my hand closed around something soft and slick. I pulled it out of the cardboard box.

I held a small, red leather book. It was bound by a tiny gold lock, which I immediately cracked with my teeth.

The first page was elaborately scrolled with Deane's ornate penmanship. She wrote all three parts of her name, and her address, including the galaxy and the universe. Then there were a couple of pages of what looked like poems, in a language I didn't understand. Deanish? Egyptian? The next page, though, was scary: a skull and crossbones, and the warning:

DANGER! TURN THE PAGE AT YOUR OWN RISK!

I turned the page.

FINAL WARNING! A CURSE ON THE PERSON WHO
STEALS THIS BOOK, OR READS IT UNLAWFULLY.

Well, I went for broke. I turned the page.

ANCIENT MAGICK & SECRETS, THE UNKNOWN

This page was even more ornamental than the title
page. I hesitated. What was I doing here, exactly?

I was stealing.

One of Deane's curses was no laughing matter—like
Stan's arm when he tripped in the grove, for instance.

Nevertheless, I wanted to steal, to steal something
important and valuable. The first step in revenge. And
the moment that I decided to go ahead and take it, I
heard the outside door open.

"Freeze, you little bitch!" The voice was rough and
male.

I froze, but was this unknown person talking to me?
Automatically, the book dropped from my hands and
back into the Kotex box.

"Get the fuck out here!"

I did that too, rounded the doorway to see two big
men dressed in jeans and black leather jackets, with
handkerchiefs over their faces, cowboy style. One looked
Mexican and had dark greasy hair, and the other had a
ducktail bob suspiciously like that of Tommy, Deane's
old boyfriend from over the hill.

"It's the bitch's sister," the one who seemed to be
Tommy explained to the Mexican.

The other guy grunted.

"What are you doing out here?" Tommy asked.

Not really scared yet, I only shrugged. The whole
thing was rolling along without me, like some kind of
James Cagney movie. Or, to be honest, what I *imagined*
was a James Cagney movie—I knew who he was only
because I'd seen him "impersonated" so frequently on

cartoons. Him and Cab Calloway. I'd had to ask Linwood
who all those mice and ducks were pretending to be.

"I said, what the fuck are you doing out here?"

"I'm only . . ." And then I felt the warm trickle down
my leg. I was mortified.

"She peed her pants," said Tommy.

"*Puta estúpida,*" said the Mexican. "Where's your
sister?"

"Not here," I managed to squeak out, sounding like
those cartoon mice.

Tommy sat heavily on the bed. There were stockings
and underwear and shoes and stuff all over it.

He pulled a large, black gun out of his jacket.

"Unless you want this stuffed up your little twat, I
suggest you tell me where your sister is."

The wet legs of my PJs were cold and sticky. I didn't
know what a "twat" was, I was scared to death, but I
was still able to figure out that these guys had better
not find out that Deane was with the police. Better for me.

"She ran away," I began.

"Yeah, yeah," the Mexican said, lighting a cigarette.

"And the policeman came to the house today"—*Always
tell as much of the truth as possible when you lie,* June
had once instructed me, unlike Xtbay—"to tell us that
they still couldn't find her."

Tommy and the Mexican exhaled simultaneously.

"Let's beat it," the Mexican said. He crushed out his
cigarette on the carpet.

Tommy stood and nodded. "What if she's lying?"

"Let's go, man." He went on out.

Tommy stood looking at me. Before I knew what he
was doing, he yanked down my pants. "Little cunt," he
said. "You bitches are all alike." He put his hand
between the Y of my legs and I felt the worst pain in
the world.

"Don't!" I screamed. My legs felt like they were
being ripped apart. I had to pee again.

He showed me his hand, covered with blood. "If you
tell anyone you saw us," he said, "I'll come and get
you, wherever you go. You think that hurt? If you lied
to me, you don't know what pain is."

"Come on, man!" the Mexican hissed from the doorway.

Tommy ran out. Then he reappeared in the doorway. "You remember," he said.

He was gone.

I pulled up my pants, curled into a ball, and things kind of stopped.

CHAPTER TWO

A week or so after The Bad Thing, I came home from school and found Linwood standing in the kitchen, arms crossed over her chest. Her presence was unusual; with low thyroid, she always took a prolonged afternoon nap. That half-hour I had to myself in the house, before June got off, was a luxury.

"Pack your suitcase," she said.

My heart sank, but it was inevitable they would find out what I had done. Guilt, horror, pain: everything bubbled up in a terrible soup. My glass of milk remained untouched on the yellow tile counter.

"We're going on a trip as soon as your father gets home." Absently, Linwood took a sip of my milk.

The convent. They were going to commit me to Deane's grisly Catholic school. Two big tears like worms rolled out of my eyes. But this was just, it was what I deserved.

"Oh, honey, I'm sorry." Linwood put down the glass and walked over to hug me.

Her skin was soft and warm. She smelled like flowers and ironed cotton.

"Deane's in lots of trouble. We've been getting phone calls from some of her, uh, friends. We're not safe here."

Tommy, I thought, my legs throbbing. But my fear was overwhelmed by my relief—they didn't know. Reprieve was a feather bed to sink into.

"I know you're worried about school," Linwood continued.

Who cared? It was so hard to pay attention lately anyway.

"But try not to think about it. Just pack a bag. Warm clothes, your heavy coat, one doll, one stuffed animal, three books. And your cigar box, of course."

Of course the cigar box. I left the kitchen, walked down the hall past June's room, and turned into mine. Were we ever coming back? The familiar pink-and-blue-flowered wallpaper, the old double bed with the saggy center, the shelves with my beloved dolls. The window overlooking the backyard. I sat down plunk on the spiny lip of the bed and picked up the box from my end table. Inside was Deane's red leather magic book. Which proved, along with that pain every time I went to the bathroom, that I really had been out to her room. Sometimes I wasn't sure. When I came in that morning, afterward, Stan was up reading the paper, as always, and I walked right by him, invisible. No one could tell I'd been gone.

In fact, no one had really noticed me since then. Stan and Linwood were wrapped up in Deane, and June had begun her new project: reading the brand-new *World Book Encyclopedia* from beginning to end. We hadn't played poodles since the police. How many volumes would they let her take?

I pulled my suitcase from beneath my bed. Ugh, dust devils. Then I opened my closet, tidy as always, and removed my best dress, a flowered lavender organdy. No, wrong season. Instead, I selected my navy sailor dress and saddle oxfords, even though my shiny Mary Janes called out. From my chest of drawers I pulled out pedal pushers, T-shirts, sweaters, and lots of socks and underwear. Everything folded neatly in the suitcase with enough extra room. I lifted up the stack of underwear and slid the cigar box underneath. I would wear my red coat.

Books were tough. *The Wind in the Willows* or *Peter Pan?* The new Nancy Drew I'd been hoarding? Strictly one-shot, but if we never returned, would I never get to read it?

Dolls were easier. I took Roberta, with her shiny cap of curls, in her brown calico travel dress. Also, I folded up her black lace blouse and the beautiful red skirt, with the huge pockets, that stuck out like a flower. And her black plastic shoes, in case she needed to dress up. And Pole, the original polar bear, naturally. Who could sleep without Pole?

Firmly back to books: *Alice in Wonderland*, my best fairy tale book, the one with "Bluecrest" and "Green Snake," and the white Bible I won last summer for memorizing the most Scripture. *Verily, verily, I say unto you, he who entereth not by the door into the sheepfold, but climbeth up some other way, the same is a thief and a robber. But he that entereth—*

"Hey, Fatso! What's wrong with you?" June walked right in without knocking. If I did that to her, she charged me a dime. "That's the third time I yelled at you."

I shrugged and closed the suitcase.

"What about the poodles?"

"What about them?" I sat down on the suitcase. It made the bed as tall and hard as it should have been.

"Where are you going to put them?" Her round face was shiny with indignation.

"Nowhere, I guess." The wrong answer.

"Leave the poodles!" Her face shifted in outrage. "What's wrong with you?"

No good answer to that one either. "All you've been doing is reading *World Book*."

"So I could learn more stuff. For them! How to make adobe, for instance, so they can have sturdier outside houses."

She was a much better person than me. I climbed off the suitcase and opened it back up. "I guess Pole's out."

But he'd slept in my bed ever since I'd gotten him, two years ago. The poodles were no good for sleeping with. Their little bodies were hard, stuffed with straw, eyes and noses made of glass. Plus, they were only five inches high whereas Pole was the size of a small pillow.

"Now I've got room for Pierre and Cherie," I said. "They're old and they deserve to travel. You know, like when Aunt Ginny took Nana to Hawaii before she died."

June looked at me as though she were about to charge me for existing. "Break them up? You want to break them up? What if I didn't take Celeste? You think Pierre wants to travel without his wife?"

"So take Celeste."

"Look." June paced to the window and turned around. "We're taking them all. If we line them up in the back window, they'll fit. In your suitcase, you're taking the photo album and the costume box." She marched back to the bed and picked Roberta up by her hair. "You don't need to take that crappy doll."

Tears stung. "She's not crappy! She's—"

"Fat!" June was triumphant. Inadvertently, I'd given her her favorite opening. "Your doll's fat, just like you. Petty's a fatty! Petty's a fatty!"

It was so unfair; Roberta *wasn't* fat. For that matter, I wore regular clothes but June had to wear Chub-Ettes.

Yet, when she shouted at me, I believed her, my resistance gone. I was fat and guilty.

Linwood chose that moment to knock and walk in. If she'd heard anything, you couldn't tell from the remote set of her face. "We're going to Disneyland," she announced.

June and I exchanged looks of disbelief. We only went once a year, at the beginning of summer.

"When?" June asked.

"Tonight."

It would be dark before we got there. Would we see the lights? Usually we left at six in the morning, so we'd be there right when it opened. Stan loved to travel at dawn and watch the sun rise. And, since it was only once a year, Linwood was a good sport, though no one was allowed to speak to her until her third cup of coffee. Used to be, you could tell you were close because of the Tomorrowland rocket, stretching up thin and elegant from the orange groves. Then they built the Matterhorn, so much more thrilling than Baldy or Saddleback topped with actual snow.

"And we'll stay tomorrow?"

"We'll stay for as long as you like." Linwood was speaking, but she wasn't there.

The three of us drifted out of my room and down the hall.

"A week?" June wasn't called Wedge-in-the-Door for nothing.

"Whatever you girls want."

"Can we stay at the Disneyland Hotel?" Shame on me for jumping in, but I couldn't help it. The Disneyland Hotel was like Oz. The monorail came right to your door. You could ride to Sleeping Beauty's Castle whenever you wanted. Snow White, Mr. Toad, and my personal favorite: Alice in Wonderland. As many times as I prepared myself for the bright colors, they were always richer, more intense, more alive. Those magic caterpillars conducted you through what was better than dreams; the new place you visited, by contrast, rendered this world pale, maybe pointless. Why play with sticks and stuffed dogs in the grove, when you could be traveling through other realms?

"No," Linwood said. "We're staying across the street."

"That's okay." I tried not to look disappointed.

"Listen," said June, furtively pressing my arm on what she called Pet's Perpetual Bruise. She always socked me on the same spot so she could exert minimal effort for maximal effect, at covert moments like this one.

I winced.

"We have to take the poodles."

"That's right," I chimed in feebly, moving out of arm range.

"You can each take two." Linwood regarded June. "In place of Pet's doll and your puzzle."

"We have to take them all."

"There's no room."

"They can ride in the back window."

"That's too dangerous. And besides, all thirty-seven won't fit."

"What if they did fit?"

She'll make a great lawyer, I thought, as I tried to

sidle back to my room. If the poodles were going in the window, there was hope for Pole.

"June, I am not in the mood to argue with you."

"Then just say we can take them."

I heard Linwood's sigh all the way down the hall.

Once back in my room, I explained the situation to Roberta. I dressed her in the black lace and red skirt and replaced her in her favorite spot. She would comfort the others for me. Then I packed Pole, the photo album, and the costume box in the suitcase. Miraculously, they all fit. There was no doubt in my mind that June would win; the truth was that nobody cared enough, whatever the issue, to wear her down. When you gave in to her, her will of steel cables, you had this sweet sense of saving your own soul, because you knew you would never be damned by stubbornness, as she was.

I lay down in the saggy center of my bed, perhaps for the last time. I thought about Disneyland, about how it took away all the sinister parts of the stories. In the book *Peter Pan*, the ending made me kind of nauseated. Wendy was this huge, embarrassed woman, trying to hide her size and age, and Peter turned out to be pathetic, unable to appreciate Wendy's desire to lead a normal life. I only read the ending once, and after that I always skipped it. Likewise, in the book *Alice in Wonderland*, the caterpillar is not a nice guy. He's cruel and sinister, and he has no sympathy for Alice. In the Disney version, he is charmingly suave, a worm version of David Niven. In fact, the books were much more like the games we used to play, four or five years ago, when we were all smaller. Deane was okay then, she hadn't started smoking yet. We used to create our own magic kingdoms. Our game of Pretend was more complicated and vivid than my illustrations of "Bluecrest" or "Green Snake." In the best game of all, we rode our tricycles in a ritualized formation at the far, looped end of the driveway. One person steered, one person pedaled, and the third person guided the voyage. The Guide stood on the back of the tricycle and described the world we were passing through. Things took shape before my eyes as I explained them to my sisters:

This is the land of Lavender and Roses. We are dressed in apple-green satin gowns and our hair is braided with diamonds and pearls. Our hair is six feet long and it floats in back of us. Now, something is coming toward us, bigger and bigger. They are bigger than horses, bigger than dinosaurs. They are huge black dogs, with eyes bigger than Ferris wheels!

" 'The Tinder Box'!" June would cry, always quick to spot when I strayed into something I had read.

If June was Guide, we heard:

We are riding into the Land of Babies. Pink and white iced animal cookies are raining down. The rivers are Hawaiian Punch and the lakes are Nestle's chocolate milk. Everyone has a swimming pool filled with M&M's.

The swimming pools filled with M&M's was her signature piece, while I got carried away with clothes and hair. After all, we were little, and we were ordinary.

And, then, nobody could guide like Deane:

We are magicians! Our heads are ravens, our wings are purple, studded with nails. When we fly overhead, sleeping women feel the breath of frost on their cheeks. Children dream of the seven tongues of fire. We fear only the Master Wizard. Now he is on us. His arms are giant radishes with revolving razor blades. Each blade can cut a piece of paper into two thinner pieces of paper. We feel the heat on our cheeks. Without the magic formula, we will be torn to ribbons!

"Say it! Say it!" June and I would shriek.

"What's it worth to you?" she'd ask.

We'd be slaves, we'd do her chores, whatever. With Deane, I swear you really saw what she saw. You didn't want to, not all the way, but you did. And it wasn't like the floating visions of princesses I conjured, soap bubbles you could still see the world through—what Deane spun out was solid, it was *there;* if only I dared, my hand would feel the keen pain of the razor.

We were grateful that she saved us from the demons she had created.

Funny. I remembered her apparitions with a sense of deep loss. Hardly conscious of what I was doing, I opened my suitcase back up, lifted out the cigar box, and removed the red leather book.

I closed my eyes and opened the book at random.

There was a pen-and-ink drawing, very detailed, of me and Tommy out in Deane's room.

For a minute, I thought I was going to be sick.

"Fatso," June yelled. "Stan's home! Bring your suitcase out pronto!"

CHAPTER THREE

My eyes were stuck together with grainy sleep, but I knew I wasn't in my own bed: the sheets were smooth and stiff-ironed, not made of the same cloth as real sheets. And then, too, I could hear the heavy, even breathing emanating from June in the next bed.

A thrill shot up from my stomach to my heart.

Disneyland!

That motel smell: air-conditioning, tiny soaps wrapped in paper, matchbooks and clean ashtrays, ice buckets, desks that were used only for storage: embossed stationery, postcards of patrons enjoying the pool or the dining room, plastic bags for wet swimsuits, shoeshine kits, and the Bible, always the Bible, patiently waiting with its unturned pages.

Quietly, I climbed out of bed and walked across the carpet, feeling guilty for being barefoot since Linwood insisted on shoes for motel carpets, breeding grounds for unidentified diseases, and slid open the desk drawer. There, cuddled in the raw wood corner, was a spanking new Bible.

I let the Bible fall open. Eyes closed, I stabbed a random passage.

> I am poured out like water, and all my
> Bones are out of joint: my heart is like
> Wax; it is melted in the midst of my bowels.

What exactly *were* "bowels" anyway? The Bible was always bringing them up.

> My strength is dried up like a potsherd.

Potsherd? Now what? This was too confusing. I scanned farther down the page.

> I may tell all my bones:
> They look and stare upon me.

I felt all creepy. This didn't sound like the Bible at all, what with the wax and the bones.

I needed something soothing, something spiritual.

Wax and bones. My arms goose-pimpled. As if it were floating before my eyes, I saw the pen-and-ink drawing of Deane's room.

I slapped the Bible shut and slipped back into bed.

What did it all mean? Did I want to understand, or did I want it to *go away?*

I had to pee. If I could get past all this queasiness, would the world make sense again?

If I wanted it to *go away*, why had I brought the book with me? It beckoned from my suitcase.

June pulled her head out from under the covers. She rubbed her eyes and reached for her glasses. "Disneyland!" she said.

"Pet, here's your coupon book." Stan handed it over, his mouth set in hard lines, contrasting with the smiles

of the other amusement seekers. We were all standing
inside the gates, right in front of Main Street. Bright
flowers and topiary hedges reinforced the atmosphere
of fun, fun, fun.

Even though it was October and Wednesday, the
place was jam-packed with tourists, especially Japanese,
the children with their neat patent leather hair and
white anklets making me feel untidy in my brown pedal
pushers and green sweater set. I'd wanted to wear my
sailor dress, but Linwood convinced me I'd get it dirty.
She was dressed in blue silk capris and spanking white
tennis shoes. She never got dirty. June was doing her
bit with the gray coat, buttoned up to the chin, and it
wasn't even cold. She looked like a nanny.

"Only three D coupons!" June rifled through her
booklet. "What a gyp!"

Stan cleared his throat and opened his mouth.

Linwood intercepted him with a look. Even through
the opaque movie-star lenses, you could feel her gaze,
heat waves rippling up from the furnace.

"We'll buy more when you run out," Stan said.

"You can have mine," I said. "I only want to go on
the A rides anyway." Why was I feeling guilty? The A
rides were pretty stupid, things you walked through
and baby rides, with the exception of the train. Maybe
I'd just ride around and around all day.

They all stared at me as if I were ill.

"I think the pancakes made me a little sick," I lied.

Linwood placed her cool palm on my forehead. "Pet,
you and June can go on the D rides together. We'll buy
more coupons after lunch. June, I don't want you girls
to separate."

"But she won't go on the Bobsleds!" June wailed.

"What about the submarine?" I asked.

June snorted. "It doesn't really go under water!"

But who cared? It was so pretty, with the mermaids
and the anemones. The squid was pretty scary, actually.

"We'll meet in front of the Castle at twelve sharp,"
Stan ordered. "After lunch, we'll make sure you each
get to go on the rides you want."

Linwood nodded.

Stan sighed. Really, he had the worst of it, because now he would have to drag around from shop to shop with Linwood, particularly all the exotic stuff over in Adventureland, and he might have preferred even the rides to that. Sometimes she made him go on the Jungle Boat Cruise, which was the only ride she liked. It reminded her of her teenage trip with her mother, a cruise to Panama. I'd seen this wonderful picture of them once, dressed in long thin skirts, each of them wearing a huge round hat tilted steeply to the side: Linwood, as slender and elegant as a young horse, and Nana, her breast the smooth round shape of a robin's. Eddie Cantor, a singer, had fallen in love with Linwood during the voyage, but she turned him down.

Stan had been to Panama too. When he got thrown out of Stanford for holding poker games in his room all day instead of going to class, he'd joined the Merchant Marines. He hated the Jungle Boat Cruise.

After Stan handed us each a dollar, June and I raced down Main Street, pell-mell for Fantasyland. The sun felt good on my face, and all the happy people made my heart lift. I tried not to think about the wax and the bones, even though I had this funny feeling, which I'd had a couple of times since The Bad Thing, that some-one was watching me. Tommy? My skin went cold. But anyway, I couldn't imagine Tommy at Disneyland.

Main Street was full of funny old shops—I barely glimpsed them as we whizzed by—that were supposed to look like the stores in old western towns, except that we'd actually gone to Tombstone, Arizona, once and I'd seen the OK Corral and the graves of Wyatt Erp and Billy the Kid. (I loved Billy the Kid. I'd had a crush on him for years, and still did, even though June had just read me the part in *World Book* where they say he was only four feet high and had a giant head and was a moron, like the guy on the cover of *Mad* magazine.) These stores were a lot nicer than the real stores in Tombstone, which were all dirty and had a funny smell, cold and sour, like the basement when it flooded. If I hadn't been following June, I would have been happy to linger inside, eating that candy that looked like pebbles and smelling the sheets of beeswax that you used to make candles. And besides, all that would come later, after dinner, when we ate ice cream cones and waited for the fireworks, strolling back home, exhausted but rich with our day full of images and feelings. For days afterward, you'd shut your eyes and see huge flowers or glowing landscapes or witches extending their long green fingers.

That's how I thought the day would go, when we crossed the moat to the Castle, and Walt crooned away about wishing on stars, and my spine itched with joy.

"Okay," June said, once we were inside the Castle.

I tried to look at her instead of the guys selling stuffed Mickeys and Tinkerbell wings.

"I'm going on the Bobsleds."

My stomach lurched. "I can't—"

"I know," she said. "Look. It's ten o'clock now. We'll meet back here at eleven. What's the difference?"

"Linwood said—"

"What are you, a baby?"

I swallowed.

"Yes, you're a baby. If you weren't a baby, you'd ride the Bobsleds."

The Bobsleds had terrified me out of my senses. My hands started shaking at the thought of going through that again.

"You're being stupid," June said, no pity in those eyes. "I'm meeting you here at eleven, and if you get into trouble or tell, you'll be really sorry."

With that, she turned on her heel and disappeared into the crowd, in the direction of the Matterhorn.

Well, it was like this. Okay, I was nine years old, but I'd never been *alone* at Disneyland before. June had always wanted me along, so she wouldn't have to sit in the carts with strangers.

For a minute I was scared, and then I shrugged. She was right; I was being stupid. I had a whole hour of freedom and a whole booklet full of coupons. What to do?

Go on a ride, obviously. And, again obviously, the idea was to pick a ride that June would never go on, in order to take full advantage of my freedom. The one ride that she unequivocally refused to take was Storybookland. What you did was you rode into the mouth of the whale, and, once inside, everything was tiny and magical, or so the postcards seemed to show. You got to see Cinderella's little cottage and the burning houses of the Three Little Pigs, and so forth. It was all too cute and sweet for June; last summer I had tried to convince her that we could pick up some tips for the poodle village, but she snorted.

The crowd seemed larger and more colorful as soon as I started moving. Hard to shake the feeling that I could vanish away, follow any other family and become part of them. To my left was a family of five buying ice cream bars. The father was chubby and smiling, holding the hand of his blond baby daughter. The mother, rounder and plainer and even happier than the father, was handing Fudgsicles to twin boys, three or four years old. Maybe they would take me on as a kind of nurse?

I pulled myself away, but couldn't really get what I was feeling. Did I want an eraser to descend from the sky, rub me out of existence?

On to Storybookland.

It was over by the exit to Frontierland, and you could hear the sounds of rifles being fired from the arcade (though I could never understand paying money so you could shoot a gun) and the shrieks of the raft passengers, floating over to Tom Sawyer's Island. Only, as I rounded the bend, there was a sorry-this-ride-is-temporarily-closed sign suspended from the whale's gaping mouth.

My eyes were full of tears before I'd even made sense of the sign. This was the ride I wanted to go on; no other ride would do. Tears ran down my cheeks, and through my mind went *No one loves me* and *I never get to do what I want* and *I want to die*.

I sat down on a Dumbo bench and sobbed away. My heart hurt, and my hands felt fat and raw. Why move? I could stay like this until someone found me.

Except that after a few minutes, you get bored with your own sadness.

What about the submarines? The submarines were okay, and June swore she'd never go on them again.

I got up from the bench, thinking about strawberry drink and a Snow White doll and whether or not Gaylin missed me at school, and glanced once more at Storybookland, but this was really strange. In front of the sorry-this-ride-is-temporarily-closed sign was a small, neat black poster with white letters:

SAMMY'S SNOWLAND

Who'd ever heard of *that* ride? Besides, it looked so fishy, tacked up over the real ride. And no one was waiting in line. Usually, at least half of the clever zigzags, designed to give the impression that you were constantly on the verge of entry, were filled. And, for that matter, none of the pretty teenagers with color-coordinated Swiss outfits (which were actually supposed to look German, but I was too young to understand why) were standing at the entrance to the ride, grinning and helping people on and off the boats. And there weren't even *boats*. There was only one long, narrow black canoe. The single attendant was a slender man dressed in a clam-colored suit, with eyes the color of ice and skin like pecans.

How long had he been standing there?

But I wanted my strawberry drink, and the submarines. I glanced at the large wristwatch of the white-haired woman who had just sat down on the bench. Ten-fifteen. Plenty of time.

I walked toward Adventureland, wanting to vanish in the crowd, thick and inevitable as a river, colorful as the flowers themselves.

Was that elegant attendant Sammy? I about-faced, until I could see him again. He waited so calmly, unimpressed by either the crowd or the crowd's neglect of his ride. It looked scary, the unpopularity, the lone man. Next door was the Mad Hatter music and the wild caterpillars of Alice in Wonderland: you could see the bright worms careening crazily on the huge leaves out front, the end of the ride, which put the riders on display—not a usual Disney feature—but was actually a play for time, my idea, to get you used to the real world again after all that wonderful stuff inside. Like being a spy and getting deprogrammed.

Come to Sammy's Snowland!

The voice was thin and eerie, like those fugues they played in Music Appreciation.

I was attracted by the same strangeness that was repelling me. And who had spoken? The impeccable gentleman was stiff and aloof, and patient.

I hesitated, listening to the wild laughter and promises of the ever-optimistic Mad Hatter.

But the mysterious lure of Snowland was too much. As though fate itself were pulling me by a steel cable tied to my heart, I marched over and sat in the canoe. *Nothing really bad could happen at Disneyland*. The elegant man did not offer assistance, nor would he take my coupon. With one gray-gloved hand, he gestured to another tacked-up sign:

SAMMY'S SNOWLAND—THIS IS A FREE RIDE

The canoe sailed into the dark mouth of the whale.

CHAPTER FOUR

I sat in the slim black boat and felt as still and calm as a rain puddle the next clear morning. Strange: the feeling of having both everything and nothing to lose. The tunnel was dark gray, almost but not quite black. The passageway curved dramatically, as if we weren't going directly through the mouth of the whale, but down into someplace else.

In fact, the canoe whizzed through a chained-off area that said STAY OUT, CERTIFIED PERSONNEL ONLY. However, that could be part of the ambience, like the DANGER, KEEP AWAY signs on Mr. Toad's Wild Ride.

It was damp, though, and the smell wasn't too great. This was probably a mistake. If only June were here.

Actually, the worst part was the lack of music or any sound at all, save the swishing of the prow through the water. In the beginning of some of the rides—Snow White, for example—it was very dark, but people kept warning you about what was going to happen, the story being narrated in this scary way so that when they told you, "The Poison Apple!" and the witch extended her hand, practically right on top of you—well, it was very effective.

Then, just when I began a little prayer in my head, I heard:

> Half of the earth's surface
> is covered with snow.

The tunnel began to lighten, as if dawn were breaking. *Oh darn*, I thought, both relieved and disappointed. *It's going to be educational, like the Wamsutta Panorama over in Tomorrowland*. The voice, though, was cold, indifferent, and vaguely British, not the jolly and paternal voice you associated with Disneyland, movies at school, and television commercials, the ones that told you how various products were good for you.

> We are like the earth.
> Snow covers us over.
> We are only half-alive.

The tunnel turned very bright, the source of illumination the walls themselves, which seemed to shimmer and swell.

Any minute now, something was going to happen.

The canoe began a long, careful curve (oddly, it didn't seem to be controlled by underwater cables, like the boats on the other rides) inside the pearly walls, and then rounded a bend. And here was Storybookland! A miniature countryside was laid out before me, a whole vista: houses, roads, stores, freight train, and lush groves, just like the ones we owned: lemon, orange, avocado. And there was this house—such an interesting coincidence—which looked exactly like our house, with the stables and the pepper tree and everything, cats lounging in the backyard and Ace nickering in his stable. In fact, the entire town looked precisely like ours . . . but weren't all small towns in Southern California pretty much alike? The ocean glimmered in the distance, beyond the rounded brown hills.

Disneyland was such an amazing place! How did they make a tiny ocean like that? You could see the waves and the sand and the minute seashells, the lank hanks of diminutive seaweed, like mermaid hair, washed up on the shore.

This is what most people see.

Well, fine. It was adorable.

And this is what could be seen.
This is what is also present.

The canoe rounded another bend, and then you couldn't tell if you were coming on the same scene transformed or a new scene that was supposed to represent the original scene transformed. (Several years later, Disneyland imitated Sammy's ride in It's a Small World, but he alone can be credited with the effect of never knowing what you are seeing. In IASW, you realize that each vision is a new scene, a partial replication of the previous one. You end up marveling not at the sheer majesty but at the expense.) The transformation was stunning! The town with distant ocean was precisely as it had been before, except that now there was a new dimension, projecting out from each object and animal—was this the fourth dimension? It was like those lapsed-time photographs of cars in big cities, and you see, besides the car, the trail that its passage made through space. No, wait, this was better than that: where the ocean had been—still was, I mean—there was now this sea of structure, like some kind of endlessly complicated illuminated molecule model, set in motion. Or it was like the surface of things had been rendered transparent, those educational toys of plastic people: Invisible Woman. The inner organs were revealed through the vanishing exterior of her skin.

But really, when you were looking, you didn't think any of these things. You just thought *wonder*.

I repeat: This is what is also present.

Three-D glasses! Linwood wouldn't let me go to any of those movies because they were about monsters and so forth, but I bet that's what they were like. Only, obviously, one dimension better.

The canoe rounded the bend again, and I craned my neck for one more glimpse of the lit-up, molecular village. Was that the end of the ride? After all, it *was* free.

Again with the slate-gray tunnel, the depressing silence. I thought about that part in the Greek myths where they row you over to Hades. Were we underground? But, as if June had been sitting next to me, I heard: *No, stupid, water can't travel uphill!*

The tunnel went on a long time. I began to get hungry. Was it eleven o'clock yet? Was June out there waiting?

Then the boat stopped. And the walls went totally black.

If I'd just eaten, I would have gone ahead and thrown up. But those pancakes were long digested. Nevertheless, my stomach hurt, and I had to pee.

It was so dark and so quiet.

Was this what being dead was like?

I started to sweat, and I never ever sweat.

Then I heard, far away, a kind of splashing sound. Not like somebody walking, but like something else—a boat?—moving over the water.

"Hello!" My voice was reedy and thin.

No answer.

"Hel—" I shut my mouth. What if it was Tommy?

But how could Tommy have found me?

I was going to shout again, and not be afraid, when I saw something gliding toward me from the far end, the direction my canoe was pointed in. It was another canoe, white, with a kind of flashlight attached to its prow.

I waited. No way was this going to be Tommy.

And, as the canoe got closer and closer, I saw that there was a man inside, a man in a clam-colored suit.

He stopped his canoe inches away from mine.

I shivered. It was awfully cold in the tunnel. Then, to be polite, "Nice ride you have here." Cartoon-mousetime with the voice again. "But my boat's stuck."

"There are laws," the man announced after a moment. His was the indifferent voice of the Snowland.

My stomach felt like Stan's shot put.

"There are laws for everything. Thieving, for instance." He leaned closer, his ice-chip eyes glittering in the flashlight.

"Deane's book." The words came out before I'd even considered them, as if I had my own fourth dimension.

"Some things can be stolen, and some things can be bought."

I saw the red leather book, felt its slick surface, even though I knew it was back in the motel room, inside my cigar box. I saw the pen-and-ink drawing of The Bad Thing, and then, presto, it was gone. My stomach didn't hurt at all. I was so calm, I could have gone to sleep.

"Children steal things. Children don't know what to do with them."

"Who are you?" I asked. "My boat's stuck, and I have to meet my sister."

"You know my name is Sammy," he said. "And I have something you need."

"Me?"

"There is great danger ahead for your family. But there is always a way around every law. Each law with the penalty attached, each system connected to another system. Because you have something that I want, I'm prepared to—"

A faint *slosh-slosh* and a trembling light could be discerned at the distant end of the tunnel.

"I'm prepared," Sammy whispered, "to offer—"

"Hal-looo?"

"Over here!" I yelled. "I'm stuck!"

Sammy gave me a look so strong, it could have been either anger or love.

The *slosh-slosh* got louder, the light closer, but then I saw that the creature was not a man at all! His head was huge and misshapen—

"Help!"

"I'm here to help," said a kindly voice. "Little girl—"

"Help!"

His nose was long and horrible. "Dumbo!" he said.

I screamed again, the air filling up with tiny red ballerinas twirling and twirling before my eyes.

"I'm Dumbo," insisted the workman. "Calm down, honey. It's only a mask."

I opened my eyes. Before me stood a workman in thigh-high waders and a Dumbo mask.

"The fumes in this tunnel are kind of bad," he apologized. "I couldn't find no gas mask." He steadied the canoe, which had began to rotate from the waves of his passage. "What on earth are you doing in here, anyway? This ride's closed. You okay?" He flashed the light in my face.

I squinted. "I was on Sammy's Snowland. The boat got stuck."

"Sammy's Snowland?" All you could see was the Dumbo mask, but his voice sounded confused.

"You know," I said impatiently. "The ride they put up while Storybookland's out."

"Look, honey. There's no ride called Sammy's Snowland. You shouldn't be back here, it's dangerous. Hang on, and—"

"Ask Sammy!" I said, then realized that he and his white canoe were gone.

Completely gone. When? How? And, naturally, had they ever been there?

"Whatever," said the Dumbo man. "Hold tight. I'm going to tow you on out of here in a jiffy."

He grabbed a rope at the bow of the canoe and, exactly as he had promised, sloshed us out of the tunnel almost immediately. Apparently, my boat had stopped right before the exit.

My eyes hurt from the light. We were over at the side of the whale's mouth. The red and yellow and blue clothes of the pleasure-seekers were too bright, the smells of popcorn and orange drink too strong, the hurdy-gurdy sounds of the rides too loud.

The Dumbo man looked at me. Without a word, I jumped out of the canoe and ran, blindly, through all the density of the people and their haloes around them.

I was back where I'd been.

No June.

"Excuse me, sir," I asked the ice cream vendor. "What time is it?"

"Quarter till eleven."

I sat down on a bench, next to an old couple holding hands. Unthinkingly, I flipped through my unused coupon book, which I still clutched in my hand.

Inside was a thick cream-colored card, embossed in chocolate brown.

SAMMY'S SNOWLAND

the card announced,

NOT A RIDE; A CONDITION

CHAPTER FIVE

"Why can't we drive through the redwood?"

June had been pressing this point for the last half-hour and we were all weary of it, even her.

"Because," Stan explained for the umpteenth time, "it's out of our way. And besides, the car probably wouldn't fit."

Apparently, the redwood had been carved out back when they had skinny cars, Model Ts and so forth. We had a baby-blue T-bird, with serious fins.

"Out of our way! That's a good one." June snorted. "We don't have *a way*."

All too depressingly true; no one spoke. Late afternoon, and we were in the northern part of the state, where I'd never been before, almost to Oregon. After a week at Disneyland and another few days at Knott's Berry Farm, with those adorable burros that move very slowly and don't eat your hair, we had all grown bored with the constant insistence on fun. And besides, they'd gotten another phone call. Or at least that's what June heard when she leaned against the door that connected our rooms.

So here we were in the gloomy redwoods, unending rain, leaves black and sodden against the gray October sky. You got used to riding in the car all the time. You stared out the window at other people's houses, grocery stores, schools. You wondered what it would be like to be them, to live the way they lived. Were they happy? Were they just like us? Was there a place you could drive to, and there you'd be happy?

"You could get arrested for depriving us of our right to education."

"Will you shut her up?" Stan asked Linwood.

"It'd be easier to drive through the redwood."

I could feel June's energy bristling at me across the backseat of the car. Times like these, it was best to be invisible. What I wanted to think about was the quick peek I'd taken in Deane's book this morning while June was in the bathroom. Or maybe I didn't want to think about it. Right after the picture of The Bad Thing, there was another one of me riding on Sammy's Snowland. And the next page—as far as I'd gotten before June returned—showed me sitting in an old-fashioned hotel room, clearly not a Holiday Inn, wearing a necklace made out of what could only be poodle toys. Something about the look of that struck me: my picture was powerful, like a hex sign in reverse. Maybe the point of Sammy was some kind of angel warning from God? Maybe I could make up my own magic and protect us? The trouble was sneaking out the toys, with old Hawkeye in the backseat, watching my every move—

"How about *that*?" June asked suddenly.

On the right side of the road, gleaming in the gray air, was a red and yellow billboard.

MADAME MIRACULO'S CRAZY HOUSE

That part was in a huge, flouncy scrawl. Underneath, the sign read:

YOU WON'T BELIEVE YOUR EYES!
SEE . . . FURNITURE FLOAT THROUGH THE AIR!
SEE . . . WATER FLOW UPHILL!
SEE . . . GHOSTLY FACES IN THE MIRROR!

"Oh great," said Stan. "Sounds like just what we need."

"My legs are all cramped," said June. "Pet and I'll probably get rickets or scurvy."

"But that's not why you get scurvy! It's from—ouch!" My bruise throbbed. Would I never learn?

"I have to find a restroom," Linwood pointed out.

Stan sighed. He took the fact that Linwood had only one kidney very personally, something she had done to spite him. Even though we were going nowhere, Stan wanted to get there with as few stops as possible.

"Oh goody!" said June.

Myself, I wasn't convinced ghosts and floating furniture were such a great idea. There was already enough stuff in the world I didn't understand.

"They'll only be disappointed." Stan's defense was weak. Linwood ignored him.

Disappointed was fine with me. A shiver twirled through my body. Best would be transparently fake, though even when we saw that magician who kept dropping the rubber balls, and the pigeon fell out of his pocket, I was still convinced he knew secret things.

June's eyes were glued to the road, watching for more signs. I took my chance and swiped Pierre's bag, dumping the contents in my coat pocket and returning the bag to his neck.

My heart pounded, my palm was sweaty. I fingered the loot inside: a pair of metal binoculars, a rubber fish, a glass bottle that I remembered had a miniature ship inside.

"Homemade fudge!"

I glanced up to see another red and yellow billboard.

"No candy," said Stan. "Not this close to dinner."

"I'd like some candy," said Linwood.

"Why do I even bother?" Stan asked the steering wheel.

"What time is it, by the way?" I liked to try to divert their attention when they got like this. Sometimes it worked.

"Three forty-three," said Stan. "I mean, why do I bother?"

Not this time.

"Stopping at some pathetic little roadside stand is the least we can do for the children," Linwood said, "after what you've put them through."

"What I've put them through."

"Who said we had to leave town?" Linwood lit a cigarette and assumed her movie star profile. "If you're in such a big hurry, for God's sake, then you might as well just drop us off. Go ahead, drop us off. We're living on my money anyway."

"I don't really care if we stop," I said. "Ouch!"

"Are we really living off your money?" June asked.

"If it weren't for my father—"

"Goddammit!" yelled Stan. "We're stopping already, goddammit! All I wanted was to get us to the hotel in Fort Bragg so *you* could relax and have your shower and your drink before dinner!"

"Well, that's no reason to shout." Linwood was all dignity. "I mean, fine, let's stop, but there's no reason to shout at us like that. Stan, really!"

There was an extended moment of silence. I looked

out the window at the dank night coming down and played with the tiny toys in my pocket. Oddly enough, they soothed me. Were they a kind of charm that could keep off the melancholy of twilight? The air was thick and misty. We were close to the ocean, not Southern California warm sand and suntan oil, but cliffs and spume and tidepools. Maybe in the morning we would go down to the shore and look for starfish and anemones, like in *The Restless Sea*.

"There it is!" June shouted. "Turn here!"

Madame Miraculo's Crazy House loomed up from a tangle of huge dark trees, dripping with evening fog. *It's perfectly spooky*, I thought, a thrill riding like a monorail up my spine. I tried to remember the lessons I'd learned from all the strange things happening lately. Don't be scared, be strong. Tommy had hurt me, I had to go to the bathroom again, but Sammy hadn't. The thing was not to be a little creep. I should be tough like June, or Deane. My weakness was my own fault. Like they said in the Bible, if you don't have very much, they'll take that away from you too. The only way to win when you're scared is to be mad and shout a lot. You can't be afraid and angry at the same time: it was like air and water—they drove each other out.

Stan pulled the car into the empty parking lot. "Doesn't look open," he pronounced.

"Oh, poo." Linwood stubbed out her cigarette. She waited, as usual, while Stan walked around and opened her door.

June clambered out after Linwood, but I waited a moment. They went up to the door, and then inside, so obviously it was open after all. For a moment, I thought I could stay in the car the whole time, no one would notice. Then I could pluck poodle toys at my leisure and avoid whatever was inside. But Stan reappeared in the doorway, glaring through his sunglasses, arms akimbo.

Reminding myself to be strong and of good courage, I shuffled across the grass, pulling my red coat tightly around me.

I pushed open the heavy door. And inside, the whole thing was right out of *Frankenstein*! High ceilings with

cobwebs, tarnished suits of armor, the whole enchilada.
Except for the gift shop, which looked cozy and familiar. To my left, through the glass door, I could see back
scratchers and beaded necklaces and those little cedar
chests like the one I got at Marineland. June was
already checking out the merchandise, and Linwood
was no doubt in the ladies' room. Stan was standing
near the entrance of the shop, glaring at a sign that
said: ADMISSION TO THE MANSION IS $2.00.

Now, I can't say exactly why I did this. Maybe I
wanted to test myself, or punish myself, or maybe I was
just being stupid. Whatever the reason, before there
was a chance to talk myself out of it, I snuck under the
chain, down the short hallway, and up the dusty staircase.

And it was plenty dusty.

Walking up the stairs, you felt yourself moving much
farther away than you should have been. So quiet, and so
remote. One of the worst things about this traveling
together was that we were always together. At night, I
couldn't play with my cigar box, never mind check out
Deane's book, with June always there. The real part of
me felt like it was shut up in a box, too.

At the top of the staircase I relaxed and breathed
deep. You were on another planet. Here were the stage
props, the filmy curtains, and the peculiar statues—
was that Artemis-Diana, huge white marble to my
right, poised before a heavy, closed door? But also the
air seemed to have a greeny glow, and I don't think it
was just my imagination. There were patches of sparkly
stuff drifting around, head-high, weird little clouds. I
fingered the poodle toys in my coat pocket.

The clouds seemed to be gathering, and in fact the
air was much greener than it had been a moment ago.

Well, I was tired of being scared. How bad could this
be? I felt that little quease between my legs, but really,
what next? I could go my whole life like this, constantly
being weak and scared.

Or I could go ahead and face up to the strange.

"Who's there?" I called.

The air got greener and denser. You couldn't even see

the black velvet chairs I'd first noticed at the top of the staircase.

"Is anybody there?"

Out of the thin air, except it couldn't have been, a middle-aged man appeared. He was elegant in a dove-gray suit with tails, a dove-gray shirt, and charcoal gloves with mother-of-pearl buttons. His skin was the color of pecans, and his eyes were chips of ice.

Sammy!

"And who's here?" he asked nastily.

"Only me."

"Precisely."

I leaned down and pulled up my anklets, then brushed off the toes of my Keds. All that dust.

"Are you ready to deal?"

I straightened up, making every effort to be calm and cool. Poodle toys and the magic book: power sources. "What about that danger you said? What about my family?"

"You have something I want. I have something you need. It's as simple as that." He smoothed down his gloves. His eyes looked like Stripey's. He was June's pet snake, until Linwood found him curled up in one of her slippers. The worst part was she found him with her foot.

"But Deane's my sister!"

"Do say."

"And what's hers should be mine. More than yours."

He straightened his impeccable tie before an imaginary mirror. "Very well. If you must be greedy. And if you want the safety of your family to be your responsibility, of course."

Globes of light seemed to spin in the sparkly air before my eyes. "How do I know you aren't making this all up, just because you're greedy too?"

"That's a chance you could take. You are the one who will have to live with your conscience."

Pang straight to the heart.

Sammy made an about-face and strolled away a couple of paces.

"Wait a minute!"

He turned back, his face a study in boredom.

"If you're so smart—"

He cocked an eyebrow.

"—why didn't you just get the book yourself?"

When he smiled, you wished he wouldn't. "You saw the hex signs in her room. Whom do you think they were meant to keep out? You? That oaf of a boyfriend?"

"*Pet!*" Stan called. Wherever he was, it was farther away than a dream.

"Are you ready to deal?"

I felt utterly paralyzed. On the one hand, how could I risk my mother, my father, maybe both sisters? On the other hand, what would Sammy do with the book? Deane must have had a good reason for keeping him away.

On the third hand, she was the person who had stuffed my sweet Marmalade.

"*Pet!*"

Sammy stared. In fact, Stripey had more expression on his face. "You have one more chance."

"*Pet!*"

"When we meet again, you had better be ready to deal."

So I ran. There was only one way to go: the stairway was behind me, Sammy was straight ahead, a stained glass window of the Last Supper was to my left. I ran to the closed door on my right, past the statue of Artemis-Diana, her bow and arrow poised, and flung open the heavy door.

Running into the room was like running on one of those cartoon treadmills, where you keep going and going but arrive nowhere at all. The white sofa I could barely see in the distance seemed to be moving farther and farther away. Of course, that could have been the "crazy" part of the house. And I was the water flowing uphill.

The effect is not so amusing if you are the water.

"*Pet!*" Stan's voice was so far away, the bottom of a well.

I wasn't ready to go back yet. I ran and ran, sticky in

the same spot, and then I was suddenly *through*. The room stopped twirling, the greeny air cleared away.

Wherever I was, it wasn't what you'd expect. This huge space was filled with bright, clear illumination. But not like I'd died and gone to heaven or *The Twilight Zone* or anything. Even though the light was strangely sharp and there wasn't any furniture, you could tell this was a real room—it smelled musty, and there were dust devils in the near corner.

After a moment my eyes adjusted to the light, and I began to feel very calm and very, well, *powerful*. As if something about the room itself were recharging something inside me, completing a circuit, like Christmas tree lights, the tricky way you have to test each bulb to make them all go on. I had this literal feeling of "a load off my chest," an image like heartache that really is what it says. But I guess everyone knows that. Every time I come up with this stuff, it's already old-hat. Like the time last year when I had the dream about the angels in the trash can, and they told me, "To err is human, to forgive divine." I thought I was really on to something! When I told Linwood, she acted impressed, said it was a lovely phrase, and the thought, too. Then I ran across the same sentence in *Bartlett's Quotations*.

The only thing worse than being a dope is being humored when you're being one.

Anyway, the room was working on me. Or maybe it was the light. I fingered the poodle toys in my coat pocket. My chest and shoulders felt free, even when I thought about how we might never go home again and about Deane's room and that night and Deane herself. And the strangeness that had been following me ever since, more closely than Tommy ever could. Even when I thought about all that stuff, I felt okay. This voice—not out loud, exactly—told me that what was past *was past*. Standing alone in the large, airy room, I knew this was true. Whatever had happened to me, it wasn't here anymore. Maybe it had happened. Maybe it had all been a dream, like the angels in the garbage.

Except I still had the book.

Or did I?

Maybe tonight when I opened my cigar box, it wouldn't be there anymore. Maybe it had never been there.

I began to pace in small circles, spiraling out from the center of the room.

Maybe I *should* trade the book to Sammy. If I didn't have it anymore, then the past could roll up and disappear, my imagination the richest fruit. You woke up from terrible nightmares all the time, relieved, you had been so convinced of the power of the other.

I stopped pacing.

I turned around and opened the door, and this time I was simply back at the top of the stairs.

"Sammy?" I called.

"Pet, goddammit, you have until the count of ten to get down here!"

"Sammy!" I cried, louder.

"One! Two!—"

I had to believe that things come in threes. Sammy had said I had one more chance. And this time I'd be ready.

"—Seven! Eight!—"

I scampered down the stairs.

All Stan said was, "Forget the gift shop."

Outside, the sky was dark, dead-dark. Linwood and June were already in the car, and they ignored me as I climbed into my spot.

We sped away from Madame Miraculo's. June gnawed on her fudge. Idly, I fingered the poodle toys in my pocket.

CHAPTER SIX

"Wake up!" June shoved me hard.

I opened my eyes. My cheek hurt—I must have been sleeping against the window. All I could see was a tall old building with shutters, which we were parked next to. Stan and Linwood were gone. The air smelled the way it did after midnight.

"You slept through all the good stuff. I must have pinched you six or seven times, but you were dead."

"Where'd they go?"

"To check out the hotel. Linwood took her marbles and she's furious with Stan because he's been driving too fast. Over ten miles an hour. It was neat! We were on the edge of this really steep cliff and the road was foggy and you couldn't see anything. Linwood kept screaming and grabbing the seat. You'd think *she* would have woken you up."

Linwood must have been mad. She only took her marbles (to make sure the floors were level; she'd once had a bad dream about shifting floors) when she was really angry. "Is this Fort Bragg?"

"Yup. And there's no Holiday Inn. Stan didn't check on the road, so it's his fault. He knows Linwood goes bananas over those hairpin turns."

I was pretty glad I'd missed this episode.

Linwood opened her door and climbed in.

"How're the floors?" June asked.

"They're all right, but the bathroom leaves something to be desired. They're waking up the maid to clean it now."

You didn't have to be Sherlock Holmes to realize that Linwood had been raised in a wealthy family. Nana had taken to bed for three months when Linwood eloped with Stan. Once I'd asked her why she'd married him. All I got back was a dark look and the promise that I would not be allowed to date until I was sixteen. As if I would ever date.

"What a perfect nightmare we've been through, Pet." Linwood smoothed her hair back on either side, fingers as combs. "I'm so glad you were able to sleep through it. Your father drove like a maniac."

"Even when we screamed," June added.

"Especially when we screamed."

Usually I was such a light sleeper. Odd. But over.

"And we never got dinner," June continued.

"How come?" I felt a hunger-tweeze.

"Nothing was open. All the restaurants are closed this time of year."

Stan opened his side of the car and leaned in. "Look," he said, "the guy said he'd fix us something right now, if we go directly inside. We can put our stuff in the rooms afterwards."

"Eat dinner without showering first? And what do you mean, 'the guy'?"

"The owner of the hotel."

We were all quiet, hoping Linwood would decide pro-food.

"I have to tell him right away if we're taking him up on this." Stan was apologetic.

"Well, good heavens!" said Linwood. "I had no idea we were in such a *rush*!"

Everybody sighed.

"By all means then, *rush* right in. Take the girls. Food, really. I prefer to shower and enjoy my drink."

I felt piggy, opting for dinner over cleanliness and everything that civilized virtue implied. I opened my mouth to say that I, too, preferred to relax rather than stuff, then hesitated. Could you really smell steak in the air? At this late hour? Steak and a baked potato, swimming in butter and sour cream and chives. Fresh green peas. Chocolate cake and milk.

But what was niggling at the back of my mind? As if in my ear, I heard: *This is your big chance to check out the book. Would you really pick food over magic?*

"I'm not hungry." Saliva was gathering in the corners of my mouth.

"Okay," Stan said. He walked around to the trunk. By the time I was out in the cool night air, he already had the bags out. June had disappeared in the direction of the restaurant.

Ten minutes later, Stan and June were occupied, Linwood was next door showering, and I was alone in the faded glory of the antique hotel room, so odd after all the Holiday Inns. The big roses on the wall were pale pink like shells, but you could tell they used to be magenta. The twin beds were high and lumpy, chenille spreads with more roses. Scattered about the room were dainty little watercolors, sandpipers and still-lifes, and a lot of old lamps with yellowed silk shades.

The room seemed peculiarly familiar.

It was the room from Deane's magic book, the picture with me wearing a necklace of poodle toys.

Hastily, I took the toys out of my coat pocket and looked around for something I could string them on. The venetian blinds had an old cord to raise and lower them, so, biting off a length with my teeth, I assembled a makeshift concoction. For good measure, I added some stuff from the cigar box: my badge from Gaylin, the piece of brick with the letter P, and a couple of seashells.

The product wasn't very pretty, yet it looked—like Deane's altar—as if it had been designed for a purpose. It looked like The Real Thing.

I put one of the lamps on the floor on the far side of the beds. If anybody came in, they wouldn't see me right away. Plus, I set some cards next to the cigar box. By the time anyone rounded the beds, I'd be laying out a game of solitaire.

Then I went into the bathroom and washed my face and hands and brushed my hair. I had that funny feeling between my legs, so I got a washcloth and washed that, too. Then I changed into my best flannel nightgown, the white one with tiny green flowers. I put the necklace on.

I started to sit down, but on second thought, the air was stuffy. With the window open, the after-midnight smell wafted in along with the sound of the sea, rumbling away far below.

The taste of the air and the night! A deep sense of excitement splashed up in me, a wave hitting a rock. My heart pounded like the surf, too, and I tried to sit down calmly, cross-legged, in front of the lamp. I opened the cigar box and took out Deane's magic journal from the very bottom of the box.

Part of me thought it wouldn't be there.

But, of course, it was. Small, red, the leather warm, as if it had been recently caressed. This time, I would see the book through. This time I was prepared, would not slam it shut in fear or horror. This time I was prepared. I would see the book through, and then I would trade it to Sammy.

I touched my necklace for security.

DANGER! TURN THE PAGE AT YOUR OWN RISK!

I turned the page.

FINAL WARNING! A CURSE ON THE PERSON WHO STEALS THIS BOOK, OR READS IT UN-LAWFULLY.

Don't farewell. Fare forward.

ANCIENT MAGICK & SECRETS, THE UNKNOWN

First there was the pen-and-ink drawing of me and Tommy. Okay. I could handle that.

I flipped the page.

Then, the picture of me riding on Sammy's Snowland. You could see the village entering the fourth dimension behind me, the bands of light that connected the trees and the houses and the ocean glittering behind them.

I flipped the page.

There I was, wearing my necklace. Deane had gotten all the details right, down to the piece of brick with the letter P. Definitely, this was the hotel room: it had been faithfully captured in faded roses and lumpy beds.

Okay, I was anxious, my legs throbbed a little, but I was handling it.

I flipped the page.

It was blank.

I flipped the next page, and the next, and the next. They were all blank!

I closed the book and tried to concentrate. This

wasn't right—if this was all the book contained, why would Sammy be so hot to get his hands on it?

You thought the book had to be full of secrets, important stuff—who knew what?—about mysterious things.

Fingering my necklace, I tried to feel important, like I was a part of everything, entitled to the book and the necklace and the cigar box and the truth, even though the air was green and cloudy, like at Madame Miraculo's, and you couldn't see the luminous fibers that connected everything the way they did in Sammy's Snowland.

Closing my eyes, I let the magic book fall open randomly.

A family was driving down the street in their car. The car was a baby-blue T-bird and the parents in the front seat looked a lot like Stan and Linwood. June was leaning forward, wearing that dumb gray coat. Out the car window you could see the sign on a shop window: MARIE LAVEAU'S HOUSE OF VOODOO.

The picture looked okay. So what? We were all in the car together, even though I was huddled in the backseat, looking alone.

Then I noticed the reflection in the store window.

An enormous truck, seemingly out of control, was hurtling directly toward us.

Slamming the book shut, I threw it against the wall. My throat felt all raw and terrible. This was the danger Sammy was trying to protect us from! Deane was going to let us be killed!

"Pet!" Linwood called through the connecting door. "Are you all right in there?"

"Fine!" I called out. What a lie.

"Okay, honey, sleep tight. Save your three good deeds until tomorrow. I'll see you in the morning."

"Good night!"

Boy, was I mad. I was too mad to be scared. It was one thing to interfere with me, and another thing to hurt them.

I was lying on my back, staring at the ceiling and wondering how I was going to do what I had to do, when June walked in. All my stuff was safely stowed away.

"Well, Fats," she said, "you missed a good dinner." She began to change into her nightgown. Her body was big, but she didn't look bad, the way adults do when they're overweight. She was all pink and solid. Sometimes I envied her size: it gave her the authority of an adult, but she still got the privileges of a child.

"What'd you have?"

"Fried chicken, mashed potatoes, and two pieces of coconut cake."

Coconut cake! "Was it fresh?"

"Still warm."

I let out a sigh worthy of Stan, and then something plopped onto my stomach. A tinfoil-wrapped slice of coconut cake.

"Thanks, June." I was humbled.

She shrugged, her flannel tent falling around her. "Didn't want you waking up in the night whining about how hungry you were."

"Want a bite?"

"Sure."

I gave her a big chunk, and we both smacked the cake right down. It had that thick, white, sugary icing that made the back of your tongue shiver.

"Want to start a game of Monopoly?"

I felt I owed her, because of the cake. On the other hand, how could you concentrate and play Monopoly at the same time? "Look." I stood up and paced a little, for drama. "I need to get my hands on some money."

Pushing her glasses up her nose, June sat down on her lumpy bed. "How come?"

"I can't tell you, but it's important."

Her mouth had that grown-up set of annoyance.

"Cross my heart and hope to die. It's very, very, very important."

She just looked at me.

"It's bad. And if I tell you, it'll be your fault too. This way, it's all my fault."

At that, she relaxed. "First, I get a consulting fee. And second, how much do you want?"

Well, I didn't exactly know. I knew what I had to do: find Sammy again, trade him the book for protection, at least. But what if he never showed up? What if I looked out the window one day and there it was: Marie Laveau's House of Voodoo? Money was what passed for power with adults. Maybe if you had money, you had power. Maybe if Sammy never showed up again, I could buy protection. Or maybe if he did, the book plus money would buy extra protection. Frankly, I was only nine years old, and money seemed like the first step, to be ready just in case. "A thousand dollars?"

"Get serious!"

"Okay. A hundred dollars."

June thought a moment. "Okay," she said. "I think I know where you can get at least a hundred dollars. But you better pick up an extra fifty for me, as the consulting fee."

"Legally, that makes you liable."

She thought again. "Okay," she said. "We'll call it a bribe."

June's idea, it turned out, was the cash register downstairs. And it wasn't even a real cash register—it was only a drawer that the guy kept his money in. She'd seen the whole thing when Stan paid for their dinner.

"But isn't that too obvious?" I asked. "Won't they know who did it?"

June grunted. "That's your problem," she said. "But frankly I think there's a few hundred dollars in there. By the time they notice something's missing, we'll be history."

I went into the bathroom to change. I didn't want June to see the poodle-toy necklace, but I knew I had to wear it under the dark sweater I'd selected as my burglar outfit. Dark sweater, dark pants, and my navy blue watch cap.

"What about gloves?" June asked when I emerged.

"I thought children didn't have fingerprints." Didn't

you get them the same time you got your social security number?

"What a jerk! Just look at your hand why don't you."

I looked. Okay, so there were fingerprints. "But I don't have any gloves."

"Come on, Pet!" June was exasperated. "You've read Nancy Drew. What would she do?"

If the queasiness in my stomach would go away, maybe I could think. Nancy Drew... "She'd take a cloth and wipe everything off."

"You bet she would."

Moments later, I found myself alone on the staircase, heading for a life of crime. *God, forgive me,* I prayed. *You too, Jesus.* You had to be careful to mention them both or someone might get annoyed.

The house-hotel was quiet, dark, and felt safe. The small lights on the stairway allowed me to see my way along the soft carpet runner. No noise. Not from me, not from anybody. The building itself seemed to be breathing in slumber.

At the base of the stairs I turned to my right and eased through the door, just as June had instructed. Inside the darkened dining room, I flicked on my flashlight.

The room was mine.

Even my queasiness subsided, now that I was committed. I opened the drawer, my last fear being a burglar alarm.

But no. The open drawer, with its cash box, was mine as well.

I selected a random sample: some bills, some rolls of coins, a little bit of everything. I piled it in my extra sweater, which I carried like a bundle. When you looked in the drawer, nothing in particular seemed to be missing. Being deceitful, cunning, tricky: how easy to learn these things. Only one step away, really, from sneaking ice cream out of the carton so no one can tell it's gone. The way you scoop a little from the edges, a tad from the center...

I closed the drawer. Then I opened it back up and wiped the cash box and the drawer itself clean, with my handkerchief.

Then I stood there. Almost as if something else needed to happen.

Under my clothing, the poodle necklace was warm and sharp.

Then, I thought I heard a laugh: a long, low, man's laugh, not amused. But when I scanned the room with my flashlight, I was alone. I was alone.

CHAPTER SEVEN

"One hundred seventy-nine dollars and thirty-four cents," June announced. "Not bad."

I shrugged. It hadn't sunk in yet.

"One hundred for you. And I'll take the rest."

"No," I said.

We were both surprised.

"Fifty for you. And *I'll* take the rest."

"Okay," June agreed, impressed. "After all, you're the criminal."

Funny thing was, I sure didn't feel like one. I knew that I'd done what I had to do. I had a good reason. Even when I closed my eyes and tried hard, I couldn't work up a case of shame.

"You don't feel guilty, do you?"

Shaking my head no, I walked around the room, trying to dispel the jittery, wild excitement coursing through my veins.

"Maybe you'll end up like Deane."

My feet stopped moving.

June was counting out her fifty, in bills.

"I'm not like Deane. Not one bit."

June shrugged. "Suit yourself. What are you going to keep the loot in?"

A good question. "The poodle bags?"

"Not my poodles!"

"Of course not."

"And what about their toys?"

"Pockets." The moment the idea came out, it sounded right. "I'm going to sew extra pockets in my red coat, and put all the toys in there."

June took her glasses off and rubbed the bridge of her nose, not a child's gesture. "Then why don't you just put the money in the extra pockets and leave the poodle toys out of this?" She hated the idea, you could tell, of disrupting the ideal order of the poodle paraphernalia.

I wrinkled my nose. "Too heavy? The money would jingle and they'd catch me?" The real reason was that I had this craving to have all the toys on my person, that much safer a shield.

June tucked her fifty dollars into the five-year diary she always kept at bedside. She recorded things like which states' license plates she'd seen and Burma Shave slogans. "Legally," her voice was reluctant, "you're better off putting the money in the bags. That way if they catch you, the evidence is circumstantial."

Well, good. "Okay." I pulled my hair back and knotted it into a rubber band. "What do you think the pockets should be made out of?"

"For ten dollars, I'll help."

"Never mind." I opened my suitcase and rifled around. Actually, a couple pairs of underwear would do the trick. All you had to do was sew up the legs and gather the waistband like a pouch.

"I'll organize the poodle stuff for free." June was magnanimous. "You'd probably mess it up."

"Fine."

She began to pull poodles from the pillowcase we kept them in at night. In the daytime, of course, they were lined up against the back of the car, and they did, indeed, fit perfectly. The only problem, which irritated Stan, was that people always thought they were for sale. The two piles grew: her poodles, my poodles.

I got out my needle and thread and began to sew up the underwear.

"We need to start making their costumes," June pointed out, once the pillowcase was empty.

"Costumes?" My index finger was bleeding already, staining the pristine white of the cotton.

"God, Fatso! For Halloween!"

That made me sit back and take pause. Halloween was my very favorite holiday, next to my birthday, and here I'd totally forgotten. How strange. Now that I knew, I didn't even really care. Holidays, poodles, it all seemed so silly. Like I'd taken a giant step into someplace I couldn't come back from.

"Each poodle has to have his own costume, better than last year. And we have . . . let's see." She began to count. "Where's the photo album?"

I pulled it out of the suitcase and tossed it. The album opened *splat*, the pages crumbled.

"Careful!" She flipped through. "We have nine more poodles than last year."

I started on the second pair of underwear. This was going to work. "Let's get a package of handkerchiefs and they can go as ghosts."

"You can act that way to your poodles, if you like. Mine are going to have real costumes." She lined up my group and began to unwrap the drawstring bags from their necks. "First off, we'll pin the matching pillows to their collars. That'll save a lot of room."

It was good to have her on my side.

An hour later, we had the whole thing set up. The money was in the bags—June had even pinned her own poodles' pillows to their collars, to lessen suspicion and because it had occurred to her that the bags were also a great place to store clandestine candy—and the toys, strung neatly on rubber bands, with name tags, were bunched into the underwear pockets. Now I looked the part of Fatso in my red coat.

Yet, even though it made me look fat and the baggage was cumbersome, I felt majestic in my supplemented garment. Dauphine's bag, for instance, had held a rubber eraser painted like the flag of Turkey, a tiny plastic frying pan with two little eggs, a red glass bead from one of Linwood's favorite necklaces, which had burst one night as they were on their way out to dinner and a play, *Cat on a Hot Tin Roof*, I think, a wiggle picture from the Cheerios package—Goofy and Pluto— and a slightly chipped seashell. Tying that bunch of stuff together filled me with a sense of peace, and energy, and bliss. Bag after bag of merchandise, gathered together in two big pockets . . . well, I felt gratified. As though this were what things were for, after all.

I hung my coat back in the niche. "Look," I told June, "thanks a lot . . ."

But she was already sound asleep, her even breathing a testimony to her clear conscience.

My heart was too restless for sleep. The deep-night air blew in from the window. I crossed over and then saw that there was a kind of shallow ledge outside the sill. Gingerly, cold in my thin nightgown, I eased myself out and hunkered down.

The black of the sky was weirdly dispersed by the bright moon, which rose like a Woolworth's pumpkin. How could you forget Halloween on a night like this? Once my eyes adjusted to the dimness, they saw the pale crescents of whitecaps far, far below.

What if you jumped? How long would it take to land? Did you die from fear before you actually touched water or craggy rock?

Or did you think you were flying? Was this the only time you could imagine yourself free?

I sighed, my breath making fog in the chill. I wasn't going to jump, even though my wickedness was spreading like a kind of infection. Sammy was sure to find me a third time.

And this time I'd be ready.

CHAPTER EIGHT

"Don't you girls care how your sister is?" Linwood's voice was disappointed but not surprised.

June and I exchanged looks in the backseat. We were somewhere in Nevada or Oklahoma or the Texas Panhandle or someplace. Who could keep track? She gave me her yarney-yarney-yarney expression.

"Your sister might be joining us soon."

Stan made that snorting sound that June had perfected. In a way, after constantly being together for almost a month, we were beginning to resemble each other. Or maybe only they were.

"Well, she might..." Linwood trailed off, lamely.

"Great," June said. "Then she can ruin our new home for us. If we ever get a new home."

Firm silence from the front seat.

"Florida would be a nice place to live," Stan suggested conversationally. Out of nowhere, they had come up with the idea of Thanksgiving in Miami. That was exactly their kind of an idea.

"Florida oranges?" June sneered.

Stan and Linwood couldn't understand that Florida was like Russia for us. The California school system indoctrinated you to resent the citrus crop, the sandy white beaches, and the tourist trade of our chief competitor.

"Where would you girls like to live?" He was trying.

"Vermont," June said.

"Hawaii," I said.

"Alaska," June said.

"Paris," I said.

"Canada," June said.

"Paris," Linwood agreed.

"Rio de Janeiro," I said.

"The Riviera," Linwood said.

"In a bank," said Stan. "The Federal Reserve."

"Anyplace with horses," June said. "And cows and goats. A real farm."

Linwood groaned.

"In coffeehouses, with beatniks," I said. "I want to wear black sweaters and write poetry."

"Me too," said Stan.

Linwood groaned again.

We all smiled and let it rest. Every now and then, you could tell we were a family. We had our jokes; we were loved. It was even rather pretty out the windows, in a chilly mid-November way. The cornfields we were passing through had been harvested. The sheaves of stalks were tied together, just like in picture books. There was a kind of rosy center to my chest. Life could be very simple and very pleasant. You didn't have to have bad men and strange rides and magic necklaces.

If only things were always simple.

But they never would be, not for me. In the last week or so, I had carried my burden of crime and secrecy. *Today*, I'd think, *will be Sammy-day.* But every place we went that looked like his sort of place was closed.

"Anyhoo," said Stan.

What an obnoxious expression.

"Anyhoo, in a week, we'll be drinking rum punches and watching the marlin leap in the Gulf."

"Pet and I get to drink rum punches?"

"Deane," Linwood said dreamily, "always loved Ernest Hemingway."

Actually, I loved Hemingway too. I'd only read parts of *The Sun Also Rises*, snuck from their bookshelf, but if I couldn't be a beatnik, I wanted to have short hair and wear men's hats. Those Paris cafés. And poor old Jake. He got around okay for a man with one leg.

"I'm sure she still does." Stan was annoyed. "She isn't dead, you know."

Not yet, I thought.

*   *   *

"Snake-A-Torium!"

June was shouting in my ear.

Was that supposed to be a word?

"There's a Snake-A-Torium up ahead!"

My head was thick, my brain groggy. I must have nodded off, as usual. The day had moved from early to mid-afternoon.

"Snake-A-Torium!" June shoved my shoulder, hard.

Sure enough, a dingy billboard advertised: THE ONE, THE ONLY, THE TOTALLY UNIQUE ... SNAKE-A-TORIUM!

> LIVE! HUNDREDS OF WRITHING REPTILES!
> GIGANTIC GATORS!
> HORRIFIC GILAS!
> TERRIBLE TURTLES!

Terrible turtles? I thought about Rose and Pansy, released into Gaylin's safekeeping.

"I need to send Gaylin a card," I said, to no one in particular.

So nobody answered.

"Are we stopping?" June demanded.

"Why break our record now?" said Stan. "We've hit every grisly roadside stand between here and L.A. We wouldn't want to miss one."

"I hate snakes," said Linwood.

"But you wouldn't want to deprive the girls, after all I've made them suffer."

Deep silence.

I started to point out that I wasn't especially keen on snakes either, when I remembered—Sammy! Of course. Where was my mind, anyway?

> SALLY THE SNAKE QUEEN AND HER DEADLY
> REPTILE REVUE!

Clearly, this was his sort of place.

Without any further negotiation, Stan parked in the gravel lot in front of the Snake-A-Torium. For a moment, no one moved. In the thin late-autumn sunshine, the spectacle before us was especially depressing.

A wooden fence, presumably surrounding the gift
shop, the snake pit, and the outdoor animals, was
painted with all kinds of cartoons. A man fell into a
cluster of alligators, and the largest one snapped, "Glad
you could drop in for a bite to eat!" Something about
the clumsiness of the drawings and the way they were
streaked with rain gave you that *uh-oh* feeling. Already
you wanted to wash your hands.

"Well?" Stan asked.

"Let's go!" June's voice sounded false.

We climbed out, staring, but we tried not to, at the
other drawings. Naked women with snakes wrapped
about their waists, children without hands or feet. One
particularly lifelike drawing—the "best"—had a big, fat
gator smacking his chops, with drips of blood.

"I don't know, Stan. . . ."

"Girls?"

"I want to go in."

Everyone was surprised at me. They stopped and
looked. Linwood placed her cool palm on my forehead.

"Life's supposed to be an adventure, right?"

"Not for children." Stan was always much more put
out by pictures of naked women than Linwood was.

"If you guys don't hurry up, we'll miss Sally the
Snake Queen!" June beckoned from the doorway.

"Just a minute." I opened the car door and pulled
Nanette from the backseat. She had the big bills in her
bag. Then I shut the door and caught up with the
others. The underwear pockets bulged pleasantly beneath my armpits. Perhaps too much so, as Linwood
had asked me the other day if I was "developing."

The first thing you noticed inside the Snake-A-Torium
was the dinginess and the powerful odor of animals,
unhealthy animals. The second thing you noticed was
the old man at the ticket counter. He was wearing a
torn Hawaiian shirt (more bare-breasted maidens) over
his considerable belly. His unshaven face was sprinkled
with gray, and he chewed on a squashed cigar stub.

"Two adults, two children." Stan's teeth were gritted.
He hated to see animals in pain. Once he caught Deane
using spurs on Ace—that was the only time he ever hit her.

"Pet!" June shouted. "Look at this!"

I picked my way through the dusty reptile cages. They were so old and filthy, the place looked like a museum and not a zoo. It's hard to feel sorry for a deadly black mamba, but you did.

In the center of the snake room there was a big hole in the floor with a railing around it. June was leaning over, gawking. The hole was The Snake Pit, about thirty feet deep and circular. The sides of the pit had been decorated with crudely painted palm trees, dinosaurs, and volcanoes. It looked like something a six-year-old might have done. There were some monkeys, too, and they were drawn so they looked bigger than the trees. I was only a child, but even I knew a little something about perspective.

"It's time for the show." June pointed at a fake cardboard clock down in the pit. It hung above the only doorway, and a sign said, THE NEXT SHOW WILL BE AT: and the clock's hands showed four-thirty.

I glanced over my shoulder. Linwood was looking into a smeared display case. Stan, a horrible expression on his face, was peering into the various snake cages. No one else seemed to be in the room.

Especially not Sammy.

"Here she comes!"

The door opened, and out stepped a large woman wearing a spangled circus costume, one of the ones that look like your stomach shows but really it's flesh-colored leotard. Her legs were heavy and her hair was an artificial red color that was almost purple. She had a lot of makeup on, but her face still looked old and unhappy. A little hat with feathers rose jauntily from her puffy hairdo.

She curtsied halfheartedly without looking up. If she'd known only June and I were watching, she probably wouldn't have curtsied at all.

Then she left for a moment, returning with a hefty black and white reptile.

"Aw, it's a king snake, like Stripey!" June was disappointed. "Anyone can pick up one of those."

An old record of tinny-sounding hootchie-kootchie music came on. "Sally the Snake Queen!" Someone announced over the loudspeaker.

I turned around and, sure enough, it was the old guy at the counter. He held an oversized microphone up to his mouth, and he was still gnawing away at the cigar.

"Every day, ten times a day, no day a holiday, Sally handles her poisonous vipers!"

Absolutely no expression on her face, Sally wrapped the lethargic king around her shoulders as if he were a stole. Then she tied him around the impressive girth of her middle. Finally, she hauled him between her legs, which gave me a twinge. What a weird thing to do.

"Now, Sally the Snake Queen serenades her cobra!"

Sally tossed the king out the doorway and reappeared with a wicker basket. June was enthralled, so I saw my chance and slipped away. Besides, I really needed some fresh air.

Following the signs TO SNAPPERS, I exited onto a catwalk.

I took a deep breath before I realized it smelled even worse outside. What was the catwalk suspended over, anyway? Alligators! There must have been more than a hundred of them, lolling only ten feet or so beneath me. Remembering Captain Hook, I did not lean over the railing, and I tucked Nanette safely into my outside pocket.

They were such sleepy, ugly things. Their "cage" was not very large, considering how many there were. A dirty trickle of water fed into a shallow concrete pool in which it looked like garbage had been dumped. Regularly. Some alligators lay in the water. Some lay half in, half out. Many lay on top of one another. Nobody seemed to care. Their tiny, sly eyes were uninterested. Unless, I guessed, somebody fell in.

Above the gator pen was a series of what looked like small shacks, the kind migrant farm workers lived in. What would they be doing here, though? Would anybody, however desperate, live in a Snake-A-Torium?

The smell was the saddest, sickest thing in the world.

"Sammy?" I called.

Only the slow splash and shuffle of the plodding reptiles below.

This seemed like the perfect place for him to show. I had my poodle toys to protect me. I had the money just in case. But, it struck me like a bolt of lightning, I didn't have the book! How stupid can you get? What good was the money without the book?

"Sammy?"

Someone grabbed my elbow—I screamed!

"For God's sake," said Stan. "Come on, Pet. We're getting the hell out of here."

Stan turned my arm like the rudder of a ship and steered me back through the snake room and out to the car. June was wailing; I could hear her as we approached.

Stan gunned the motor and we tore out of the parking lot.

For a moment, everyone sat tense. Linwood smoked, June snuffled, and Stan . . . why, he was crying too.

"People like that should be shot!" he said after a moment. Since I was sitting in back of him, I couldn't see the tears, but I saw his hand go up to wipe his eyes.

"I wanted to see the show!" June lamented.

"Here," said Linwood. She turned around so she was facing the backseat. "I bought you girls each a present."

June abruptly stopped crying.

What could she have found to buy in that terrible hole? I patted Nanette in my pocket, melancholy with the sunset, the failure to make contact.

"How could you give that bastard any more money?"

"Your language, Stan. Maybe if he had more money, he'd take better care of those poor beasts." Linwood dropped a small white object into each of our pairs of cupped hands.

"A tooth?" June held hers up.

Mine was a small triangle, very white, and hot. Hot? Not heat-hot. Instead, it emitted a radiation of sorts. *More power,* a voice whispered from nowhere.

"Those are alligator teeth," Linwood said.

"Oh, great!" Stan exhaled loudly through his nose.

"And I want you to use them to make wishes on. If you ever see an animal in pain again, or if you find yourself thinking about the poor creatures we just saw, I want you to hold the tooth and wish that their pain will be healed."

"Tonight," said Stan, "I'm reporting that bastard to the SPCA. That's the only wishing that'll work around here."

I turned and stared out the back window. If I'd had the book, would Sammy have been there? Did I need more money too? Or was it possible that expecting him kept him away?

CHAPTER NINE

June and I were busily making Pilgrim hats in the backseat. We were in Alabama somewhere, and Stan claimed only two more days to Miami. I was cutting out the shapes: circles of brown cardboard for the top, larger circles with that hole missing (you had to fold the cardboard; June wouldn't allow a slit) for the brims, and strips to support the space between the brims and the tops. June was on stapler detail. She had a definite way with these things.

Linwood fooled with the radio until she got the news, a Florida station. A balmy eighty degrees in Miami!

"The poodles will swelter in these costumes," June muttered. Always the traditionalist, she'd like us to sit on Plymouth Rock while we ate our turkey.

Stan was trying to sing something, even after all the times Linwood had tormented him about his voice.

"I'm trying to hear the news."

He went on singing, so she shut off the radio.

I cut out another circle and brim. "How many more?"

June did a quick head count. "Seventeen."

Linwood turned around. "Why do you have their pillows out like that?"

I kept my head down. My cheeks grew hot.

"They like to sleep while they're riding in the car." June was cool as sherbet. "It's so boring and tiring for them. They're used to playing outside and seeing their friends."

"What other friends do they have besides each other?"

What Linwood was getting at was that June didn't have any friends. I mean, every now and then she caught one, but she scared her away almost instantly.

"How would you know?"

Linwood turned back around, restless. She thumbed through an old magazine, threw it on the floor, lit a cigarette.

"Do you think we should call her tonight?" Stan seemed to know what the problem was.

June and I froze, soundless. It was beneath our collective dignity to ask about Deane, but that didn't mean we didn't want to know what was going on.

"I'd like to," Linwood pleaded.

Why did they have to be so caught up in *her* always? We were here. They never agonized about us like that.

Stan sighed. "She won't be any better."

"You don't know that."

"But I can make an educated guess, can't I? Unless they move the court date."

"When *is* the court date?" I had such a big mouth.

"We'll discuss this later," Stan said.

"As if I'd brought it up," Linwood said.

"I didn't say that."

"Well, you implied—"

Oh, just shut up! I felt vicious, the thoughts screaming in my head. It was like cabin fever in an automobile. I wanted everybody dead, but the instant that thought wheeled into my mind, I wheeled it right out again. I really wanted . . . what? I really wanted to stop making these stupid Pilgrim hats, for one thing.

Out the window was green grass, green trees, an occasional white farmhouse with a car or two in front. The way you could tell it was cold out there was that bruised color to the sky. That, and the shade of green, not the blinding vibrant one of summer but the resigned shade of autumn.

"Keep cutting."

"Yassah, boss-ma'am. I'sa gwine keep cuttin' dem hats, awrite."

June punched me on the bruise, but at least I got a chuckle out of the front seat.

"Let's stop there," said Linwood.

A bright pink billboard announced cactus candy, cold lemonade, and "the world's cleanest restrooms."

"Not much cactus around here," Stan observed.

Running Redskin's was the name of the curio shop, and it was twelve or so miles away. That gave me time to cut out at least six more hats. But what I wanted to do was watch the billboards, to see if Sammy might be there. This time I'd be prepared: my pockets contained poodle toys and money, and, burning against my thigh, the book.

Every mile or so, another billboard appeared, but food seemed to be the main order of business. Coney Island hot dogs, homemade apple pie (like "Mom's"—except Linwood wouldn't have baked an apple pie if her life depended on it), frosty old-fashioned root beer, on and on. I hadn't been hungry when the signs began, and now I felt a little sick.

Then, when I was resigning myself, came a new enticement:

> HUMONGOUS HANNAH
> WORLD'S STRONGEST FEMALE
> SEE HER LIFT 1000 POUNDS!
> ICE COLD LEMONADE, ETC.

"That's half a ton," said June.

Half a ton sounded like even more than a thousand pounds. How could anyone, a woman, lift that much weight? "Maybe she weighs a thousand pounds herself," I said stupidly.

"Like you," said June.

"I don't either!" Usually this conversation didn't bother me, but, like I said, my nerves were frayed.

"Close to it, Fatty."

"Linwood," I said, clutching the back of the front seat, "tell June I'm not fat!"

"Goddammit!" said Stan. "How many times do I have

to tell you not to hit the seat when I'm driving?"

"Fatty," said June. "Lean on the seat and you break it!"

"I'M NOT FAT!" I wailed.

"Absolute silence," Linwood said. "Total silence for fifteen minutes or no allowance and no sweets this week. Do I make myself clear?"

"Are we stopping at Running Redskin's?" June demanded.

"Yes, if you shut up."

Totally silent, afraid to breathe—had I gone too far?—I snipped away at my hats. Deep shame. Shouting and shoving and evil thoughts. No wonder Sammy had abandoned me.

I glanced out the window and watched the network of electric poles, mean cats' heads, strung on silver up to the sky.

We only passed one more sign for Running Redskin's: no Hannah, only creamy fudge. June poked me in the side and mouthed "Fatty," but I kept my dignity. And, even when the fifteen minutes had passed, we were both wise enough to maintain our silence until Stan was pulling the car into the parking lot.

Two enormous plywood figures dominated the front of what was only a small, concrete building. The figures towered at least three stories high: the wily Redskin and the resplendent Hannah. When you first saw them, they were as impressive as cartoon gods—his blue and yellow loincloth, his feathered headdress; her pink and green polka-dot bikini, the flowing mane of platinum hair. But also their bodies were godlike, his sleek and linear, a runner this Indian, and hers all curve and muscle bulge. Slave bracelets on her upper arms emphasized the power of her biceps. Her thighs reminded you of Paul Bunyan, of Viking legends. Stan snorted when he saw them; June and Linwood laughed.

But I wanted to cry. Okay, she was silly, but that's who I wanted to be. A woman like that: she had *power*. She could protect people. This was what Sally the Snake Queen intended to be, and failed so dreadfully. Could I ever grow up to look like that, with my slight build and my hair, thin as water and brown as mud?

Stan opened his door and I weaseled out of the backseat.

"I'll meet you inside," I called over my shoulder. They probably thought I had to use the ladies' room. But what I wanted was to see Hannah before they all had a chance to make fun of her. I had a mission, and this time it was all for me.

Inside was nothing special, just a long lunch counter and the usual rows of dusty trinkets. Where did they keep the world's strongest woman? Behind the counter, a redhead in a bowling shirt (MOLLY) was reading a movie magazine.

"Excuse me," I said. "Where's Hannah?"

Her eyes lifted from the movie magazine in surprise.

"You know, *Hannah*. Who lifts a thousand pounds."

"Why, out back," the woman said. Then she winked.

I raced out back at the same time I heard my family walk in the front door. But outside was nothing except a kind of stable. Inside the stable was a scruffy old mule.

I ran back inside. The woman was reading once again.

"All I see is a mule."

"That's Hannah," said the woman. "And she's carried a thousand pounds before."

I merely looked at her.

She looked right back: in her stare there was both sympathy and daring. My mouth opened and I meant to say that I was angry, I had been tricked, I would make a citizen's arrest for false advertising, but nothing came out. My mouth slammed shut like a trapdoor.

The woman nodded sagely. Her eyes were the no-color of ice. "The sign didn't say Hannah was human." Her voice turned kind. "It's a sort of a joke."

But not my kind of joke. "Then who's the lady out front?"

"Lady out front?" She shrugged. "Why, it's nobody. It's just a pitcher."

"But—" What was the use? "Well, who painted it?"

She shrugged again, and her face looked a little older.

"Guy name of Fred? He does all the billboard stuff around here."

"Did he have a model or anything?"

"Honey, forget it," said the woman, losing patience. "It's just a pitcher. It ain't alive."

Ka-boom! Stan put his hands on my shoulders. This gesture was meant to look friendly but felt like the yoke of doom. "Leave the lady alone, Pet."

"Hannah's a mule!"

"So what?" He tightened his hands around my neck. "You and June can each pick out whatever you like, as long as it's under two dollars."

I couldn't quite give it up. I sensed it was hopeless, but I still couldn't quite give it up. "Is there any woman in the world who can lift a thousand pounds?" I asked the two adults.

"Your mother," said Stan. The woman laughed.

But even as we drove away, and I realized that once more Sammy had failed me (though to be frank, it didn't seem like his sort of place), or I had failed him by expecting him, or simply failed because I was a child, without power, and couldn't understand, I stared out the back window at Hannah in her pink and green polka-dot bikini, white-blond hair wafting around her powerful chest and shoulders, and I *knew* she was around somewhere. Maybe not there, maybe not then, but she damn well existed.

"Piece of fudge?" June offered her box.

"No, thanks."

She looked relieved.

I opened up the bag with my trinket. It was a copper bracelet, a big one. I pulled up the sleeve of my sweater and fastened it to my upper arm, the left one in hopes that June wouldn't see me. Furtively, I raised my arm muscle-man style. Wasn't that just the barest bulge of a biceps?

"You won't believe what Pet's doing!"

Linwood whipped her head around, so fast I didn't have a chance to resume a normal posture.

"Honey," she was trying not to laugh, "what's all that?"

Talk about feeling like a dope. Coolly, I rolled the sleeve down over my bracelet, crossed my arms, and stared out the window. Green trees and more green trees.

"She thinks she's that Amazon on the billboard."

The front seat snickered.

I wasn't going to cry. I felt the warmth of my new bracelet spreading energy through my upper arm. I should have gotten two. But never mind. This was only one more thing nobody understood.

June beat her chest and yodeled. "Me Tarzan," she said. "You Fatso."

But out in the greeny woods I thought I saw the shadow of a great big woman, climbing the trees as easily as pie, her broad back fit to carry the weight of the world.

CHAPTER TEN

"What do you girls think about spending Christmas in New Orleans?" Stan asked.

We'd both been asleep in the back seat. It was late afternoon somewhere in Florida. The sky was all light blue and the palm trees had squirrel-colored stalks and dusty green fronds, but you could still tell it was winter. The ocean looked sort of lonely.

Miami at Thanksgiving had been kind of neat and kind of odd. The wind always blew, like the breath of South America calling you down, and everybody walked around in Hawaiian shirts. Stan and Linwood had been dead set on Cuban food, but it turned out to be like Mexican only beanier. Except for the fried plantains. Nobody but me liked them, so that's what I had for

Thanksgiving dinner. I let June eat the whole rest of my meal, including the mango ice cream.

"Christmas in New Orleans!" Linwood echoed Stan, sounding surprised and delighted, though no doubt it had been her idea in the first place. Stan wouldn't dare make something like that up all by himself.

Funny, I had this bad feeling about New Orleans. Why? I'd certainly loved it last summer.

"What about *snow*?" June had been making this point for weeks. She wanted one of those old-fashioned sleigh-ride holidays.

"Children." Linwood used her Hollywood voice. "They're the most conventional people in the world, don't you think, Stan?"

I looked out the window. We were driving up the east coast, along the beach. The sign said twelve miles to Daytona. A man in blue jeans was walking five tiny French poodles, which had been dyed, I guess, all different pastel colors: they looked like one of those special desserts, five different flavors of sherbet. I nudged June but she ignored me.

"What's wrong with that?" she asked. "What's wrong with wanting to be normal? Why can't we ever, ever be like other families?"

"When you grow up," Linwood said coldly, "you will be surprised to discover that there is no such thing as 'normal.'"

Was that true? Gaylin's family seemed exactly like the people on television: they didn't have expensive stuff around their house like we did, but they always had lots of regular food in their refrigerator. For instance, Mrs. Rezek let Gaylin eat cookies and cake for dessert, instead of fruit and cheese like we did. We even had wine. Linwood would give us tiny glasses of sweet sherry because, she said, that's what children drank in Europe. And sometimes there wasn't any actual food in the house at all. Linwood hadn't felt like shopping or cooking, so we'd eat out every day until that phase passed and another began. Also, obviously, other children generally called their parents "Mom" and "Dad."

"Not in this family, that's for sure."

"Very well," said Linwood, fitting one of her new cigars into the rhinestone holder. "I suppose you'd all like me to be exactly like that dreadful Mrs. Nutter everyone's so wild about."

Mrs. Nutter had been June's 4-H leader, and a drabber, better-natured woman didn't exist in the world. She smelled of flour, and her stomach was soft like stuffed animals. Pole, that is, not the poodles.

"I suppose you'd like to move up to one of those remote villages in New England and sit around singing hymns and making ornaments out of apricot pits or whatever."

Stan sighed, right on cue.

"And that's just fine with me." The cloud of smoke she exhaled hung around her head. Alice's Caterpillar. "Far be it from me to try to make you girls into interesting human beings. The world is rife with mediocrity, and it can always use plenty more Mrs. Nutters."

"What's wrong with Mrs. Nutter?" June demanded. "Why does everybody always make fun of what I do? Nobody ever makes fun of Pet—"

Ha.

"—I suppose it isn't stupid for her to take those tap-dancing lessons? And ballet and acrobatics and *Hawaiian*, for God's sake!"

"Goddammit, don't swear!" said Stan.

I felt a real pang, thinking how much I missed those classes. Not that I was any good. I only won that talent contest with cuteness and spunk. Plus, adults like to see kids making total fools of themselves.

"*EVERYTHING I DO YOU MAKE FUN OF!*" June started in with the shriek and the wail. She hadn't had a major fit in a long time.

I looked out the window again: a pink stucco house, with a tile roof and big pots full of geraniums, right on the water's edge. A young girl, her brown legs sticking out of perfectly faded blue jean cut-offs, was pinning a few pieces of fluffy white laundry to the clothesline. Her blond hair hung down her back like a sheaf of wheat.

I wondered where I could buy some hair dye. What

would they do if my hair was bleached to look like Hannah's? Shave my head? No one had seen Linwood's real color in years. I never had. But then I remembered that dyeing her hair had been one of the things that upset Linwood the worst about Deane.

Deane, darn old Deane. Everything revolved around her, even though she wasn't there. If nothing changed, she'd be like this great big tree hovering over the landscape of our lives. Everything we did or didn't do would get measured against her shadow.

"And Deane," said June, as if reading my thoughts. "You're so wrapped up in her, you're so worried about Deane. You spend all that money on clothes and records, and she's no better than a convict!"

No response from the front seat. Apparently, Stan and Linwood were going for Freeze Her Out, the stance they adopted when they hadn't the inclination or the energy to out-yell her. Casually, they both scanned the landscape, shoulders relaxed, as uninvolved with June's ranting as with the upholstery of the car or the signs we passed advertising Wonder Bread.

"How much farther to Saint Augustine?" Linwood inquired pleasantly.

"Thirty-five minutes, hon."

"What about the golf clubs you said I could have on my twelfth birthday?" June insisted. "The archery set? What about how you said I could redecorate my room? A new carpet? Bedspreads?"

I decided to stop listening, watch the ocean and detach myself from my surroundings, exert an invisible control over my natural environment. Lately, I'd been getting these peculiar thoughts about the way in which the world worked, things it seemed I hadn't made up by myself, and I hadn't read them. Maybe they came to me in my dreams? Every now and then, one of these tidbits would pop into my head, like: *Show your own energy by holding your hand like a goblet in front of you.* Things like that.

The ocean looked solid, metallic. I missed the way the sun would not set beneath it, as it did in California, but only reflect a faint rosy glow from the other side of

the sky. The beach itself was visible from time to time
through clumps of palmetto and sea oats. The sand was
white, holy, untouched by human feet, or so you wanted
to imagine. But every now and then you saw a woman
and two black dogs bounding into the waves like big
rubber balls; or a father and his twin daughters, tiny,
their chubby knees scarcely able to support them. They
held hands, for balance.

Then, for a few minutes, the scrub brush opened up,
and there was a vast stretch of sand with nobody on it.
You wanted to lie right down and go to sleep in the final
bit of sunlight.

But then I blinked and there was somebody on it.
How could I have missed her? She was dressed in red
and purple robes, and a shiny gold sun, moon, and
stars glimmered from the back of her outermost cape.
Raven hair, flashing like glass in the last of the light,
shot out from her head in a tangled vine. A small dog
followed along beside her, its neck decorated with an
orange and green ruffle, except that as I watched, I saw
it wasn't a dog—it was a cat, a white Persian cat, her tail
as fluffy and upright as sea oats. Lately, I'd seen all
kinds of things.

"I . . . WANT . . . SNOW!" June was winding down,
her voice desperate and sore, and at these moments
you had to feel sorry for her, for how much she exhausted
herself.

But I had lost my focus. The woman and the cat were
gone. Were they ever there? Automatically, I felt for
the clumps of poodle toys in the coat draped over my
knees, for protection.

"Ha," said Stan.

The sign for the Holiday Inn had appeared.

"The girls can get a swim before dark," he pointed
out.

"I hear my scotch calling me," Linwood concurred
gaily.

They were always so happy to reach the end of the
day. You wondered why we stayed on the road if they
were always so anxious to find a comfortable harbor. We
didn't have to get up the next morning and go any-

where, but we would. Then, when the day wound down into twilight, they would sigh with relief, as always, as if they had accomplished something.

I was a child, and I didn't understand the principle of staying in motion.

"The Fountain of Youth is in Saint Augustine," Stan said.

Understandably, this attraction didn't hold much appeal for me and June.

"I better buy a gallon," said Linwood.

"Hell," said Stan. "You still don't look a day over thirty."

Linwood smiled. "Oh, honestly," she said.

"I'm being honest." Stan clicked his ring on the steering wheel, he was so delighted he had pleased her. But—and this was such a regular occurrence you could practically tell time by it—he would go on and on, go overboard, until his exaggeration had succeeded in irritating her again. You'd think after all those years, he'd understand her a little better. "Twenty-five," he amended.

Linwood gazed out the window. There were scattered houses, the first motels in the town: Sea Breeze, Ocean View, The Vagabond.

"Twenty-two." There he went.

I would have kicked him under the seat except he would have ignored me, definitely.

"Twenty-two—if you'd let your hair go natural. Wear it long again."

Linwood sat bolt upright, as if injected with a shot of helium. "Good God!" she said. "What on earth do you think you know about how I should look? Men! They get these sentimental notions about 'long hair'—probably from some damn Bing Crosby song—and that's that! No eyes in your head, just these half-baked notions of what you *sentimentally* think women should—"

"Ripley's Believe It or Not!" shouted June, recovered from her sulk.

Sure enough. A lurid yellow billboard advised us that the Ripley's Believe It or Not Museum was in Saint

Augustine, right smack across from the Fountain of
Youth.

I got the cold creeps just thinking about it. June
always bought the books, reading outloud the parts about
two-headed sheep who lived longer than real sheep, or
precise replications of pre-Revolutionary Paris, constructed
entirely from swizzle sticks provided by Harrod's—"Reno
or Bust!"—in Nevada. Naturally, the man who had built
the model had also consumed the drink that went with
each swizzle stick.

"Listen to this!" she'd say, and I'd get queasy even
before she read it, from the ugly look of the book and
the cheap quality of the paper. It smelled funny.

Actually, her attitude toward Ripley-type feats was
totally in accord with her attitude toward the encyclo-
pedias. The sensational. What she loved was that a
billion meant dollar bills placed end to end, stretching
four and a half times around the earth at the equator.

"We have to go!" June was even more worked up
than usual. "Can we go tonight?"

Please no.

"I'm sure it isn't open at night, June." Stan's voice
had a steady, even tone. Although she was behaving
again, she was still, as they say, at a combustible
temperature.

"What if it was?"

"Well, then . . ."

"Oh boy!"

We passed a billboard that was delighted to inform us
the museum would be open until nine every night,
in honor of the holiday season.

"You can take them," Linwood said. Her tone of
voice clearly indicated her position on the subject.

"Actually," I began. But then I stopped; my mouth
snapped shut with sudden force, like a Chatty Cathy
doll's.

I had to go.

Destiny, in the form of Sammy, could be knocking
one more time. There was always the chance.

"Actually what, Pet?" Linwood turned around. Her
lovely face looked concerned.

Had my voice given me away? "Actually, that sounds like a lot of fun."

Linwood watched me for another moment, then turned back.

My chest felt heavy. I didn't want to think about any of that stuff, but where was the choice?

"We need to take the poodles in tonight," I told June. "I want to check through their bags."

CHAPTER ELEVEN

Stan dropped us off after dinner, right at the entrance. After double-checking the price of admission, he'd given us each an extra dollar. Of course, he didn't know that we had quite a bit of money with us, mine cumbersome in the underwear pockets beneath my armpits, crowding the poodle toys and the magic book. June brought her money hoping that she could buy Stan and Linwood something really gross for Christmas so she could get to keep it herself.

I stood on the heavy stone steps a moment, watching Stan pull away in the pale blue T-bird. He said he was going Christmas shopping and would pick us up at nine, when the museum closed. The car tooled off into the flamingo streaks of sunset.

June was already inside the huge stone mansion. You could tell from the outside that the inside was monstrous: odd rooms and towers and staircases that led up to nothing. Fifth-floor doors that opened onto mysterious drops. Perhaps the grisly Mr. Ripley had spent his last days here, exhausted from his cross-continental travails, aged, with his last breaths, hobbling from room to room to survey the masses of weirdness he'd accumulated at what risk to his personal psyche. *Whoever has the most things when he dies wins*. Maybe he was right—maybe it depended on *which things*.

I shrugged and went inside anyway. No choice.

Was Sammy somewhere here, waiting?

"Speed it up, Lard Bucket!" June yelled from the other side of the ticket counter.

I counted out my three dollars and crossed over. No one but us seemed to be going in tonight. Perhaps this was not the right kind of festivity for the season.

June pointed to the map, prominent at the base of an enormous, curving marble staircase. "It's by country," she informed me. "Not by type."

No comment.

"And the best thing is this." June opened up the brochure that they gave you with the ticket. I'd already dropped mine. Inside was a picture of a grinning short man next to a glittering mass. The caption read: JOSEPH VON SCHMULO AND HIS CITY OF ANCIENT ROME, OVER FORTY YEARS IN THE MAKING, CONSTRUCTED ENTIRELY FROM THE PARTS OF BROKEN FOUNTAIN PENS.

Still no comment.

June shrugged. She knew I had no taste. "Okay. Here's what you have to do—" She pointed at the map again.

I could never read maps. I'd wait until she was out of sight and then go ask the people at the information desk.

"You cover the South Seas, the Far East, and Africa. I'm going to do Europe, Russia, and North America."

It sounded like one of our interminable games of Risk.

"What about South America and Antarctica?"

June squinted at the map. "You'll pass through them on your way. What you have to do is make sure I'm not missing anything. We'll meet back here at eight-thirty, and if there's anything special, I'll have time to go see it." She was really excited. Her eyes shone behind her glasses, and her smile was genuinely pretty.

I smiled back. Even if this wasn't my cup of tea, I was glad to see her so happy. "That sounds fair."

She grabbed me by the shoulders and pointed me in the direction she wanted me to go. "You know the kind of stuff I like!" With a gentle shove, we were both off.

As soon as I rounded the curve of the winding hallway, I stopped. After a few minutes, sure the coast was clear, I backtracked to the information booth. June was long gone to the fountain pen Rome.

"Which way to the South Seas?" I asked.

The woman behind the counter had silvery hair that parted like stage curtains. "It's in the annex," she said, pointing in the same direction June had pointed me in. "You have to walk all the way down the hallway until it becomes a tunnel, and then you follow it until it rises up again, and then you go down into the basement, and that's the South Seas."

"Thank you." I started off.

"Little girl?"

I turned back.

"Do you want me to check that coat for you? It looks so heavy."

"Oh, no," I said, feeling a light sweat break out on my forehead. "It's so chilly in here. But thank you."

The hallway, once I rounded the various beginning turns, was immensely long, like the voyage into the underworld that had been so tough on Orpheus or the distance they always had to travel in fairy tales, East of the Sun and West of the Moon. No one else was around at all, and the air smelled musty, as if no one had been breathing it for a while. My Keds made no sound on the shiny linoleum.

The walls were decorated with various posters from around the world. They looked like circus posters, in all kinds of foreign languages. Except not regular circuses, of course.

Chinese flea circuses, Spanish freak shows. The posters had that lurid look Ripley seemed so keen on. You saw armless people smoking cigarettes with their toes. Not the happiest sort of decoration on an isolated December evening.

And the hallway began to slope down. This must be the tunnel to the adjacent mansion.

The skin over my stomach tingled, as if spiders were dancing across it.

In a few minutes, a few more steps down the tunnel, I would be okay. I wasn't going to be scared. I was going to be free, instead.

But I wasn't prepared for the sight that greeted me in the room the tunnel emerged into.

What were those things? Carvings? Statues? They were as tall as a three-story building, taller than Hannah, and they loomed above me, great skinny totem poles. But all weird and lacy, as if wood had been turned into cloth and then into leaves or webs. Figures with lanky legs and spindly knees balanced on the heads of other figures, and the guy on the very top, at least on the pole closest to me, held out a mysterious triangle, oddly protruding from between his legs, and it was carved with curliques and whirligigs and slithery little animals gnawing furiously at their own tails.

I walked around the towering figure next to me and stared at what was on the ground. Canoes, every bit as long as the several dozen figures were tall. They were carved to resemble enormous lean alligators, lizards, dragons, crocodiles, and carved men sat inside, with extra spaces beside them for the "real men." Were they meant to sail on regular water?

What an enormous dusty room, an airplane hangar as still as a closed book, but with that about-to-wake-up quality that lifelike dolls have. Any minute, I figured, one of these statues would creak to life, like the Tin Woodsman after oiling.

Or, Sammy might pop out. I adjusted the unpleasantly heavy bags. The poodle toys gave off a pleasant energy, but that energy was somehow blocked.

Stupid money. I waited.

Nothing happened, and then I began to adjust to the carvings' sleeping presence. It was peaceful, soothing, and my eyelids grew heavier, like the bags.

To keep awake, I walked over to the far wall and read the sign, moving as slowly and carefully as I would in a library or a church.

SOUL SHIPS

Soul Ships resemble dug-out canoes of normal size, complete with carved prows, but are made *without bottoms*!

I glanced back at the boats. Sure enough, no bottoms. Perhaps that was the strangeness.

Soul Ships are used in ceremonies to expel the souls of recently dead people, and in coming-of-age ceremonies: young boys are scarified *while floating in the canoe*!

Well, big deal. I was scared looking at those bottomless boats. No doubt it was much scarier riding inside.

These canoes are considered the medium for passing from this world to the supernatural!
BELIEVE IT OR NOT!

What wasn't to believe? They looked the natural vehicle. No one else was around, seemed like no one else ever would be around, so I went ahead and climbed into one of the Soul Ships. Maybe this was the way to find Sammy. Actually, it was pretty comfortable, the alligator. And I wasn't afraid. All I felt was this deep, sweet urge to let go and give up, float on away into the air.

CHAPTER TWELVE

The jingling sound I took to be Stan clicking his ring on the steering wheel. We were in motion, always in motion, across the endless pancake of land.

But when my eyes squinted open, I realized that I was not sitting in the backseat of the car or in any car at all. The bottomless boats, the dusty statues of the

museum—it all flashed clear except that I'd been asleep.
And the jingling sound.

"Sammy?"

"Who's there?" called a gruff male voice. Footsteps
jingled closer.

I pried myself from my position, a fetal curl inside
the Soul Ship.

"Miss," said the guard, hovering over me. "We closed
an hour ago."

I swallowed. My throat felt ragged and dry. "Is it
nine o'clock yet?"

The guard, an old man with a dark, sad face, scrunched
his white brows together. "I told you," he said. "We
closed at nine. It's almost ten-thirty now."

June would kill me. But, I wondered as my limbs
stretched out and I climbed free of the boat, why hadn't
anyone come looking for me?

"You go on out the way you came," the guard
recommended, not unkindly. "A lady there'll let you out
the door."

Back down the tunnel, my mind was still groggy. A
flash of something—what was that, a dream? This amazing woman decked out in layers and layers of clothing,
all covered with objects, tiny dolls and glass beads, her
face was cloudy, but it was . . . Deane! Deane? Deane
wasn't an old lady, she was a kid.

And this was funny too. My shoulders were aching, as
if I'd lifted something heavy. Another dream, and I was
all grown up, pulling a bar loaded with weights from
the ground up to knee level. Why would I do that?

Besides, my shoulders hurt because I was carrying all
this *stuff*.

I knew it was right to carry the poodle toys, and the
magic book, though I could never open it again, had to
be on me to be sold, but maybe my big mistake was the
money. Ever since I'd stolen the money, no Sammy.

The same old circus posters in the passageway, only now
they didn't seem strange or scary. Only useless and old.

Cold sweat began to bead on my forehead. What
if—what if my theft had driven Sammy away? Then the
death of my family would be all my fault!

My stomach roiled up with guilt. Strong and powerful as I felt, I knew nothing at all, really, about the
world of magic.

Then, for some vague reason, I had this strong sense
about New Orleans. Maybe I could buy my own charms,
my own amulets.

Didn't they have voodoo shops in New Orleans?

The next thought after that was too horrible. *Don't
farewell, fare forward.*

At the entrance, the information lady was waiting for
me. "There you are," she said. "Your sister's waiting for
you." She turned the key and I walked out into the
cool, damp night.

June was all huddled on the steps, a forlorn ball of
misery.

"I'm sorry," I said.

She looked over. "At least *you* showed up."

The mourning wasn't for me; my automatic guilt
rolled away like a backpack with a broken strap. "Where's
Stan?"

The streetlights were bright. You could tell she'd
been crying. "I don't know! And where were you,
anyway? I thought you went back to the motel without
me."

I sat down beside her on the steps. The granite was
cold through my pants and coat. "I wouldn't leave you.
I went to the South Seas, like you said, and there were
these huge boats...I guess I fell asleep. I had the
weirdest dreams! I dreamt Deane—"

"There's no answer at the motel," June said. "Do you
think they ran away?"

Such a picture wouldn't materialize. "Maybe separately,
but not together."

"You've got a point."

June pulled her coat tighter around. A wind was
picking up off the ocean, which we could see glimmer-
ing in the moonlight, right past the palm trees. The
view was really fine. The dark, the breeze, the water.

Those canoes gliding off into the swamps, transporting the souls of the dead.

"What're we going to do?" In situations like this, it was better to be the little sister.

"We'll walk back," June announced. Her voice was filled with confidence again, now that she had her troops to order.

"Okay."

We marched down the stairs, full of purpose and direction.

"It's about five miles," June said. "We've walked that far before. Remember last year when we snuck out at Aunt Edith's?"

"The good vending machine?"

"That was over three miles each way. From the Mission Beach pier to the Pacific Beach pier."

Aunt Edith had been more angry at what she perceived as our lying—that we had walked so far, even that we'd been able to find our way to the drugstore with the good vending machine—than at our disappearing during "nap time." Nap time was what relatives made up when they tired of taking care of you.

The beach air and the late hour, reminding me of grunion runs, suffused me with sweet homesickness. "Remember Moni?" I asked.

Brad and Kirk, our cousins, were Aunt Edith's sons. Brad was only a month younger than I, but he already had a surf board, which he stretched between his twin beds and slept on at night, complete with blanket and pillow. I'd always called him Bread, because he was nice and squishy like a loaf of Wonder. Kirk, though, was a whole other story. He was a year older than Deane—seventeen—and he never wore shoes. Moni, his girlfriend, didn't either. Kirk had his hair in a blond ducktail and he smoked cigarettes like someone in the movies. Moni wore her hair with the top part teased up in a beehive and the bottom part hanging down, like Kim Novak in *Bell, Book, and Candle*. Deane said that Moni was a goody-goody, but everyone else said she was cheap. You could tell Aunt Edith wasn't too keen

on her, just by the tone of voice when she offered
potato chips or Cokes.

"White jeans," said June.

Kirk and Moni liked to wear tight white jeans with
their bare feet.

"I wish we'd move to the beach," I said. "Any beach."

We rounded the corner of the cobbled street we'd
been walking on. There was no traffic in sight, though
you could hear it whooshing nearby. An old fort stood
elegant in the moonlight. The give and take of the
waves was soothing.

"I'd like to ride a horse on the beach."

"Or run with a big dog." I'd like to have one of those
furry white ones, the kind that pulls sleds. "Maybe
we'll move here."

Then we'd never go to New Orleans.

"Maybe we've been left here." June dug her hands
into her coat pockets.

My stomach queased. "Do you think they found out
about the money?"

"I don't know." June's voice indicated that was exactly
what she did think.

Maybe when we got back to the motel, Stan and
Linwood would be long gone, and the police would be
waiting instead.

Or maybe they'd decided to turn us in, in trade for
Deane. Two little ones for a big one...

"June?" My heart was really pounding. "What if they
liked Deane so much more that—"

"There's the car!" June shouted.

Sure enough, there was our car, pulled halfway off
the road. Stan's form slumped over the wheel.

"He's dead!" I cried. But it didn't seem very real.

June was already running toward the car. I ran after,
our footsteps crying out on the concrete.

She sure could run. The bags of money pounded
painfully against my chest. "Stan!" she shouted.

I kept running, running, the heavy bags beating with
each stride.

"Pet!" she yelled. "He's drunk!"

Abruptly, my feet stopped. When I looked up, the car was only ten feet away.

June stood to one side, under the streetlamp. Her arms were akimbo, and her face was set in a perfect mask of indignation and disapproval. And rage. You didn't want that face mad at you.

He was drunk, all right. A loud, contented snoring issued from his slumped shape, arms hugging the steering wheel, face pressed into the spokes. The bourbon fumes were impressive.

I shook his shoulder. "Stan?"

"Wazzat?" He jerked upright a moment and then collapsed again.

"Now what?"

June shrugged. "Let's go back to the motel."

"And leave him like this?"

"Why not? He left us." She was strictly Old Testament.

I looked around. A phone booth gleamed about half a block away. "We should call the motel."

June shrugged again but handed me the matchbook with the telephone number.

The desk rang Stan and Linwood's room. The phone was picked up on the ninth ring.

"Yes?" Linwood's voice was sobbing.

"This is Pet. We're—"

"Honey, are you okay?" She could barely get the words out.

"I'm fine, but—"

"Is June all right?"

"She's fine, but—"

"Oh, honey, isn't it terrible!" Her voice choked on hiccups and tears.

"Stan's not *that* drunk," I lied.

"Our beautiful house," Linwood moaned. "My paintings! Nana's wedding veil. Your baby books."

A terrible cold chill racked my body. "What do you mean?"

"Didn't Stan tell you?"

I couldn't breathe.

"Oh, honey!" Linwood was choking again. "Our house! They burned our house down!"

All I could see was Roberta, her beautiful body melting in the flames.

"Everything's gone," she said.

"But who . . ."

"Those boys did it! Those terrible boys who ruined Deane!"

Tommy.

"Her trial . . ." Linwood trailed off. "It was sort of a warning."

June wasn't going to take this very well. I wasn't taking this very well. "Look," I said, suddenly as clear as a piece of Saran Wrap. "We're stuck up here and Stan's too drunk to drive."

"Very well," said Linwood. "You girls stay right there. I'm calling the police."

CHAPTER THIRTEEN

Outside of Mobile, on the old road along the Gulf, you really begin to feel you're on your way to New Orleans. All those enormous houses, white columns, and golf course lawns. And the peaceful, disinterested water to your left. No waves, no noise, only flat glimmer.

A grim Linwood was at the wheel. Stan, whose license had been suspended, was snoozing away in the passenger seat.

Christmas was the day after tomorrow, but nobody had bought any presents yet. The idea was that we'd all go shopping tomorrow in the Quarter, but I wondered. It was as if we were complete strangers, bound together on this journey by an odd twist of fate.

"Look," said June.

A couple of boys in black rubber wet suits were trying to ride what passed for waves, little ripples. Bread would get a good laugh over that. He had pictures of those real surfers in Hawaii, their boards sliding diagonally down what looked like mountains of water. That's the way the world would end: wiped out from ocean to bay by the great looming giant of a wave.

Only 156 miles to New Orleans. We'd only been there in the summer, it was such a warm-weather city. Even now when I could see the cold wind blowing the trees, I assumed it would be hot in New Orleans. Balmy air, lazy sound of insects. The mosquito trucks would glide up and down the streets at night, spraying their smoky odors.

The French Quarter was the best. The painters at their easels around Jackson Square (though Linwood sneered at what they did, calling it "craft" rather than art) wearing berets and blue jeans with splotches of color. In the center of the square were sheaves of flowers, pink and yellow and red. Farther down was the coffee place and the thick warm doughnuts covered with powdered sugar, like the talcum powder you pour over yourself after a bath. (Maybe I used too much? When I got talcum for my birthday, it never seemed to last very long. I wanted to make my skin white so I'd look Japanese.)

The doughnuts were great, but so was the just-sitting-there, watching how bright and lively everyone was. Linwood would smile and turn her sunglasses toward the light. She liked to explain how black people were the prettiest, the gleam of their skin, the firm line of their bones. When she'd started sculpting a few months ago (everything destroyed now), it looked like that's who she wanted to shape. Always her ideas were so much larger and grander than real people. The men were warriors, the women were curvaceous and fruity, like Betty and Veronica in the *Archie* comic books. There was no way I'd ever look like that. Even Deane, who seemed to have a lot going on in the breast department, routinely stuffed Kleenex in her bra.

Linwood had showed me once how men could be drawn as a series of triangles and women as a series of circles. Even then, I knew my body would be straight lines all the way.

"I sure wish we were going somewhere else." June's sigh was profound.

"Me too."

"Pet?" Linwood was surprised. "I thought you liked New Orleans."

Jackson Square, the smell of coffee and doughnuts, and the women sashayed by, orange bandannas over copper skin, turquoise skirts, red and yellow blouses. "I do, but I have this, uh, bad feeling."

"What kind of bad feeling?"

All I could see when I thought of New Orleans was this big red schmear all over everything. But who knew?

"Fatso has dreams," said June. "Even when she's awake!"

Where did that come from?

"Let's all have an awake-dream," said Linwood. "I'll start. I see us . . . oh, sailing off on a boat. . . ."

Stan was wearing a jaunty nautical cap, Linwood sprawled on deck in a flowered bikini. June was fishing. They were all neatly tanned, waving, waving to whoever had come to see them off. The sun hot and calm, they were about to sail away . . . forever. The bright white of the sky was like a Band-Aid over everything that had happened before.

But where was I?

"No," said June. "No boat! How about just a regular house . . ."

They were all in the backyard barbecuing hamburgers on one of those big round grills. Stan was wearing a jaunty chef's hat and a silly apron. Linwood reclined in a chaise-longue, a frosted drink poised in her beautifully manicured hands. June was on the lawn, playing in a sprinkler, and she was much younger, maybe four or five.

No me again.

"A 'regular' house?" Hurt in every syllable. "What was wrong with the house you grew up in, now that it's gone?"

"The Buddha, for one thing."

"My glorious Buddha!" Linwood was trying not to cry. "That's a very Zen way of going, though, fire."

"Regular people don't have Buddhas and they don't talk about 'Zen' and they don't have witches for sisters."

"Don't exaggerate," said Linwood. "Deane may have her problems, but there's nothing wrong with Pet."

"That's what you think," June muttered.

I silently agreed.

"And we may as well all enjoy each other now," Linwood continued, as if to convince herself. "We're all we have. The insurance paid off generously. We have no ties. We're free as birds—it's a wonderful feeling, really. . . ." She began to sob quietly.

"We could go to Alaska!"

This looked bad; this picture, I was in. We each had our own dog sled, and we were each wrapped in thick fur coats against the snow. Sundown. We were heading off into the cold and the dark, no one knew where. Huge rounds of mink haloed our faces, which were lonely and afraid. Somehow I knew that each of the sleds would end up going in a different direction, the four points of the compass. We would never meet again.

Alaska was cold. Alaska was bleak. It was like the snow of the spirit, covering everything over. Maybe the tropics were better, after all.

"New Orleans is wonderful," I said. "It'll be great."

After all, I had no proof that the picture in Deane's journal was New Orleans. It could be Haiti or Havana. I'd never seen that voodoo shop.

"Do you really think so?" Linwood's voice was child-like now.

"Yes." I wanted to be very strong, for all of them. "We'll have a terrific time. A real adventure. And then we'll buy a new house, just for the four of us."

"We've got lots of money for Christmas," Linwood added.

"Oh yeah?" June asked.

"You girls can each have fifty dollars to buy presents with."

That would have seemed like a ton of money, once.

"Won't that be fun?"

*   *   *

"What's so great about Antoine's?" June asked me.

We were sitting in our room, putting off getting dressed. No matter how long we delayed, we'd still be ready before they were. "I don't know."

"Plus it's after nine. I wish we could order sandwiches and ice cream from room service."

I did, too. We were staying in the Hilton. What good was staying in the Hilton if you didn't get to do all the different stuff? We'd already been down to the indoor pool, and the sauna, ordered Shirley Temples from the downstairs bar and charged them to our room, ridden up and down the elevators a dozen times, and watched the color television. But room service!

The phone rang. June picked it up and said, "We already gave at the office." She hung up.

"That was them," I said.

"I know."

When it rang again, I picked up. Stan told me we had ten minutes and he didn't appreciate being hung up on. "We better get dressed."

I put on the outfit Linwood had bought me for Thanksgiving: a black velvet dress with a white lace collar, white tights, and short black patent leather boots. Then I brushed back my long, straight, thin hair and tied it with a green ribbon. When I put on my red coat, I'd look festive.

You had to try.

June put on her new gray wool dress, which looked exactly like her coat. It was the only thing she let Linwood buy.

"Why don't you put something in your hair?"

She looked in the mirror at her round face. Last year, she'd chopped off her thick, wavy chestnut hair above her ears, and had taken to wearing it combed straight back with a hairband. Now, at least, it had grown out a little.

"Like what?"

I opened up the suitcase and pulled out the present I'd gotten her in Miami. It was a straw hairband with little white shells glued all over it, in flower patterns. "Merry Christmas."

"Oh." She looked at the hairband as if it were an object from Mars. Then, shyly, she plunked it on her head.

"Like this." I rearranged her hair so there was a kind of wave over her forehead. "See?"

Well, funny thing, it worked. Her face looked longer and less moony. In fact, without the glasses, you could see that in a year or two, she would be even prettier than Deane. But *pretty* was the wrong word for Deane, anyway.

"Thanks, Fatty," June said. She said it nice, though, so that was okay.

We got our coats and went out into the hallway and knocked on their door.

"Just a minute," said Stan.

"What a surprise," said June. "They aren't ready."

Then the door opened.

"Don't you girls look cute," Stan said. "Eggnog?"

We walked into their room and found Linwood sitting at the table, in some kind of black dress that made her skin look like milk. Her rhinestone earrings were big as Christmas tree ornaments. Stan was wearing his usual dark suit, but he had a red carnation in his lapel.

The best part, though, was the eggnog! Four motel glasses were laid out with the thick creamy stuff.

"Oh boy!" said June.

We all sat at the table, and they didn't even *like* eggnog. It was really just for us.

We all raised our glasses in a toast:

"To our new home, wherever it may be!"

We headed down Bourbon Street in the cold December night. We'd avoided this area after dark before, and you could see why. It was solid bars, all of them packed with people, their doors open wide. Sailors moved freely and frequently from place to place, tall drinks in funnel-shaped glasses balanced precariously in their hands. Right to our left, a window above a bar opened, and a nearly naked woman glided out on a swing. Her breasts bobbed up and down, only the very tips protected from the cold by silver-tassled decorations. She was lovely, really, but she looked awfully cold, with her long blond hair swept over one shoulder. You could see the goosepimples on her thighs around the G-string.

"Gross!" June said.

Stan and Linwood were striding ahead, perhaps pretending that we were not their children trailing past strip-tease joints and gawking.

"Look at that!" I pointed to the other side of the street, where the saloon doors were swinging open and shut so you could see a woman taking a bubble bath in a great big champagne glass. She had one of those big sponges like you wash the car with, and she was merrily squeezing it over her astonishing chest.

"Yuck!"

"Don't you think she's beautiful?"

"With those great big boobs? She looks deformed!"

I made a protocol decision in favor of clamming up. It was almost Christmas; why bicker? I kept my admiration to myself, but these big sleek women filled me with awe. Real live naked women! The closest I'd ever gotten to seeing Linwood naked was one morning, mid-makeup, when she dashed from bathroom to bedroom—but even then she was wearing a brassiere and underpants and a full-length slip over that. Still, I remember being delighted by the round curve of her arms and shoulders, and the place where the breasts meet.

"Why don't they have hair there?" I asked June. Deane had explained to me about the hair.

June ignored me. She wasn't trying, like I was, to catch glimpses of Naughty Nan through the swinging doors. Instead, she was watching a trio of tap-dancing boys, shuffling dutifully along on the street corner. An older man, probably their father, played the harmonica with no great show of enthusiasm.

"Pet," she said. "You can dance as good as *that*. I could be your manager and we could—"

Stan materialized before us. "What in God's name is

taking you girls so long?" Arms akimbo, previous good humor only a memory, he glared down at us. "Pet, this stuff is strictly for adults. Do you want to end up like Deane?"

I didn't quite see the connection. What I did see was the threat, so I squared my shoulders and we marched along in two neat rows of two, like Madeline. I tried to close my ears to the sound of low-down music, the wailing trumpet and the raspy beat of the strippers' snare drums.

Stan and Linwood veered abruptly off Bourbon, and here it was quiet and dark, only a few couples strolling past the antique stores, their windows filled with shadow puppets from Bali, carved jade Buddhas, Mardi Gras clown masks, jeweled boxes with hidden interiors, spilling enameled beads.

Forgetting my resolution, I stopped to stare in the window of a particular store. There was a carved wooden face, with Spanish moss for hair and big carved mouth, eyes, and nose, a little like the stuff at Ripley's. And there were also all kinds of colored candles in the window, and tiny baby dolls, the plastic kind painted black and gold. They were all bound together with rope and crow feathers.

Not very pleasant. It reminded me of... Deane's room. Gone now, dust to dust.

I glanced at the sign above the door.

MARIE LAVEAU'S HOUSE OF VOODOO

My whole body wrenched, like I was about to throw up. Then I looked both ways on the street, quickly: *no truck hurtling toward us*.

My heart slowed to normal. No truck, and no family either. They'd already turned the corner to Antoine's. Plus, we weren't in the T-bird.

"Goddammit, Pet!" Stan's voice carried well. "You've got exactly thirty seconds to—"

But I was already running. Next morning, I'd be back, alone.

CHAPTER FOURTEEN

As soon as the first pale gray rays of light filtered through the white curtains, I was up. I emptied out the poodle bags and counted $112.39. That meant I could spend a hundred dollars in the voodoo shop. Twelve dollars plus the fifty for Christmas presents left sixty-two dollars, which was enough for three of the good kind of plastic horses for June, a real silk tie for Stan, and something wonderful for Linwood, if I found it and it was under forty.

I put the hundred dollars in a Hilton wet-laundry bag. But what about the toys? My gut feeling was: carry them with you. Afterward, they'd go back in their individual bags. And Deane's book.

I dressed quickly, hoping to beat the storm. The gusty wind might wake up June, but actually people always seem to sleep later when the weather's bad, as if it prolongs their dreams.

I grabbed the sack and my coat and an extra room key and stealthily slid out the door. Outside, the cold breeze was flattening down the green bushes, fluttering their tendrils.

But this would be okay. I felt powerful and rich and strong. Whatever the disaster was, I thought I could avert it.

Down on the street, the world was stormy and wild, and you couldn't smell that usual day-before-Christmas odor. Bourbon Street, from my position at the far end, appeared deserted. Discarded cups, rolling about, cocktail napkins, bits of foil blew everywhere, an urban snowfall. Yet, as I passed one grimy bar after another, I saw they were still open—there was always one old guy talking to the bartender—but not alive, and the sour whiff of last night's drinks and cigarettes kept hitting me smack in the face.

A group of photos with a woman and some snakes caught my eye, so I stopped to look. No one else was nearby, and the icy wind blew up the bottom and sleeves of my coat.

"Suzanne" sported a dimpled waist, hammy thighs, and two of the largest, firmest breasts I'd seen this side of a Barbie doll. Poor old Sally. *This* snake didn't have a chance, even though he was as big around as her arms, which were decorated with slave bracelets, like the one I wore now over my biceps. Once you got your eyes off the breasts, you realized that her arms were amazingly strong. No Hannah this, but nevertheless there was real strength there, especially in the photo with the hapless serpent stretched over her head.

"Really something, hmmm?" One of the overcoat types was standing next to me on the sidewalk.

You could smell the liquor and the cigarettes, and there was another smell too, the one Tommy had that night. It was the way men smelled when they didn't mean you any good.

Acting out of some new instinct, I reached down into my pockets where I could feel the poodle toys lumped together in their underwear bags. I thought about my cigar box, and I thought about Hannah.

"That's a man, you know," the old guy leered. "Would you like to meet him in person?"

I thought: *strong*.

I thought: *power*.

I said it over and over in my head: *strong-power, strong-power*, until I forgot where I was standing and everything. It was like that weird light on the second floor of Madame Miraculo's. My hands began to tingle, and then my forearms tingled, and then my elbows, and then my shoulders, and then my whole body felt warm and pure and chock-full.

When I opened my eyes, nobody was standing on the street next to me, but out of the corner of my eye I saw a light-suited man with pecan-colored skin.

Quick as lightning, I was after him. He turned, I

turned. He was fast, nothing but a shadow. He disappeared inside a shop and I whipped in after him.

It was the voodoo store, of course.

"Where's Sammy?" I panted out to the very fat man behind the counter.

"No Sammy here."

I caught my breath. "Yes, there is," I insisted. "I was right behind him."

"There was nobody in front of you and there's nobody here." His voice was as cold as Sammy's but he was so different. First, he was fat. Second, his skin was pale yellow, like the inside of a banana. Third, he was all decked out in scarves and green velvet pants, like a gypsy. I'd only met Sammy twice, but I knew that wasn't his style.

I scanned the store. Herbs and dolls and trinkets and candles. No Sammy, no visible truck. No nothing. What was I doing here, anyway?

"Besides, little girl, we aren't open yet."

"Oh." But the door had been open, hadn't it?

"In fact," he continued, "I'm just cleaning up, then I'm on my way to bed. We open after twelve." He began to shoo me in the direction of the door, as if I were a stray cat.

Strong-power, strong-power. "Wait!" I cried, on the threshold.

"Yes?" His hand was on the knob.

"I have to buy something."

"Well . . ."

"I have to," I said. "I have to get it now, before it's too late."

"Do you have any money?"

I held up the Hilton wet-laundry bag.

"Okay," the fat man said. "Ten minutes. What do you want to buy?"

I started to say I wasn't sure, but then I figured that would be a strategic error. "I need to keep something bad from happening."

The fat man resumed his stool behind the counter, a professional look on his face. "What sort of bad thing?"

"A wreck. And I also need to disappear my, uh, sister. And I need to get this man to come see me again." Go for broke.

A wrinkle of intensity appeared between his eyes. He rubbed his earlobe, where a large gold ring appeared painfully heavy. "You want Uncrossing. You want Disappearance. You want Attraction. Am I right?"

"Yes." I swallowed hard.

"Okay." His voice was reasonable. "What makes you think there'll be a wreck?"

"My sister predicted it."

"The sister you want to disappear, I presume?"

A hint of temptation, but no. "Yes, that's the one."

"And how does this man figure in all this?"

The whole thing sounded pretty stupid, but I plugged on. "He has something he wants to trade me." Something to make Deane go away, which would make the wreck go away.

It all came clear.

"Look," I said. "I'll make it easier. I want the best, most powerful thing you have that will make somebody appear, no matter what."

The fat man narrowed his eyes. "How much have you got in that bag? All pennies, I bet."

"No, sir. It's a hundred dollars."

He smiled, and I saw the sharp tooth, like the alligator's. "I believe we can help you," he said.

Stupid me. First I'm only a child, now I'm a chump. Yet, what else was the money for, except the off chance that magic might work?

After rifling around under the counter a moment, the fat man produced a large key. "Follow me," he instructed.

We went through a curtained niche with the sign: VOODOO MUSEUM $2.00, over the archway. Inside was dark and glitter and candles, and the smell, thick as destiny, was exactly like Deane's room. For a moment I felt scared, and I had to pee, but it was all reflexive and my eyes adjusted to the dim.

The fat man went up to the altar, which Deane might as well have designed, and produced a small, iron box, which he unlocked with the key.

"Is this place still used?"

He looked at me. "What makes you think that."

Not a question. I let it go.

He pulled a little pouch out of the box and then relocked it. He hesitated.

I tried to ignore the peculiar vibrations wafting off the various witchy-looking machinery against the walls.

"What the hell," he muttered as he plucked an object off the altar itself. We went back into the shop.

He locked the front door and then motioned me to an alcove behind a small partition. A grubby pack of cards with funny symbols on them lay on the small table next to a crystal ball.

"This is very serious stuff," he said, once we were seated. "I've decided to believe that you're sincere, so this is the real McCoy."

I nodded, impressed in spite of myself. On the other hand, this fat guy didn't have the same kind of pizzazz I'd come to expect. "Are you sure you don't know who Sammy is?"

"Little girl, I never said that." His small dark eyes looked like raisins in a golden bun.

"Then you *do* know who he is!"

"I never said that either."

Instinctively, my hand fingered the poodle toys. I plopped the wet-laundry bag full of money down between us and slid it over. For some reason, my energy felt cleaner, fuller, as if the money had been blocking something. "Do you or don't you know him?"

"Look, kid." The man fingered the ring in his lobe. "You've already got five more minutes than I promised you." He took the bag and secreted it behind the counter. "Plus, there's this stuff I got off the altar at great personal risk."

Strong. Power. "Do you or don't you?"

A fine sweat misted over his forehead. "Let's say I might know about this guy. Wait!" He held his hand up in protest.

I swallowed my excitement.

"Let's say I do know who he is. You want him to come see you. This stuff, she'll do the trick."

"But—"

"And just to show you what a good egg I really am, let's say I throw in a coupla lucky amulets, to keep harm off in the meantime. At no extra cost to yourself. How's that sound?"

"Four of them."

"Fine." He studied my face. "Four of them."

"And how soon will Sammy come see me?"

He shook his head. "You don't want to do this here spell until the next full moon."

Would that be too late? What if Deane turned up before then? Everything was all jumbled in my mind. For instance, I had this idea that if Sammy got his hands on Deane's book, we were through with her. But when you thought about it, that wasn't necessarily so.

Trouble was, I knew I had power, but this magic world was too much to understand. Where were the rules? It was like trying to control a bunch of tiny, lively rodents, all scrambling off in different directions. All you could do, finally, was put out some cheese and hope most of them stuck around.

You could purchase the spell, get your family to wear the amulets, and make positively sure, come hell or high water, that you never, ever drove by Marie Laveau's Voodoo Shop.

"When's the next full moon?"

"Last night was full moon." For some reason, he avoided my eyes.

"Okay." I sighed like Stan. "What choice do I have?"

"Don't farewell," he said.

"Fare forward."

CHAPTER FIFTEEN

When I opened my eyes, we were all in our usual places, speeding along the highway. The light was early morning gray and the landscape was becoming increasingly hilly. You could tell an immediate difference between Louisiana, with its swampy flatness, and Arkansas, with its rolling hills and pine trees and piles of stones, which were turned into houses with an irregular, patchwork effect. They looked like the kind of place Hansel and Gretel would find.

Signs for restaurants advertised all kinds of odd food: chicken-fried steak, collard greens, sweet potato pie. We were going to have lunch at a place called Hot Springs and then go see the house Stan and Linwood had bought. Day after tomorrow, we'd drive back to New Orleans and pick up Deane at the airport.

My amulet hung around my neck, my bracelet sat on my biceps, and my pockets were filled with poodle toys, the magic book, and the new spell to make Sammy appear. Trouble was, tonight was the *new* moon! What could you do? Stupid old Deane was coming back too soon, and I'd have to talk everybody into wearing their amulets again, bad enough a scene the first time. For all my personal power, I felt pretty depressed and hopeless. The whole thing had gotten away from me somehow.

"Pet's awake," June shouted.

"That's nice." Linwood turned around and smiled.

"Where are we?"

Stan consulted his odometer. "Just about exactly halfway between Texarkana and Hot Springs."

The Holiday Inn in Texarkana was where we'd been staying the last ten days. Every day, Stan and Linwood would go house hunting while June and I stayed at the motel. The coffeeshop had been told that we could charge breakfast and lunch, and even dinner if they weren't back by seven, but no room service and no candy bars. Also, we shouldn't get any ideas about ordering a succession of desserts.

There wasn't a lot to do. In the first place, we were the only children. In the second place, what is there to do in a motel in the dead of January, the pool covered over, the swing set too chilly to sit on, the slide coated with a slick sheet of ice, after you've read all the postcards and ordered everything on the menu? Heavy celebrations for Christmas and New Year's had burned us out on the poodles.

June made up a new game at the Holiday Inn called: I Will Only Do What Is Good For Me. It went like this: It's good for me to play solitaire and watch *The Price Is Right* because when I do these things, I'm not eating. (Years later, I can see the exquisite logic here, but it eluded me at the time.) You could mold this game to cover eating as well: It's good for me to eat this candy bar because it will spoil my dinner and I'll lose weight.

June was also crocheting an afghan with yarn and hooks she'd gotten for Christmas. It was very pretty, black and white and green squares manufactured painstakingly one at a time, the same kind of obsession for detail she brought to the poodle paraphernalia. And, of course, crocheting was Good for her since she wasn't eating.

So, basically, between the deck of cards, the game shows, and the afghan, she was pretty well amused.

I, on the other hand, was sure I was going mad or coming down with leprosy, whichever came first.

I'd always enjoyed stories about people going mad, and particularly the tales of Edgar Allen Poe, a big volume of which I'd gotten for Christmas. I looked forward to the day when I'd go mad, but I figured that day would come after I blossomed into a buxom beauty; with snow-white skin and long black hair, and after I'd been betrayed by love and locked in a castle. You could see how it would be: sleeping on pearl-colored sheets, never knowing if it was day or night, summer or winter, your cheeks flushed, and you couldn't tell waking from sleeping, it was all strange haze.

But there was no glamour to going mad at the age of nine, nobody weeping or gnashing their teeth over you. It was true that I could hardly tell day from night or morning from evening, but that was because it was all endless monotony, perpetual boredom.

When you went mad, I thought, you would be taken away from yourself. You would sleep and remember nothing. But in the madness I was in, the world was right there on top of you, each minute an hour in passing, each hour as long as a day.

Each morning Stan and Linwood would sally forth, armed with local papers and jotted-down telephone numbers of various realtors. They'd hooked on to this idea of buying a farm, though neither one of them had ever lived on one or wanted to. They thought a farm would be wholesome. And it was an improvement on their original plan, which was to buy a rundown plantation and transform it into a guest ranch. No way would Linwood take care of guests, and Stan wasn't what you'd call handy. He always expected applause when he changed a lightbulb.

Arkansas, they explained to us, was a more regular (read *remote*) place than Louisiana. Since Deane had ratted on Tommy and friends and there wasn't going to be any trial, we had to get located quickly, and start pretending to have a normal family life. Then she could come back and upset everything again.

So they set off each day determined to find the dullest, most isolated house in the world, plunk on its own little farm. Linwood took her marbles, of course. No tilting floors for us. Each night they'd explain the disadvantages of what they'd seen that day, until last night.

"What's so hot about Hot Springs?" June asked.

"Whichever one the crippled Roosevelt was," Linwood said, "he used to bathe there."

"He had leprosy," June told me.

She'd been putting leprosy in my head ever since we'd passed that leper colony on the way to Baton Rouge.

"June," said Stan, warningly.

Leprosy. It made your nose fall off.

"It isn't really contagious," June explained. "People who are destined to get it get it. Even the tiniest—"

"That'll do," said Stan.

"It'll be better for Pet if she knows these things. If she doesn't know what to look for—"

"Let's decide where we'll have lunch," Linwood suggested, pulling out the Automobile Club dining guide.

I looked down at my hands. Was the skin really yellower around the nails? Didn't the tips of my fingers look a little strange?

"Ben's Bar-B-Q. Casual attire, good country . . . Forget it. Morrison's Cafeteria. I loathe having to carry my own food on a tray! Fat Boy's—I don't—"

"Pet would like that!"

Stan sighed deep and long. "June," he said. "Take a good long look at your little sister."

I wanted to disappear.

"Do I have to?"

"Yes."

June stared at me with real fury.

"Now then. Do you really believe that she's fat?"

"Yes!"

Even though I hadn't had breakfast, my stomach began to swell like a balloon.

"You need stronger glasses then," he said. "The problem is in your eyes and not in her body."

"I suppose you're going to say that *I'm* the one who's fat," June said.

"Well." His voice was mild. "Well, yes."

"*YOU DON'T LOVE ME!*," June screeched.

I closed my eyes and willed myself into another dimension.

"We're here," said June. "And it's a real dump."

I opened my eyes and found that we were driving down one of Hot Springs' ancient city streets, the elevated sidewalks three steps above traffic level. Elderly couples in long, shapeless overcoats strolled so slowly that they seemed hardly to be moving at all. The glass storefronts, which seemed to comprise the entire downtown, were filled with odd merchandise, not the kind of stuff you see in regular shops—cupids with clocks in their stomachs, mismatched china, old jewelry and tools.

"Are those antique shops?" I asked Linwood.

"They're auction houses," said Stan.

Auction houses! So exotic. They reminded me of Bob Barker on *Truth or Consequences,* the only game show of June's I could watch. I thought Bob Barker was really handsome, and he'd make a great auctioneer.

"The guidebook," said Linwood, "says they're over-

priced and the merchandise is defective. But once this
was supposed to be charming, part of the whole resort
bit."

Well, who cared about the dumb old guidebook?
Something about the ambience got my attention—the
strolling couples, the charming sense of days, years,
eons gone by.

And then I saw a familiar-looking figure duck into
one of the auction houses. A pecan-skinned gentleman
in a clam-colored suit.

My arms prickled up and blood danced through my
body like those waltzing flowers in *The Nutcracker Suite*.

Our car zipped around the corner, but not before I
took one last look at the building:

SMILING SAMMY'S SHOWROOM

Maybe you didn't have to *use* the spell to get Sammy.
Maybe you just had to *have* it.

"There's the hotel!" June pointed.

"The Hotel Roosevelt," Linwood explained. "That's
where we decided to eat."

She took out her compact and began to powder her
nose. It had a funny blunt end, overly round, like the
edge of a shelf that's been painted too many times. The
story went that she'd been in two serious car wrecks,
both with sports cars and drunk dates, before she was
seventeen. One of the boyfriends had read to her every
day while she was in the hospital, stopping from time to
time to weep because of the pain he had caused her and
how he had ruined her nose. But I liked the bump
particularly; I wished I'd been born with one too.
Because of Deane, I would never have teenage boyfriends, never go cruising at night on the fire-fast
freeways, hair streaming out behind you.

My fate was something entirely different.

"After lunch," you could hear the weasely caution in
my voice, "do you think we could go to one of those
auction houses?"

Stan pulled the car into the hotel parking lot. "We're supposed to meet the realtor at three."

"Just for a minute?"

"They've just got a bunch of crap in there, Pet." Stan used his authority tone.

"It looks like a haunted house!" June was staring at the spindly, dark, multi-eaved old ramshackle building. Spooky, but that's all.

Somehow, I knew I'd get to Smiling Sammy's Showroom.

We paraded in the front door and were all struck dumb by the opulence, gold as the treasure room in *The Seventh Voyage of Sinbad*. Stan had taken us to see it one night last week in Texarkana, and it was even better than *Jason and the Argonauts*. I liked the part where the princess was tiny and Sinbad carried her around in the special box—sort of a chair—that he'd made specially for her. Six inches tall, really cute. She wasn't even upset when she discovered she'd been shrunk. All she did was tease handsome Sinbad about how he couldn't still love her if she was so small. But her size didn't make any difference to him. He was nice to everyone and said his prayers to Allah.

June's favorite part was the Cyclops, either when he had his eye put out with fire or when he wrestled to the death with the dragon. The Cyclops had a log cage full of skeletons, but the dragon reminded me slightly of the sweet beagle we used to have, Freckles.

Anyway, what with the gold cupids and the lamps encrusted with glittering stones, you could see that the Cyclops would have considered the hotel lobby as loot. Except this place was dingy and tarnished, if you stared a moment. As if the party had left already and been gone awhile.

"Can I help you, ma'am?" the bellboy asked Linwood. He was decked out in a green velvet suit with gold trim. His young face was an even, all-over pink, very pleasant, but one eye seemed to focus away, as if he saw a spirit hovering behind you.

"The Arabian Room." Linwood reserved that lofty voice for waiters and sales clerks.

"Of course." He bowed and we followed him.

"Dressed up like Jocko," June muttered in my ear.

Obediently, I winced. On my fifth birthday, someone had given me a monkey with a hard plastic face and a heart-shaped felt pad on his bottom, and he, Jocko, looked evil to me. There was something terrible about animals with human faces, not to mention the disconcerting combination of stuffed-toy softness with plastic-face hardness. The worst was the grisly story *Stuart Little,* in which a human couple give birth not to a real baby but to a mouse!

"Lordie," said Stan.

We were in the Arabian Room. Enormous gilt pineapples topped an impressive series of windows, and colored silk drapes wafted out from them, pink and coral and flamingo and salmon. The velvet booths were patterned in purple brocade, a little worn but still pretty.

"It looks like a harem," said Linwood. "Or should I say bordello."

The waiter seated us and the bellboy vanished. You expected those brocade cushions to sink you like a stone, but actually they were rather hard.

"A vodka martini. Very dry." Linwood looked right through the waiter, but you could tell he loved it. The meaner she was to people like that, the more they seemed to love her.

"Double bourbon on the rocks," said Stan. "And two Shirley Temples with extra cherries."

June beamed.

Linwood allowed Stan to light her cigarette and then surveyed the room in that chin-high, non-looking way she had, which made everyone stare at her as if she were famous or beautiful. "Everyone" in this case turned out to be two or three aged couples, their jewelry showing more light than their skins.

That aloofness, that was a kind of power you'd think I could create for myself. It was attitude, separation, indifference. I straightened my spine and surveyed the room with equal dignity.

"Why did the moron throw the clock out the window?" June asked me.

I ignored her, my chin up like Linwood's.

"Say 'Knock knock,'" she suggested to Stan.

"Knock knock."

"Who's there?" June asked.

He looked surprised and then annoyed. I couldn't believe he'd fallen for that one again.

She turned to Linwood. "Why did—"

Luckily, the drinks and menus arrived, which were beautiful. Pink water the color of roses and big velvet books, tasseled in silver. To be fair, the Arabian Room was more like the treasure house of the gods in *Jason and the Argonauts* than like the Cyclops's cache. My bias against the Jason story, all that stuff about Hera and so forth, was that it was real—I mean, it was an actual myth. Hercules getting stranded because Zeus had something better for him to do and the clashing rocks and Neptune and all of that. You couldn't enjoy the story because it was preordained. Like when they tried to snazz up stories from the Bible and make believe they were real stories. But Sinbad. He could have done *anything*.

"I'm having Sultan's Ecstasy," June announced.

I scanned the menu.

SULTAN'S ECSTASY!

Succulent roast baby piglet seasoned in mouth-melting spices. Festive pilaf rice with plump raisins complements this Far-Eastern taste pleaser. Just the thing to tease and tantalize the palate, whether you be sultan or peon!

The description gave me a headache, and there were dozens of them. So I applied the same theory I used on all random choice: rely on the name. Persian Prince was my selection, and I didn't care what it was.

"Well," said Linwood gaily, after ordering Serendipity in the Seraglio, "tonight we'll be in our new home!"

"Tonight we'll be in another motel," said Stan. "Tomorrow we look for something to sleep on."

A glum silence fell over the table. I was sure they
were all thinking what I was, that we no longer had any
furniture to have shipped. We would have to fill the
house with new things, strange things.

"We'll order some stuff in New Orleans," Stan pointed out. "When . . ."

"When we go pick up stupid old Deane." June
pounded her fist on the table. "I wish she'd burned up
with the house."

Nobody answered. Nobody told her it was a bad
thing to wish.

CHAPTER SIXTEEN

"Look," I said, after picking at Persian Prince for ten
minutes or so. "Can't I just run next door to one of
those auction houses and meet you back here in fifteen
minutes?"

Stan consulted his wristwatch. "It's after one now."

"It only takes half an hour to get to the house,"
Linwood said. "You said we weren't meeting her until
three."

"June'll go with you," Stan ordered.

"And miss dessert?" Her outrage was mortal.

"I'm nine years old," I announced, chin high. "I don't
want dessert. I want to go to the auction house right
next door," I pointed, "on this side of the street.
Fifteen minutes."

Stan and Linwood exchanged looks. Perhaps they
were remembering how I'd gone into the Quarter and
back that morning, without mishap.

"Okay," Stan said. "Meet us in the lobby at one-
thirty." He wiped his mouth with his napkin. "There's a

shop your mother wants to go to on the other end of
town."

I pulled my coat around me, taking pleasure in the
power the toys gave me. Then I made tracks.

Back through the golden lobby, I walked swiftly and
keenly, vanishing out the front door in jet-powered
haste. Right next to the hotel was the dusty storefront,
shabby oriental rugs and bronze candlesticks shaped
like cobras.

I pushed open the grimy glass door. A bell jangled
from a knotted rope.

Rows and rows of metal folding chairs were facing the
far end of the rectangular space, marked by a card table
and a podium of sorts. Festoons of bric-a-brac cluttered
the swaying shelves on either side of the seats.

But nobody was inside. No auctioneer, no audience.

My heart sank with disappointment, the way I'd
thought my bottom would sink into the brocade pillows.

I went up to the front row and sat down anyway,
clutching my treasures about me. A clock chimed and I
glanced at its broad, cracked face: one-fifteen.

From behind a curtain at the far left end of the room,
out walked a dapper gentleman in a suit the pale shade
of lettuce, those white leaves close to the core. His
pecan-colored skin set off the grim cold of his ice-chip
eyes.

He walked to the podium and banged the gavel.

"Let the auction begin."

I was calm, calm and strong.

"For sale today," said Sammy, "I have your heart's
desire. I have what you need to set your troubles to
rest. I can make the worst fear in your heart turn to
dust and sift through your fingers. I can ease your pain,
a silk cushion you eternally sink in."

I cleared my throat. "I want protection for my family."

Sammy nodded his head. He moved like water.

A moment passed.

"It's yours," he said. "I start the bidding at one red
magic book."

The gavel rang out.

When my fingers touched the book, it was warm and

lively, the leather living and breathing. What did the book contain that had never been found? What could he find inside it that was lost forever to me?

But there had to be more courage in trading its mysteries and receiving the lives of June, Linwood, and Stan.

I held the book aloft.

After all, the spell was still mine. Things got bad, I could make Sammy appear again.

"Sold!" The gavel rang the third and final time.

Sammy walked around the podium and stood before me, palm extended.

"Protection first."

Sammy smiled, and it wasn't a pretty sight. Those eyes were like an Arkansas pond right after it frosted over. "You already have protection," he said, vanishing the book from my hand.

Right then, I knew I'd been cheated. "Those amulets?"

His smile was gone. "The spell," he said. "The one you purchased to make me appear."

My head clouded up like bumblebees, and all the bad things that had happened to me danced before my eyes like a circle of crazed Apaches. "But who needs to appear, besides you?"

"You want someone to disappear."

Deane, of course.

"You want someone to disappear, you do the spell backwards. Instead of the night of the full moon, you do it on the day of the new moon."

That was today.

Sammy scanned the room, full of gew-gaws but empty of other people. "You can do it right here, right now if you please."

I started to feel relief, like the whole shebang was finally over. Then suddenly something niggled at the back of my brain. "But does making Deane disappear mean that the stuff in the book won't work anymore?"

Sammy had already turned his back, walking away from me. The energy of Deane's magic grew fainter and fainter. The power of the toys and my individual person grew stronger. "That's a chance you'll have to take, isn't it?"

What other chance was there?

He vanished behind the curtain. You knew there was no way he was coming back out.

I sat in the chair, puzzling it all out, even past the chiming of the weird old clocks for one-thirty. They'd still be drinking their coffee, anyway.

The book was gone, Sammy was gone, and there wasn't anything to do but try the spell backwards. So Deane would disappear, and maybe the bad stuff with her. What if I'd never stolen the money? When I had the money, Sammy had never appeared to me. But then I never could have bought the amulets or the magic spell.

All there was to do was fare forward.

I took out the spell.

Seemed like the opposite of love was always disappearance.

PART II

*

CHAPTER SEVENTEEN

The alarm clock clicked pre-ring, but I shut it off just in the nick. If only it were the kind with the radio— *c'est la vie*. Best not to clutter your life with material details, anyway. Bad enough that the orange juice cans I rolled my hair with had come loose in the night, gouging a touch-noticeable dent in my forehead. Plus, I was a tad hung over.

No matter. There was a dilly to record in my dream book! My hand groped around under the bed before encountering the embossed cover that distinguished the dream book from the other books. I flipped to the motto page: "Ennui is the greatest evil." That was from the kid story, "The Most Dangerous Game," and never failed to cheer me up, an inspiration for the life I'd lead when my circumstances improved. You had to keep visualizing what you wanted, put some images into motion. Sure, you could do the hatha yoga bit all you liked, practice eating a slice of whole wheat for an hour, chewing each bite until it dissolved into nothingness. But beyond the discipline, you had to keep on dreaming yourself out the other end of the tunnel.

May 6, 1967. Trapped in a coffin on a hillside. The coffin is slanted on an angle so I can see grass and flowers all around me. This is kind of like Apollinaire's "Cows grazing there/ Slowly are poisoned."

This was my book, so I figured I could be as pretentious as I liked.

"My life from your eyes slowly takes poison." In another coffin propped next to mine—

*   *   *.

The Beach Boys blared out from Bread's room, so
scratch the dream book. In five seconds I was in the
bathroom with his door locked and the shower steaming
on. Then I took a piece of Kleenex and lowered the
toilet seat before sitting down. Afterwards, I took some
more Kleenex and wiped some of the black gunk out of
the sink. He must have been working on his bike again
last night. However, one peek in the mirror revealed
black gunk on my face, too, but not from bikes. The hair
had gotten rolled but the mascara hadn't gotten removed.

I slathered on some Noxema as the room filled up with
steam. The smell of camphor was queasy-making. Darlene
never felt sick the next morning and she said it was
because she stuck to Bacardi and Cokes. Wine was my
choice, more continental, but it did fight back. If only
absinthe were legal! I could always drink less and feel
better, but how could you do that and still live life to
the fullest? Look at Thomas De Quincey. Look at
Baudelaire. Look at the Marquis de Sade, for Pete's sake.

The shower was full of sand, as per usual. My skin
was the kind of sore where it bothered, but you had to
move right on through pain. And besides, if I didn't
hustle, there wouldn't be time for my makeup. Without
makeup, there was absolutely no point in going to school.

After a quick toweling, I wiped off the mirror.

"Pet, I've got to take a leak!"

"Five minutes!" I hollered back.

Cover Girl base went on first—who cared that it was
made out of beeswax? It covered up zits like nothing
else. And if you used a dark enough shade, you looked
really tan, especially if you left some white space around
your eyes, where the sunglasses would have been. If
you were really into that, you could even leave a little
white strip across the bridge of your nose.

After all the peaks and valleys were filled in with the
base, you put on lots of loose powder, just in case you'd
missed something. Plus it would sop up the oil that
started oozing through within the hour.

This moment after the powder was always my favorite; I could have been anybody. The face was like a

package that hadn't been unwrapped yet. It was still possible that I might turn out to be really beautiful, or at least wildly exotic. Not just the same old dumb Pet-face with the small nose, brown eyes, turned-down mouth . . .

"Pet!"

"Three minutes!"

Black Maybelline eyeliner framed my eyes, skyblue shadow on the lids, and a heavy coat of mascara. While that was drying, I quickly contoured my cheeks. What you do is make the bottom of your face even darker so that it recedes and then put light blusher high up on the cheeks, for that hollow-face model look. I alternated coats of mascara and dustings of blusher until they balanced out. I could always add more at school.

Last was the lips, and I liked my mouth to kind of disappear. Not only did it turn down but it was also on the large side. First you powdered the lips, to give the gloss something to grip on to, then you slathered on the Yardley slicker in superpale pink, for that Jean Shrimpton appeal. However, she had those terrific eyebrows that arched up like bridges to—

"Pet, dammit!"

And I hadn't done my eyebrows! Quickly I added in the little strokes that are supposed to look like fake hairs, except that my pencil must have needed sharpening or something.

Bread rattled the doorknob of the door that connected with his room.

"Alright already!" I pulled out the couple remaining juice cans, and my long blond hair, artificial but pretty anyway, fell relatively straight past my shoulders. My bangs had a hump in them but that would fall out.

Bam! Bam! He was pounding on the door.

"It's all yours, Slick!" I unlocked his side and dashed out mine. The lock clicked from inside and he sighed loudly. Now he'd take twice as long as I did, coaxing his hair into that wavelike pouf that all the surfers affected.

The next production was picking out what to wear. I put the Doors on the stereo for inspiration and Bread

yelled *"Gross!"* from behind the bathroom door. He
was beach music all the way.

"Turn it down!" yelled Aunt Edith from the hallway.
"Come and eat your breakfast or you'll both be late!"

God, it was such a drag having all this chaos in the
morning! And breakfast, forget it. What was I going to
wear, for instance? I'd already worn my two favorite
dresses Monday and Tuesday, and this was only Thursday. My new pink skirt had a rip in it, and the only
other cool outfit was the wide-wale corduroy vest thing,
but the blouse was dirty. My flowered suit felt too
dressy: it was sunny out. The Mexican skirt—

"Breakfast, now!"

They were always yelling at you around here. I'd just
have to wear the Monday dress. It was real cute, short
with orange and purple stripes. If the gladiator sandals
looked okay, no need for pantyhose since my legs were
only a little stubbly. I grabbed my purse, sprayed some
Oh! de Love under my hair and around my neck, and
ran down the stairs.

Aunt Edith was frying eggs. As usual, she was all stiff
mouth and neat hairdo.

I grabbed some coffee and added a bunch of milk and
sugar. It tasted okay, which is to say not actively disgusting. What would be great was a cigarette.

Aunt Edith slid a couple yellow and white eyes onto
my plate and returned to the stove to do Bread's. "I
don't believe I heard you come in last night, dear," she
observed.

"Oh, really?" I concentrated on cutting up the eggs
and swishing them around so they'd look eaten.

"You know you're not supposed to stay out late on
school nights."

We both sighed, it was so hopeless. Sometimes I
wondered how Linwood would have liked me as a
teenager, but mostly I never thought about all that.

"And, dear, your makeup—" She swung around with
her spatula in hand, the very picture of a Mom.

"—is totally bitchin', fab, boss, far out!" Bread sat
down across from me and forked some egg off my plate.
The smell of English Leather was staggering.

"You know how I feel about that makeup," Aunt
Edith persisted, sliding more food onto both plates.

I concentrated on my coffee and perpetrating a kind
of Zen negation around me. It's so effective to refuse to
respond, and besides, Bread was there.

"All the chicks look like that." He overdid it on the
slang, but that's hard to tell somebody. He was always a
degree or two off, close but no cigar. "Pet looks practically natural compared to the rest of them." How could
he eat so much? We were at the same party last night
only he'd been twice as wasted. But, of course, his body
was much bigger and absorbed all those poisons. Besides, if he were feeling all that great, he'd have been
out surfing at dawn. Or maybe there weren't any waves.

"What's up at the beach?" I asked, giving him more
of my eggs.

He turned his handsome, plump face toward me.
Like his brother, Kirk, Bread had Aunt Edith's swarthy
skin, tanned to an elegant strong tea color, and heavy
straight eyebrows that gave him an honest, Gregory
Peck look. His bleached hair was combed forward into
that amazing cascade I mentioned, a coif possible only
through genetic good fortune, great patience, and the
wonders of technology. "Glassy as get-all." So were his
eyes, actually. He must have popped one before breakfast.

"Pet, you aren't going to school until you eat something." Raisin toast descended before me.

I nibbled and chewed slowly, thinking about *prana*
instead of barfing.

Darlene honked and Bread and I leaped up as if
cattle-prodded.

"Have a nice day," Aunt Edith called after us. "Brad,
honey, tuck your shirt tails in!"

Darlene was smoking a cigarette in her red Mustang
convertible, short platinum hair gleaming in the sun.
"You wore that dress Monday," she said as I climbed
into the backseat. Even though she was my friend, I let
Bread have the front so he could stretch out a little.

I put on my sunglasses and lit a cigarette.

Darlene burned rubber.

Bread turned up the radio.

We screeched around the familiar streets of Mission Beach, all the little houses nestled as close together as possible so that as many people as possible could live there. Our place was on the bay side of the skinny peninsula and the bay stretched out, flat and gray. The ocean side was prettier—I preferred the sight and sound of the waves—but more popular with the tourists, so Aunt Edith opted for relative quiet.

"Big party tonight," Darlene shouted over the music.

One good tsunami and the entire place would be wiped out. One mediocre tsunami, for that matter.

"Wanna go?"

"Sure!" I yelled back. After all, it was practically the weekend, and it was so depressing around the house at night. Aunt Edith watched television all evening while she knitted, and if Kirk and Moni dropped by, it was even worse.

"Count me out," said Bread. "Surf's supposed to be up tomorrow."

Darlene sighed. She never counted him in.

Everybody was hanging out in the parking lot, as per usual. The tough guys smoked by their choppers and the more respectable types lurked in the passageway to the main building. The really respectable ones, of course, were already in front of their homerooms.

"See ya." Bread hopped out. He always ditched us before we parked the car so he could have that extra minute jawing with his surfing buddies. They huddled to one side of the choppers, peroxided shocks of hair glinting in the sunlight.

I climbed over to the front seat and Darlene and I sat, as we liked to when there was time, at the far end of the lot, listening to the radio and smoking. "This Magic Moment" was on, a song that depressed us because of that guy Scott Darlene'd been so wild about. She'd slept with him a bunch of times and everything and then he up and joined the navy. He was in Vietnam, if you can believe that. She sent him peanut butter fudge once, but I don't think she was a real whiz at letters.

"You got a date this weekend?" Her pale lavender eyes were rendered eerie by her purple glasses.

"Nope." Three calls for last Saturday, and this week a big goose egg. "But it's only Thursday."

We both sighed. Life was so depressing.

"Maybe Friday—damn!"

Jefferson Airplane's "I Saw You Coming Back to Me" came on the radio.

"I can switch stations." Darlene knew how the song affected me, far beyond "This Magic Moment."

I felt that black melancholy drop over me like a paper bag. My heart ached, my stomach knotted up, and my hands went weird. "No! Leave it on."

My depressions were sort of famous, but I hadn't realized that I'd been hovering so close to one, like a hole you fell into. The song brought it all out, though, the whole thing about time passing and somebody's gone and you can't go back and all that jazz. *Where are the snows of yesteryear?* and so on.

The first bell rang and people began to get out of their cars as if they had a real place to go to and that, their destination, meant something.

Inky black trouble, like something from another world come to swallow you up.

"Hey!" Darlene tapped me gently on the wrist.

"You go on," I said. "I'll be in in a minute."

"A bad day to ditch," she opined, climbing out. "That trig test?"

I produced my best metaphysical shrug.

"Okay for you," she continued through the window. "You can make it up. But if I don't have Danny to cheat off of, I might as well start pumping gas tomorrow."

The second bell rang and Darlene shot me a sympathetic look and hustled off. Then that weird silence, peculiar to the space surrounding a school in session, filled the parking lot. I turned off the radio. Homeroom. Then the first-period bell rang and five minutes of cacophony ensued. When the late bell rang, I accepted the fact that makeup or no, no way was I going inside.

At least I wasn't letting a new outfit go to waste.

But what to do? The day spread out before me like a new carpet you were afraid to walk on. Scratch going home, where Aunt Edith and her friends were no doubt scarfing down a bunch of coffee cake and gossip. The movies? The mall? The beach? Nothing appealed to me. I felt like the guy in one of those existential novels, I can't remember which one, who's repelled by the doorknob. He looks at the doorknob and goes: *Blaugh!* How can I bear to touch this and what, besides, is the point in going through the door?

I lit another cigarette, slid over to the driver's seat, and tooled out of the parking lot.

I drove north, along the coast. The immaculate community of La Jolla sped by like an oversized Barbie's Dream Village. All that artful bougainvillea and red Spanish tile. Next was Del Mar, with the slate-blue sea on one side and the race track on the other. It had been a long time since I'd been up this way—the track was where they held the county fair, and that was where June and I had made Stan spend twenty dollars in quarters, procuring for us Cherie and Mimi, the Original Poodles. They now resided in cardboard box tombs, collars and special toys around them, as if they were Egyptians and needed treats for the Other World.

Past Del Mar was this wonderful white building with a dome painted gold, like a huge gilded onion. There were gardens around it, red begonias and yellow marigolds and blue lobelia and sweet white alyssum. Maybe Paradise looked like that.

North of here, I wondered where there was to go. It crossed my mind to go to Vista and check out where the house had been.

After all, I was getting closer and closer. Once through Cardiff-by-the-Sea, where our beach house had been and where June used to make me glue shells to pieces of cardboard and give them names, all that was left before Oceanside—and Vista was only seven miles inland from there—was a short drive through Leucadia.

This morning it was beautiful! The sea was bright blue to my left with choppy whitecaps, and the hills rolling upward to my right were covered with wild mustard. The breeze felt so good that I almost didn't mind that my hair was probably ruined for life. Better have it ruined, though, than wear one of those nerdy little scarves.

The miles passed all too quickly. Seedy Carlsbad, with its Twin Chicken Inn adorned with giant plaster fowl, another childhood delight, was upon me, and then the outskirts of Oceanside, the down-and-out beach town responsible for most of the dope traffic between San Diego and L.A.

I was out of cigarettes and energy, so I steered my car into the parking lot of The Surf Burger, just the sort of place you'd expect to see along here. A bell went off in my head, and then it came to me that this was one of Deane's old hangouts.

Well, so what? They weren't going to have fan pictures of her on the walls, that was for sure. And besides, too much time had passed. I should have done this a long time ago—but I'd only had my license for a couple months.

A few older guys, of the burnt-out variety, were hanging around inside, scuzzy beards and hair. They were too out of it even to give me a hard time, so I ordered my cheeseburger, fries, and shake, and got a pack of Kools out of the machine. My table was one of those rollers they wind telephone cable on, and it had been treated like a surfboard so that there was this glassy surface about an inch thick. I lit a cigarette and relaxed a little, looking out the window toward Coast Highway. You couldn't see the ocean, but there was a nice view of the cars whizzing by and some dusty eucalyptus trees in the background.

Everybody else was probably taking the trig test right now. That was okay. Poetic spirits didn't need stuff like mathematics; math eroded you and made you ordinary.

The waitress plopped a very ordinary burger et al. in front of me. Well, the body had to be fed.

Into my second bite, the door opened and some more has-been types shuffled in. They were apparently having a kind of convention at the far table, the one away from the windows and the doors. Every now and then a piece of their conversation floated toward me, a "shit, man, no!" or a "fucking A!" But then a new voice spoke.

I put down my burger. The words were indistinguishable, but the sound of the voice . . . *where had I heard that before?*

Suddenly I had to pee, bad. The ladies' room was right in back of the losers' confab, but that was okay. They didn't scare me, not much.

And, in fact, they ignored me when I passed by. I took care of business, but then hovered in the hallway, right in back of the door that led into the room, only a few feet from their table. The guy with the familiar voice was talking again.

"No fucking way, man!" he said. "You want that kind of shit, you do it yourself."

Who was that? I closed my eyes tight and concentrated. I did the Zen flower thing, for improved recall, and then I tried to relax various of my muscle groups, in unusual sequences. But when he spoke again, the venom with which he shouted, "Screw that lousy bitch!" brought it all home.

Tommy.

No doubt about it. Tommy!

My solar plexus went *oomph* and that whole lower part of my body, and all these sort of sick and bad shadows flickered up and down. Tommy.

Did I think he was dead? Vanished? Never had been?

Guys go to jail, guys get out of jail. That was the world and the way that it was.

But you know, this was the weird part. Right while I was standing in that stupid burger place, listening to this creep carry on, I had this tremendous rush of excitement, totally 180 degrees from my previous mood.

The thing was: if Tommy was around somewhere, maybe Deane was too. *And Sammy*.

Then all kinds of conflicting feelings, a whole flock of birds, flew up in my heart, and I stood there, hovering by the restrooms, until there was a shuffling of feet and chairs, some grunts and slaps. Tommy and whoever went away. Not a single greaseball remained.

Scratch lunch! I went up to the waitress behind the counter. She was doing her nails.

"You know those guys who just came in?"

She stared at me vacantly. She had lifeless brown hair but one of those deep tans that looks like dyed skin.

"You know a guy named Tommy?"

The light went on. "You trying to score?"

"Uh, sure. Right. I'm trying to score."

She went back to her nails. "Tommy's your man, all right."

"Yeah, well, you wouldn't happen to know where he lives, would you?"

She snorted. "Those scumbags! They don't *live* anywhere!" Her splayed fingers, half-varnished with violet, seemed to please her.

"Well, where does he hang out?"

The look she gave me was well-earned. "Here, obviously."

"Obviously." This seemed pretty hopeless. "You mean if I wanted to find him tonight, this would be the place to come?"

She shrugged. "Why didn't you talk to him now? When he was here?"

"Okay." I raised my palms in defeat. "Another time."

"Wait," she said, when my hand was on the doorknob. I turned around.

"There's a big party out to Petey's tonight. Everybody's gonna be there. You might try that."

"Where's Petey's?"

She told me.

"Thanks," I said. "You've really helped me out. Think there's any problem crashing?"

"Shit, no!" She laughed, for the first time, not a happy sound. "They never complain about extra girls."

CHAPTER EIGHTEEN

"What'd you tell your aunt?" Darlene asked when I picked her up that night in her own car. "Got any reds?"

"Studying at Shaun's."

"I said Casey's, but it's the same difference. Let's hope the old bat doesn't check in with the old bitch."

"Who cares?" Maybe this was existentialism, my current frame of mind, or maybe it was Buddha resignation. At any rate, my mind was unclouded by trifles. "Look in my makeup bag."

"Oh, good." Darlene popped some. "So where is this party anyway? It better be good because we're missing the one at Mark's."

There was a lot of traffic, mostly kids racing around in beach buggies, throwing beer cans and stuff. I lit a cigarette and concentrated on driving carefully. "Oceanside."

"Oceanside! Look, Pet, what if—"

It was only fair to let her know what was going on, so I gave her the whole story. Well, an expurgated version anyway. By the time we were in Del Mar, she was sympathetic.

"One thing I don't get, though."

"What's that?"

She raked back the top of her hair with her hand. "What are you gonna do when you see this Tommy?"

Good question.

"You go up and accuse him of all that stuff, he's not too thrilled to see you."

Not hardly.

"Aren't you scared?"

"Yes." Why was the drive taking half the time it had

earlier? We were nearly to Leucadia already. At night, it was this terrific expanse of nothingness.

"Or," Darlene mused, "maybe he knows where your sister is."

"I told you she disappeared." My hands were very sticky on the wheel. "Besides, why would he know anything?"

"Geez, Pet, I don't know! Don't yell at me. I just said *maybe*."

All these things to think about. Darlene turned up the radio, clearly annoyed with me, and I lapsed into speculation. There was the old Best/Worst conundrum to ponder: in any situation that you find yourself unduly anxious over, you could ask yourself what was the very worst thing that could happen and what was the best. In this case, the worst was that Tommy would remember me. No, the worst was that he would somehow hurt me again. No, the worst was that it hadn't been him and he wouldn't remember me.

The worst was what Darlene suggested: that he would lead me to Deane?

But wasn't that the best as well?

Damnation, I hadn't a clue. I mean, the whole thing was beginning to wear on me, and if I'd been in the car by myself, I think I would have gone ahead and swung the sucker around. But somehow, after dragging Darlene out, quitting didn't seem right. With another person, you could always believe you were in the midst of adventure, an attitude often difficult to sustain alone. Alone, for instance, it often felt like regular old danger.

"This must be Petey's."

Darlene snorted through her nose.

The ramshackle old beach house was not a pretty sight. First off, several of the windows had been tinfoiled over, and one window just had cardboard where the panes used to be. Second, the porch steps were missing. And the guys hanging around on the porch looked like rejects from the Salvation Army. Third—well, what was the point? This place was a real armpit.

"How much will you pay me to walk in there with you?"

"Let's reconnoiter." I drove us around the block and parked in an inconspicuous spot, where we could watch the ocean. The white edges of the breakers glowed.

Darlene was fidgeting a little, probably from the reds. "Cold feet?"

"You betcha."

"What have we got to lose?" Mostly, she just wanted to get out of the car.

"Our lives and our good looks. Maybe both."

"Oh, Pet."

Then I remembered something. Not a coincidence exactly—why else was I carrying the things around in my purse? "Here," I said, handing her one after rooting around for them. "Put this on."

"What the hell is it?" Darlene held hers up to the car window, trying to get a good look, but the streetlights weren't very bright.

"It's a sort of a necklace."

"Who made it—Dracula?"

I hadn't really looked at the gris-gris in a long time, and maybe never very closely. Mine was mostly feel to me: it felt right when I put it around my neck, so right that the question was why it had ever been off my neck. Yet, all four gris-gris had been sitting in my cigar box ever since the day Deane walked past us in the airport. That was my big mistake, letting them take theirs off. If only—but I couldn't think about that stuff. I'd gone over it and over it in my head all these years, and it didn't do me any good that I could tell. All I knew was that this afternoon, without even thinking about it, I'd put June's and mine in my purse.

"God, that's two favors you owe me. Going in that dump and wearing this creepy bit of weirdness."

"Just put it on, okay?"

"I hope I don't catch something from—"

She was getting on my nerves. "It's an amulet, okay? And it happens to be very powerful. And it just so happens that you'll be very sorry if you don't wear it. So just shut up and put it on or stay in the car, okay?"

"What a bitch! And it's *my* goddamned car, in case you happened to forget! And who needs you to tell me what to—"

Were any of the old powers left? I shut my eyes and fingered the gris-gris.

Darlene quieted down. Her platinum hair glowed in the dim light, like a ball of heat lightning.

"We'll stick together," I said, after a minute.

She shrugged and climbed out her side of the car.

The first trick was climbing up onto the porch, but luckily we were both wearing jeans. Nobody paid much attention to us, and that was a break at least. Inside, the scene was what you'd expect, except more so. The music was loud, the lights were dim; the smell of cheap wine and marijuana was a record-breaking contact high. Many bodies were crowded into the two rooms you could see into from the front doorway. There were groups standing and talking, groups in cross-legged circles, and groups sprawled in corners. "Inagadda da vida, wah-wah" boomed out from the stereo, the bass turned up so high that the drumming felt grooved into your skull.

Darlene disappeared in the crowd, the drop of water sent back to the sea, but I felt like a visitor from Mars. A thin green shield separated me from regular life-forms. I was oil, agate, and could not be absorbed.

"Hey, chick."

My spine went cold. The face the voice issued from appeared close to mine. The smell of his breath and skin roiled the bottom of my stomach.

"That's right, babe, you."

Tommy stood in front of me. Deep lines in his pale skin connected the edges of his nose with the edges of his mouth. But the deepest line of all was the scar etching a swift diagonal across his left cheek. His pale eyes looked at mine, but there was nothing you could read there, no person home. Recognition? Curiosity? Anybody's guess.

"You alone?"

"I'm with a girlfriend." *Stick together, dammit, Darlene!*

"Now you're with me." He touched my arm, and I jerked back, as if burned.

The expression on his face chilled me into silence, and I allowed my body to be directed over to the far corner of the living room. That's when I realized I was really here, and didn't know why. You think bad stuff is better than nothing happening. Then you remember what bad stuff is really like.

When we were seated on big pillows covered with tatty fake fur, he pulled a reefer out of his shirt pocket and lit up. Though clearly, by his lack of tan and unbleached hair, he was not a surfer, his body had the same lean tautness, and was dressed in the typical Mexican shirt and faded bellbottoms. From the neck up, he looked to be over thirty, and his forearms, where the shirt cuffs were rolled, sported tattoos, the kind you do yourself with razor blades and ballpoint pens.

Part of me wished I were strong enough to strangle him with my bare hands. The other part—well, at least he existed. And again, somehow that meant everything else might, too. For instance, that night—

He poked me with his finger, so I took a long drag on the dope, immediately feeling gooey-limbed and soggy. Great: who knew what kind of horror it was laced with. In another moment I'd be hurtling through the galaxy, an unhinged Catherine wheel tumbling over itself in the stratosphere.

My skin seemed to shrink away from him though I was doing my best to hold in there. I felt like one of those plants, you touch the leaves and they wrinkle up.

"Where do I know you from?" His speech was a little slurred and he took another hit on the reefer. "Why don't you show me your tits, maybe I'll remember you."

Now I was offended. I mean, really! I ducked back just in the nick as the greaseball made a lunge for my shirt.

"Awww, got her little feathers all ruffled! Well, let me tell you something, bitch. You look just like this other bitch I used to know, only you're a rotten bag of bones and she was some stacked . . . " He trailed off, not even looking my way anymore, and took another hit.

Then my anger really hit me, like ten tons of bricks.

The reality of it all hit me, too. This fool, this wicked
and repulsive animal in front of me, was Tommy, *Tommy*, the creep who hurt me when I was little, and
probably burned down our house. Maybe it was even
all his fault that Deane was the way she was.

Men! All I'd ever seen of them, they were scummy!

"I'd sure like to get my hands on that bitch," he
mused, idly inhaling another half-inch of marijuana.
"I've been meaning to track her ever since I got sprung."

"Oh?" It was hard keeping the emotion out of my voice.

"Nobody's left from the old gang, you know?" Tommy
shook his head sadly, like he was missing his old Cub
Scout troop or something.

"Anybody seen her around?" I aimed for a tone of
utter nonchalance.

"What the fuck is it to you?"

Okay, so maybe my acting wasn't quite what it should
be. "Nothing! Just making conversation, that's all. Geez,
I love this song." I made drumming motions on my leg,
to demonstrate that I was really grooving on the music.

Tommy, the idiot, relaxed. He lit up another reefer,
which he hogged, but that suited me fine. "Heard she
was down to New Or-leans not too long ago, but fuck
that shit. I can't be traveling down there, man, with
that cocksucking parole fuckhead. . . ." His eyes were
getting so glassy, you could practically apply your makeup.

"Way down yonder in New Or-leans!" I beat on my
leg some more but the whole display was pathetically
phony.

"Working in some queer-ass voodoo shop, the lousy
bitch."

First I wasn't sure I'd heard right, but the next thing
was this feeling *of course*. The voodoo shop—that was
the answer. It was like all along, this was exactly the
only possible way things could be: you saw the great
steamroller of Destiny coming squash down on you.
"Working in a voodoo shop, huh? Did somebody actually see her there?"

Before I could even inhale, Tommy was on me, his
forearm pressing into my windpipe, the steely muscles
in his body wound up like so many Swiss watches. "You

tell me," he hissed in my ear, "what your connection is or you won't have a face left to talk out of."

"Hey, Pet!"

My body was frozen with fear, and anyway my neck was positioned not to swivel. But obviously Darlene had come to my rescue.

"Hey," she said. "I'm going to split with Jerry here. You gonna be okay?"

Was this for real?

"Tell her to have a nice time," Tommy hissed in my ear.

"Pusher Man" was droning away on the stereo, and it added that extra, surreal gloss to the whole scenario.

"Have a nice time."

"Thanks! You too, keep the car 'cause Jerry said he'd drop me home. Sure it's okay?"

Tommy increased the pressure of his forearm, ensuring an emphatic nod.

"Listen," she said. "Did you find that friend of your sister's?"

CHAPTER NINETEEN

There must be a way to stop time or so many different groups of people wouldn't claim they could do it. At least that's the way I look at life—I know you could argue the opposite more effectively. Why long for something so much if you've got it already? But, and here's my point: look at the total lack of imagination going on around you: how is it possible for so many people to have the same vision? The thing envisioned must exist.

The aborigines for instance—that dream-time exists. Plus, I've seen some of that stuff myself; Sammy could do it. You could argue that I was a kid and didn't know what I saw, that my state of mind was weak and all that jazz. But that kind of reasoning, if you ask me, gets you exactly nowhere.

Time is stopped right now. Tommy has his forearm at my jugular and Darlene has just said the wrong thing. Nobody moves. Here's what I see: the voodoo shop glittering in the sunlight as if washed over by a magical powder. I see the ghosts of myself and my family driving past. I see the whole picture, but not the sense of it.

For instance, the last time I saw Deane.

She was disembarking her plane in New Orleans. We stood expectantly in the airport, Stan and Linwood expecting Deane to arrive, June expecting continuing misery, and me expecting not to see Deane, that my spell would have disappeared her. Hadn't I reversed the love spell just like Sammy told me to?

But Sammy or no, voodoo or not, Deane got off that plane. Her hair was dead black and teased into a beehive that would have put the Supremes to shame. White lipstick, tight skirt detailing her rump, she looked at her family as if observing specimens in an ant farm.

I took a step toward her. I stepped back. My anger over what she'd put us through and my horror over what she'd done to Marmalade, never mind my night in her room, weighed against the sway of my love.

She was my sister. And she walked right by.

"Where the hell is she?" Stan scowled. By now even the most crippled passengers had hobbled off.

Linwood was ominously silent. Her Hollywood shades and sapphire-blue turban left nothing on her face except expertly outlined lips and a small nose with its auto-accident bump.

"She flew the coop," June opined. "Where are we going for lunch?"

I opened my mouth to say *but she was here*. The words stuck to my teeth like licorice.

Stan marched off to consult with the airline desk and Linwood lit a cigarette. I moved over to the plate glass windows, where you could see all that flat murk surrounding the airport. Looked like a plane could just dive right into that swampland, terrain neither entirely liquid nor entirely solid either. Vanish without a trace. Distant white specks of bird flew up and over, winging their feathered way over the bayous.

"This is the best thing that's happened yet," June said following me. "Maybe she's dead."

Maybe what I'd seen wasn't Deane at all. If that was Deane, for instance, how come nobody else saw her? She'd passed within inches of Linwood, the masklike expression of teenage indifference freezing her striking features.

On the other hand, it was a well-established fact that I had a tendency to see things that other people, for whatever reason, didn't. On the other hand (that made three hands), with a little effort, I could conjure up whatever spectacle was necessary. If it's true that the mountain could come to Muhammad, Deane could have come to me, figuring the strength of what I was feeling.

Or, the spell had worked, for everyone but me and Deane herself. She was disappeared to the others.

Whichever way the dial swung, it was all my fault. Or my triumph.

"What's eating you, Lardo?" June munched on a Snickers bar. The machine must have been out of M&M's.

I shrugged her off with a pained expression and gesture I'd picked up from an old Garbo movie, another thing you thought you'd discovered but were only a kid cottoning on to.

"Tubs vants to be a-lone," June concluded, having seen the same film. She licked the candy wrapper.

With a great show of personal dignity, I redirected my gaze to the swamp.

You could blink twice. Those birds rising up were maybe not birds at all.

"June, Pet. Let's go." Stan stood next to us, massaging the bridge of his nose, where the sunglasses cut in.

"Was it a clean getaway?" Worry shone under June's voice.

"The airline said she was on board." Stan sighed.

She was on board. I almost said it. *She was here*.

"So how come—"

"How the hell should I know?" Stan snapped. "We called the police and they're checking it out. If you've got any bright ideas, let's hear them."

We all waited a minute, listening to the announcements of arrivals and departures.

"No point hanging around that I can see." He turned away from us and started toward Linwood, who appeared to be carved out of marble.

"Where to?" June asked once we were all in the car.

Stan turned on the ignition. "We're spending the night at the Royal Orleans. In the Quarter."

"That ritzy hotel?"

Nobody answered.

"Kind of a celebration, huh?"

"She'll turn up," Stan prophesied grimly as we drove out of the airport parking lot. "No doubt some technical error."

Linwood maintained her silence.

"So what about lunch?"

Nobody answered that either.

Idly, as if my involvement were purely coincidental, I toyed with the amulet around my neck. Everyone else was wearing theirs. "Listen," I said as we drove down one of those endless streets full of hamburger stands, on our way to the ancient part of town, "could I have my necklaces back do you think?"

If Deane was disappeared, then so was her book. If her book was disappeared, then so was Sammy. If the necklaces were disappeared, then none of it ever happened. If none of it ever happened, then nothing was my fault.

Silently, they removed their necklaces and handed them over. Warmth surpassing simple body heat wafted out. I wanted to toss them then and there, and should have, but instead I put them in my coat pocket, figuring they were bound for the cigar box.

"Stan," Linwood said as we turned off Canal Street and headed into the heart of the Quarter, "you take the girls out somewhere to eat. I'm getting a kidney infection."

Her kidney infections were always well-timed.

"Oh great." Stan took her infections, like any ailment of hers, personally.

"We get to pick where," June said.

I stared at the random, oddly angled streets. This

was a city that could lose anybody. And keep them lost until they desired to be tossed up on the shore, chance disclosure of effluvia coughed up from the deep.

CHAPTER TWENTY

"Listen," Darlene said. "Did you find that friend of your sister's?"

I expected severe bodily pain from any of these: strangulation, knife through the heart, hand between my legs.

But instead, almost disappointingly, Tommy's grip relaxed. When I swung around, he fell down like a freshly cut tree. We should have called out *Timber*!

The guy was such a loser, you almost had to feel sorry for him. Some master criminal: a little pot and a burst of anger, and that was it for the evening, all tuckered out.

"Was that him?" Darlene had her arm wrapped around her catch of the evening. Outfitted in body-glued worn denim, chestnut mustache scintillating like the fuzz of a spiny caterpillar, this specimen looked like he'd be hard pressed to cop a whizz.

I stood up and brushed off my jeans. Little flecks of marijuana fell to the floor. "Thing is, he's not supposed to know who I am."

"Whoops!" Darlene covered her mouth cartoonishly.

"Not that he could remember, even if I told him." Oddly, a bunch of stuff roiled up in my chest: relief, that the guy was a goner; excitement, that at last, at last! something was about to happen; and then the odd one—a feeling of anticlimax, like this confrontation that was always there for me, wasn't there for me. Someone that had haunted me for so long—Tommy—and this was all there was to it. I had my lead to Deane. What else was there to do? Kill him? Follow him home and burn down his house? Besides, like the girl at The Surf Burger said: scumbags like him don't *live* anywhere.

You had to know when to walk away.

"About my car . . ." Darlene said.

"I'll be fine driving back. You sure about bozo here?"

"Sure enough. Anyway, he lives back at the beach."

"Jerry" just sort of swayed, like a feather in the wind.

"Do me a favor?"

Darlene nodded.

"Keep the thing around your neck on."

She winked. "Pretty kinky!"

I waited a few minutes after they left, thinking something might happen, like who knew what, but the scene was strictly a scene.

And Tommy snoozed on, just another dead-beat gone dumb.

What was the point? I went back out into the beachy night, inhaling the moist salt air as if for the last time, knowing I was *on my way*. I had what I came for: a direction, a place to go to. Most of all, this feeling that once again, any old damn thing in the world, or not in the world, was possible.

But first, there was an important stop to make.

My dream sense of what had been led me over the railroad tracks, up the hill, past the fields, and up the other hill, where the proud yellow house should have risen up in the moonlight. Or, you'd have thought something else would have been built in the ruins. Instead, as the Mustang pulled into the driveway, I saw—ruins.

Even the cypresses were gone!

One of Stan and Linwood's few attempts at landscaping had been the planting of a dignified battalion of cypress trees, which shielded the front side of the house from the passerby. Now, the foundation was simply there, right next to the road, as unprotected as a child with a new haircut.

I lit a cigarette and rolled down the car window. At least the baby redwood was still standing; perhaps being of a grander line than the cypress, it was more resistant to fire. I climbed out of the car and walked over, crunching snails like Rice Krispies beneath my feet.

The moon, crescent and orange, came out from behind a cloud.

The avocado trees that separated our house from the DiBordios' were there, slightly worse for the wear. I wondered if they still raised peacocks, and if the peacocks still escaped and shed their glorious feathers for the lucky to happen on.

I picked my way around to what had been the rear of the house, Deane's room. Everything was so small and hard to believe in—this overgrown slab of concrete the floor on which so much had happened to me? I just couldn't get it.

The pepper tree was a stump in an ex-lawn the size of a postage stamp.

The question was: what were you supposed to be feeling in this situation? What was there before your eyes seemed to have no real connection to what you remembered. What do you believe, then, your senses or your memory? Listen to Jean Genet or Gertrude Stein, forget your real experiences. You make it art and then it achieves artful reality.

But I wasn't an artist. And standing there in the moonlight, the house, the whole thing—it didn't mean beans to me.

There was only one place to go and that was New Orleans.

CHAPTER TWENTY-ONE

It took me about ten minutes to pack my duffel bag. What was there to take? Underwear, makeup, a few pieces of clothing. The cigar box. Four hundred-odd dollars, not much dough but it would have to do. The dream book I'd been keeping. Departing my room was nearly as weird as seeing the old house— you get stuck in things and they seem so important to you. But, like the existentialist said, *Blaugh!*

I walked into Bread's room and shook him on the shoulder. His sheets smelled like kelp and sand and zinc oxide. Or maybe that was him.

"Go away," he mumbled into the pillow.

"I need you. It's important!"

He halfway sat up and did routine wake-up behavior, the eye-rubbing and so on. "Huh what?"

"You've got to take me to the bus station." I lit us each a cigarette. "And it has to happen now because Aunt Edith won't want me to do this."

"You in trouble?" Light from the bathroom reflected phosphorescent on his hair. The nicotine was hitting his brain.

"Not exactly." I gave him the story synopsis. "But knowing she might be there—well, I have to go."

He nodded. "Mom's gonna kill you."

"She'll have to find me first."

"You better leave a note so she doesn't call the police. Need some money?"

I accepted a hundred dollars and promised to repay and then composed my remarks while Bread pulled on his clothes. Trouble was Aunt Edith had never been what you could call enthusiastic about Deane, and it seemed she kind of blamed Stan and Linwood somehow. After these years of putting up with me, she probably figured the flaw was genetic. I tried to express my love and appreciation for what she had tried to do, and also she was my legal guardian and I wanted to make sure I got that money, from the sell of the ex-house in Vista and the farm in Arkansas plus what was left of Linwood's inheritance, when I turned twenty-one in five years. Provided my life continued that long.

"Okay, sport," I sealed the envelope. "Let's head into the night."

After wishing me good luck and retaining custody of the car, Bread dropped me off at the San Diego bus terminal. The inside of the station was almost as bad as the area immediately surrounding it. Besides the sailors, relatively inoffensive, there were clusters of tough-looking teenage boys, hookers (which explained the presence of the teenage boys), pimp types in silly-looking hats, foreign families clustered together in fear, and women padded in all the layers of their clothing, raving as they clutched their pathetic bags of God-knows-what to their persons. The smell, which you don't want to even try to break down into its loathsome components, was one of melancholy, disenchantment, and out-and-out ugliness. Classic stuff: Eau de Bus Station.

I bought my ticket, two hours predeparture, and tried to find a plastic chair relatively unstained by urine, gum, or spit. The bum two chairs away kept coming to and muttering *muthafuckah* and then resubmerging himself in his dream, or whatever it was.

I lit a cigarette and tried to think like Kerouac or even Henry Miller. This was all *material*, see, except that I wasn't a writer. But what about my journal, the dream book? The last entry was the one about the coffin on the hillside, and did that ever seem like years ago! But it was less than twenty-four hours. The last line read: "In another coffin propped next to mine—" Gone. No relationship. The dream was what they say about dreams, smoke and nonsense.

I sat there, pen poised, and then must have drifted off a little because next thing you knew, the page was covered with densely packed script.

Owl flew but not with wings. You find yourself selecting new objects with which to surround yourself: a pitcher, an ashtray, an unknown Expressionist print. Soon you discover, perhaps in the dream-return as you tack that print above the chair in your room, that you have owned this item before. As you watch, its colors become clear to you and then obvious: what could ever have made you imagine that you come fresh to any purchase? That choice is not entirely dependent on what you have selected before? And you say: Oh, yes, this pitcher with its blue and yellow garland of roses . . . how much it resembles . . . of course! You have owned this pitcher before, or one so much like it that you doubt two such identical objects could co-exist in the world. You were in Italy at the time or perhaps living in a loft in New York City. Now you have a room in Seattle. It is all the same.

At the moment one thing becomes clear, the next becomes clouded.

Owl flew. You are sitting in a restaurant where you have never dined. To your friends, you say that you have never eaten Javanese food. How odd that its flavors swell in your mouth with familiarity. As you reach your bamboo spoon toward the milky salad, already you anticipate the sharp thrust of the anise. You look around the small, sparsely decorated interior and the faces you encounter strike the base of your throat with their inevitability. How odd that you do not embrace these others as your kin. That you have never entered their houses and crossed your legs upon their living room mats. You know without asking that the dessert will include guava, lichee, mango, and you know precisely how the flavors will burst. Still you maintain you have never dined here before. With wings, you stretch out the coiled tendrils in the tips of your fingers: they shine out, the exiting ectoplasm.

There is shame in release, whatever the nature. You zap the space between you and the danger. Is there danger? You have always imagined there was. Even in the most innocent street, you have always rushed, as though you can feel the chill breath of your pursuer. Have they caught you yet? Even now, do you sit in your chair while strange flowers bloom and wither on the pearly lattice of your garden trellis? Is the air thick beneath your feet because the ground eludes you? Over and over, you attempt to walk as if what gives way has not always done so. You remain sure, and the snowy wings behind you unfurl like the banner of a proud conqueror, that there is a place to begin and hence

*to end. You are strong and noble, and the profile of
your face glints behind the eclipse like the bright
exploding gas of the stars.*

To tell the truth, it pretty much flipped me out. The
content was weird enough—the bit about buying stuff
had its moments, but all that jazz about foreign food
tended to lose me. And then about walking, and the
space between you and the danger...

But the definite worst, or best, part was that *the
handwriting didn't look like mine!*

It looked, from what I could remember, exactly like
Deane's.

"New Orleans, Houston, Austin, El Paso, Tucson,
points in between, now boarding Gate Six!"

I hustled on board, if that's what you call it with a
bus, and situated my duffel next to me, hoping to
discourage any goon who might try to get cozy. There
was serious thinking to be done, no doubt about it. For
instance, where had all those words come from? Actually, that part was the least worrisome: every one of those
Surrealist guys got messages this way; it was just French
for automatic writing. The part that bugged me, that I
needed to consider, was the overwhelming feeling that
this really was a message from *Deane*.

No doubt that was all a construct of my own brain,
though.

I wanted—

The bus pulled out into the grubby streets, past the
X-rated theaters and the gloomy near-dawn of the night.

I wanted to believe, obviously, that Deane not only
wanted to see me but somehow knew I was on the way.
Was that so dumb?

Soon we were well on our way into the desert. The
minute you leave the ocean behind, you realize that all
this land is supposed to be bare and dry, not irrigated
into emerald lawns and precious flower beds. If the

earth had its way, for instance, stark bare land would
roll right up to the edge of the sea. Except, of course,
the earth doesn't have its way.

· The sun was coming up all right and the sky was rosy
pink, tinted by layers of dubious gunk that had collected on the window.

It was a good thing I'd never washed off my makeup
because it would act as a protective shield, warding off
the icky air that everybody else was breathing out.

Not a pretty crowd. The usual harassed mothers with
noisy kids, the usual middle-aged men slumped down
in their seats, faces concealed by lumpy fedoras. Though
the only reason they seemed *usual* to me, who had
never ridden a genuine bus before, as opposed to the
school variety, was from reading too many books. And
over us all was that weary pall of suspension, unlike the
control you have in your own car, when a simple steer
from the road will propel you from the magic of transi-
tion to normal old stasis. Here, we were like in the web
of some pitiless spider. Either that or procured from
central casting, since I no doubt looked every inch the
part of runaway teenage girl.

The only person who didn't quite fit the bill was the
guy sitting catty-corner across the aisle from me. At
first he looked okay, and then the shininess of his suit
fabric, the frayed cuffs, and the worn-down heels gave
him away. He had this briefcase on his lap, but on top
of the briefcase he'd propped a Bible, which he was, if
you can call it that, reading.

Even looking out the window, the oddness of his
movements disturbed me, so I watched more carefully.

He opened up the Bible at random, or so it seemed,
scanned a column or two frantically with his index
finger, then slapped the book shut. Brief pause, eyes
turned beatifically upward. Then he flipped open the
Bible again—you couldn't tell if it was the same place or
not but looked like not—scanned another column, shut
the book again. Wait. Then, he relaxed his shoulders
and put the Good Book away in the inside pocket of his
shabby overcoat. He settled the briefcase on his lap,
centered it, and opened it up with a body-language show

of anticipation, but what I could see over his shoulder gave me a chill.

The interior of the briefcase appeared to be pure jumble. You could detect pens and scraps of paper and rocks and sticks and the odd plastic dinosaur. A couple M&M's wrappers, a crushed milk carton, a brown apple core, a ragged bit of stiffened sandwich. Who knew what all else . . . my stomach went queasy.

He reminded me of something but I couldn't put my finger on what. So I decided to ignore him and look out the window instead. It wasn't all that far to El Centro.

A minute later I was watching him again.

He combed through the junk for a minute or so and extracted a ballpoint pen, a piece of string, and a couple pages from a *Little Lulu* comic. He put the pen inside the pages, rolled it up, and tied it with a piece of string. Then, as quickly as he had created the package, he took it apart and tossed everything back into the stew of weirdness inside the briefcase. Pause. He rifled through again. Now, the worst part was he wasn't looking at the stuff with his eyes. He was feeling it. Both hands tossed up bits of debris as if sorting through sand for shells, or mud for bits of gold. He hit upon a used kitchen match and the apple core.

Then it sort of clicked, what the display was reminding me of. First idea: *voodoo altar*. Then, *poodle bags*. And finally, let's call a spade a spade, *cigar box*.

Certain accumulations of objects produced, like bizarre batteries, certain charges of energy.

And that's a fact.

Okay, so used matches and bits of string and tuna-fish sandwiches may not create the most exquisite of voltages. But they did create *something*, according to who selected them and how they were collected. This bozo with his briefcase was essentially no different from me and my cigar box. He just didn't have very good taste.

Outside the window, in the middle of the desert, a large black dog, sleek as the wind and shiny, trotted along with a three-foot stick in his mouth.

I shifted my butt, trying to get comfortable. My jeans felt heavy and clammy and my hair felt lank. I was

plunging back into all those things that scared and
intrigued me, so I might as well get used to the idea.

What else was voodoo but the combination of powerful objects?

I stroked the gris-gris around my neck, feeling momentarily comforted. Voodoo, the voodoo shop. Now
was as good a time as any, and it had to be done.
Closing my eyes, holding the gris-gris, and whispering
a prayer, I made myself remember.

"So what do we do today?" June demanded over
breakfast.

Stan and Linwood exchanged weary adult looks.

We were sitting in the sunlit courtyard of the Royal
Orleans, eating breakfast. Green plants glowed greener
in the humid air and the fountains rippled. White linen
tablecloths. I'd ordered waffles, though, and they were
always a big mistake. The idea, *waffle,* was great, but
all that syrup and the constant soggy texture made me
feel tired and cheated. At least if you ordered eggs, you
got to break up the monotony with potatoes and ketch-
up and toast, never mind jam.

"Are we going back to Arkansas?"

"Do you want to?" Linwood sipped her coffee.
It was amazing how much lipstick came off on the
cup.

June hesitated and then her face started to go pink
like she was going to cry. "I don't know."

"Pet?" Linwood asked.

I pushed a square of waffle raftlike around the shallow lagoon of maple-and-butter gunk. "Everything drags
on and on," I said. What did that mean? "It seems like
one day lasts more than a week. How come third grade
went by so quick and this year is so slow?"

Stan snorted that unfunny laugh through his nose.
He rubbed the sides of his head with the flats of his
palms. "Damn good question. Let me know when you
figure out the answer."

"The tin soldier store," June said. "We could go buy
some tin soldiers."

"What for?" Linwood asked curiously.

"For the poodles."

"For the poodles?" Stan repeated.

June's face was pink, and then the tears started oozing down. None of that wide-mouthed bellowing stuff—this was real pain, the genuine article.

This was what I felt: *We can't take any more.*

You looked around the table at us and you saw the deflated appearance we had acquired, that of people who have moved to a foreign country and can't find the things they are used to, not only clothes but also food and sleep. June and I seemed like those kids raised by wolves in the forest, abandoned in the wilderness. We were at the end of some invisible rope. Without thinking, I touched the amulets still in my coat pocket. The rope floated literally before my eyes. There was a cliff too, and then there was nothing. Just an end.

Stan shook his head and lit a cigarette. "That's a nice idea, sweetheart. But—"

He never called her *sweetheart*.

"—but the poodles already have so many nice toys. Those soldiers cost a lot, and I'm not sure the poodles would really play with them very much."

June snuffled glumly. None of this was really about soldiers or poodles or any of that.

I touched my amulets again, wondering why I'd forgotten to put them in the cigar box. I'd do it tonight, without fail.

Linwood freshened her lipstick and shut the compact with a click. "Well, what *do* we do next?"

It was a good morning for prolonged silences.

"I can call the police again," Stan offered. "And the airline. I can call Edith and see if she can find anything out from that end."

Linwood paled. "Not Edith! You know how she feels about Deane. And us."

"How does she feel about us?" June seemed to have recovered.

Linwood sat up straight and tossed her head as she lit a cigarette. So much for the fresh lipstick. "She thinks

Deane is hopeless. A bad seed. And she thinks your father and I are terrible parents."

Neither June nor I said anything. Stan and Linwood looked kind of expectant, like we were supposed to protest.

I had to say something. "Uh, what's her idea of a good parent?" I looked down and pushed the disgusting waffle-mush around with my fork.

More exchange of adult looks.

"Church!" Linwood finally snorted. "Sunday school, Bible groups. And we're not supposed to drink liquor or coffee or smoke cigarettes!"

My heart went out to them. What on earth would they do with all their free time?

"What's wrong with that?" June demanded. "Think of all the money you'd save."

The truth was secretly I agreed. But more secretly, I knew that finally I didn't agree. How can I explain this so it makes sense? The deal was, as a child, you could see that what they did was silly, pretty disgusting, and useless. Who wanted bourbon when you could have a chocolate shake? But sure as anything, this was one of those situations where you just agree that you don't see clearly. And you hope that one day you will.

"Mrs. Nutter doesn't smoke or drink."

There was another silence and then Linwood burst out with one of those noises that you think is a sob but is really an hysterical laugh. "Mrs. Nutter!" she cried weakly, her sides kind of heaving. "Mrs. Nutter!"

Stan joined in, going all red in the face. He had to take off his sunglasses and rub his eyes from merriment, the tears rolling down his face just as June's had a few minutes before.

They tried to support themselves on the table but they were laughing too hard. One of them would recover a little and then the other one would say "No alcohol" or "Sunday school" and off they'd go again.

We watched. I think both June and I were glad they were having such a good time, but the punchline was lost on us.

Wild hyenas, they kept it up for a full five minutes. It

was getting fairly boring, but you knew they needed to do this. It was similar to the time Linwood told June and me that Nana had died and we fell over laughing.

"Boy," Stan said, finally getting a grip on himself. "Lordie. I needed that."

The corners of her mouth still inclining upward, Linwood got her compact out once more. Even though her eyes were all red, she looked a lot better.

"What was so funny?" June inquired in hurt tones.

Stan and Linwood deliberately avoided looking at each other. It was a struggle to control their mirth but they succeeded.

"Just life," said Stan. "Hell, you might as well laugh at it."

"Now what?"

"Now—how about if we all go to Florida and go to the beach!"

June and I groaned—what was it with them and the beach?—but Linwood looked pretty happy.

On our way out of the Quarter an hour later, this truck ran a stop sign, plowing into the front end of our car. Linwood died instantly, as did June, who had been leaning forward in her seat. Stan lingered on for a day or two.

I was the one who survived. Is that supposed to be first prize? Once Deane had disappeared, I had thought the whole deal was settled. I was wrong. The last thing I noticed, before the screams and the shattering glass and the car whirling like a top into oblivion, my hand unthinkingly holding the too-warm amulets in the pocket of my coat, was the glittering window: we were right in front of the stone-cold eye of the voodoo shop.

CHAPTER TWENTY-TWO

"Tucson!"

I woke up hungry, sticky, dry-mouthed. Total yuck.

The gluey window revealed Woolworth's, a pawn shop, a greasy spoon. The cumbersome bus pulled into its station.

"Fifteen minutes in Tucson! Next stop El Paso!"

The man catty-corner in front of me, the guy with the briefcase, had disappeared.

It was going to be tough recapturing some zest for this whole pathetic enterprise. Back at the beach, school was just getting out. Friday afternoons, Darlene and I generally walked down to the beach to meet surfers and smoke dope. It was warm enough to lay out—would I even get a decent tan this summer? Did anybody besides Darlene miss me? Bread loved me but he probably didn't miss me. And Aunt Edith was no doubt washing her hands with relief: like bad parents, like bad sister. Who knew, if I went back now, she could slap me into Juvenile Hall.

I let out a sigh worthy of Stan.

Don't farewell, fare forward. I put my money in my pocket and left the duffel to guard my seat, repel interlopers, and then went into the bus station, passing through one clean swath of downtown Tucson air, which was nevertheless redolent with the far-off odor of desert verbena. Out there somewhere, cactus were blooming. After all, tonight we'd be crossing Texas.

"Fifteen minutes," the bus driver reminded me as I entered the terminal. *Terminal* was a good word for it.

"Coffee with cream," I told the woman behind the tiny counter. "Do you have any pie?"

"Cherry. Lemon. Apple."

"Are they fresh?"

She gave me a wiseacre smile.

"Apple. With a piece of cheese?"

She produced a soggy wedge, deplasticked a sheet of American cheese and slapped it on. The coffee was something you don't want to discuss.

I stirred in a bunch of sugar and played around with the goopy pie. Besides the unpleasant feel of my jeans, my bra straps were cutting into my shoulders. Some adventure. One day out, I hated the life of the road. No Beat poet, me. The way to go was to have your parents

do the driving and stay in Holiday Inns every night.
The shower. The clean white sheets.

"Cigarette?" a male voice asked.

Over to my left was what looked like a cowboy-
Indian. He had copper skin, broad cheekbones, and
heavy black hair, slicked away from his face with oil, but
he was dressed more like a bronco rider: low-cut jeans,
battered boots, neckerchief.

"Do you want one or are you offering one?"

He briefly dazzled me with his teeth. "If you're
offering, I'm taking. If you're taking, I'm offering."

Settle down, Sam! I ate a bite of pie before answering,
to show my cool. "Have one of mine."

He helped himself to my pack, which was sitting on
the counter. His long frame was perched on the stool
like a crane on a spool of thread. After exhaling the
smoke in an impressive stream from his nostrils,
dragonlike, he emitted even more from his mouth and
then inhaled it back through the nose, very French.

"Are you from El Paso?" I asked.

He stared first at my face and then at my neck.
"Same as you," he said. "I'm going to New Orleans."
He pronounced it Nu-Aw-Leans.

I was outhipped, no doubt about. Not only was my
cigarette expertise outclassed, but also the smoke tasted
both oily and chalky, the same way my face felt. Coffee
coated my tongue like tar.

"El Paso!" the driver called.

Time flies when you're having fun.

The cowboy-Indian tipped his hat to me and I figured
that was that, except he stuck close boarding the bus
and two minutes later was settled next to me in the
seat. He removed his sunglasses and we exchanged
looks: his eyes were a clear dark brown, strong tea in a
white china cup.

The bus pulled away from the terminal and out into
the afternoon dust.

"Alonso." He touched the base of his throat with an
index finger.

"Me Jane."

Alonso put his glasses back on.

"Sorry," I said a minute later. "Happy to meet you. My name's Pet."

He smiled and his profile lost that cigar store Indian look. "Petunia? Petrina? Petulia? Wait, Petroniski!"

My cheeks flushed; he had a strong effect on me, but also the fatigue of the trip was taking its toll. "Just Pet. My family nickname."

"Okay, Just Pet." He took off his sunglasses again and put them in the front pocket of his workshirt.

That was when it occurred to me that the odd feelings welling up, strong but not emanating from any particular part of the body, might be what they called *sexual attraction*. Maybe. How old was this guy anyway? Under thirty, but so what.

"Since we're going to *travel* together"— the innuendo was peculiar—"why don't you tell me about what you have around your neck."

So that was it. He wasn't taken with me: he was taken with the gris-gris. Typical, and my chest felt a little sad.

"Who made it?" he asked after a few minutes had passed.

I shrugged.

"But you remember where you got it."

"Oh, sure." We were out of the city already. Sagebrush, saguaros, little yellow flowers just like always. And the looming presence of endless distant mountains.

"Do you want to tell me?"

"Not particularly."

"Uh-huh." His voice was unsurprised.

A few minutes passed. Alonso tilted his hat down over his eyes and slumped back in his seat and I turned away from him, trying not to be alert to how close he was, the nearness of skin and all that skin contained. No way was sleep going to come, that was the last thought before my head plopped against the thick glass and it seemed like my body floated out over the desert somewhere, riding along while the first crayon streaks of sunset advertised the approach of night.

*   *   *

We were riding along on a dirt road, the pure solitude like a chaperon between us.

"Look," I said. "I don't want to go to your village."

There was no village in sight, nothing but a distant pile of low hills like rubble.

When we got to the edge of the pile of rubble, you could see that we were suddenly on the edge of a large canyon. The truck descended a bumpy dirt road that sloped gently into the mouth. The sky was turning rosy, and in spite of the dust the air was cool and smelled like water.

"My mother will want to meet you."

You want to drink the last drop of wine in the cup. But if it spills, it spills. "What for?"

"Because she can help you." Alonso raised his right arm aloft and pointed at the side of the cliff, where the canyon wall rounded to accommodate the bend in the stream. There was not much of a stream now, but later in the season, when the snows melted, the snows of yesteryear, perhaps the river would run.

I studied the side of the cliff, and then realized that what you took for an interesting rock formation was really a stack of pueblos.

"Cliff dwellers!" I was excited. The concept had always had charisma for me, like the Bay of Fundy.

"We are Pueblo People."

After the truck was parked at the base of the main pueblo, we hopped out. Several people stood around the brace of ladders. Two Indian girls about my age were wearing bellbottomed jeans and smoking cigarettes. A couple of older men greeted Alonso in whatever the language was, the tone of voice and mock punch to the shoulder seeming familiar enough.

In response to Alonso's nod, I followed him up the first two ladders and past a group of older women, who were slapping together tortillas and chit-chatting by the open fire. We crossed some roofs and then Alonso stopped before a doorway and motioned me inside. "You can sleep here," he said. "You can wash down there." He spun around and pointed back to the valley, where *the trickle of the stream was a silver thread on a dusty tablecloth.*

Then I was down there on the edge of the stream. The sun passed over the lip of the canyon wall and the sky bruised up like grapes.

I took off all my clothes except for the gris-gris around my neck. The water was warm against my skin and the brace of cottonwoods shielded me from anyone in the pueblos who might be looking down. The stream, which had appeared larger from above, was actually only a few feet across and shallow. When I sat down, the coarse sand was pleasantly rough.

But suddenly someone was standing there. You couldn't see anyone but my vertebrae prickled, as if the air had become thinner.

"Who's there?"

KEE-AWK! A huge bird winged out of the branches and took to the sky.

"Who's there?"

BA-ROOG! An unseen animal cried out from the other bank, scuttling of stones.

I stood up and the water rolled like silk off my body.

Standing across from me was Alonso. He stretched his hand out toward me, I thought he was going to touch, but then he opened his palm and there was my gris-gris.

The air was dark all around us, as if it were an infusion of foreign, inky matter.

"That's mine!"

He held it aloft, like a star. "Now it's mine."

"But—"

"Shhh!" He held his finger to his lips.

"But—"

"Ask my mother!" he cried, swinging to the left and pointing his arm. His body followed and so did mine and then suddenly we were back at the pueblos, only they felt different. The old same-but-not-the-same.

A woman stood by the campfire, if that's what Indians call it, and her face was lit from below, like the witches in Macbeth. She threw something on the fire and it poofed up into colored clouds of smoke.

She muttered in whatever their language was, monotonous and guttural.

"She says you're on a journey," Alonso explained.

Then I realized I was still naked, and then I wasn't entirely naked anymore—I was wearing black bikini panties. Great way to impress somebody's mother, *I thought, trying to cover my breasts in a casual way. The gris-gris was there again. Had it ever left?*

The old lady shook her head, mumbling. She wasn't all that old but the dignity imparted her in being foreign made her seem wiser and therefore older.

She flung her arms open wide, as if catching a beachball.

"What's wrong?"

"Shhh," said Alonso. "She's receiving."

"She wants to change me into an owl!" I screamed. The whole thing was so clear—my feet ran desperately but there was that sick feeling you get when you know you're going nowhere, when the legs propel you forward but, it's impossible and it happens anyway, you stay right where you are.

"No!" Alonso shouted, holding on to my bare arm. "Don't run! Don't run away!"

I was sweating hard and my mind screamed RED.

"The nineteen layers of the soul!" he shouted. "My mother wants to trade you for the juju!"

"What's a juju?" I yelled, running harder, feet sinking in.

Bingo! I was awake. The bus was dark gray inside with all the different shades of gray representing many bodies sleeping in many postures.

A smoky headache, like a marijuana hangover, hovered on the edge of consumption. Also, my legs, and the edges along my inner thighs where they touched, throbbed slightly.

Alonso—then he wasn't imaginary!—was still slouched down in his seat, hat shading his eyes from nothing.

Now, this was a dilly to record in my dream journal. Trying not to disturb my companion, I reached down into my duffel and rifled around until my hand closed on the familiar slick cover. I also pulled out my fountain pen with the tiny lightbulb.

Carefully, I printed:

THE NINETEEN LAYERS OF THE SOUL

Then my eyes got real heavy again.

CHAPTER TWENTY-THREE

THE NINETEEN LAYERS OF THE SOUL

1. *The blue membrane*
2. *The hypnotic shell*
3. *Memory*
4. *Leather extremities*
5. *The fatal body*
6. *Red eyes*
7. *Interplanetary travel*
8. *Hair*
9. *Moving through the seven colors of the wind*
10. *Mathematics*
11. *The hysterical wall*
12. *Sex*
13. *The odor of trees*
14. *Walking as if on feathers*
15. *White noise*
16. *Owl*
17. *Serendipity*
18. *Astral emissions*
19. *Mud*

CHAPTER TWENTY-FOUR

"Wake up!" I shoved Alonso hard on the shoulder.

Instantly he was alert. You could feel every cell at attention; he was either entirely asleep or entirely not-asleep.

"What's all this stuff?" I demanded, pointing at the entry in my dream book.

"How should I know?" he replied craftily.

Good question. It wasn't my handwriting, but it probably wasn't his either. Once again, the script was suspiciously similar to Deane's. "Sorry." I felt sheepish. "I had a rather powerful, uh, dream."

"Can I see that?"

"Oh, you wouldn't—"

He took it out of my hand and borrowed the penlight. After studying the list for a minute or two, he handed the book back and lit us each a cigarette.

"Where'd you learn all that?"

"That's the point. I didn't. It isn't my handwriting. It's . . ."

We let a moment pass.

"You have to sneak up on things," he said, after a while.

"Come again?"

"Watch your language!" He grinned wolfishly.

It took me a minute. "Oh, right. I mean, what are you trying to say about sneaking?"

"I'd rather talk about coming."

I gave him a full dose of my steely-face, a face devoid of all humor and gamesmanship. Not that you could get the full brunt of it in the dim, but anyway.

"Okay," he said, inhaling mightily. "You know that bit in the Bible about walking in the front door?"

I knew that Bible school would pay off one day. "John Ten. Something something the same is a thief and a robber. But he who entereth through the front door is the shepherd of the sheep!"

"Right, that. Well, in a way they're right, but actually they're wrong."

"This is making like no sense whatsoever."

"You sure you want to talk about this shit?"

"I'm sure."

"All right." He took off his hat, which he'd shoved to the back of his head, and placed it on his knees. Then he stroked back his hair with both hands, as if the gesture stimulated his brain. "Maybe *sneak* is the wrong word. What I want to say is that one way you go in directly and the other way you go in indirectly."

"Go in where?"

He seemed surprised. "The voodoo shop, of course. What did you think we were talking about?"

I held my hands up, palms facing Alonso, like *Back off, Jack!* I took a minute to organize my thoughts and during that minute the gris-gris, which was still secure around my neck, emitted a warm, pleasing sensation. "Supposing we *were* talking about the voodoo shop. I want to know how you knew."

"Snickers?" he offered, pulling the candy bar from his pocket.

"No, thank you."

"The juju around your neck, man." His bite of candy muffled the words slightly. "I know where you got it. And I know who made it."

"I see." Actually, this was a transparent stall. But what was the point in being cagey? "Okay, who made it?"

"A guy named Sammy."

Now, you'd think that would have flipped me out. Sammy! But, of course, this Sammy might not be my Sammy. It wasn't like it was a weird or unusual name.

"Cold eyes. That's what you notice first. And then his clothes—quite the snappy dresser."

"And I suppose his skin is sort of pecan-colored?"

"You got it."

"Uh-huh . . ." A simple case of subjective reality in-

truding, that was all. Happened to André Breton all the
time. In fact, this was precisely that sort of dream state
that those guys clamored to be in. The idea was to
enjoy it, I sternly pointed out to my body as the
shoulders, stomach, and calves remained tense. The
idea was to relax. "Do you have any drugs?"

"Life is a drug." He touched my forearm. "Sex is a drug."

It was like somebody had thrown a medicine ball at
my belly; this *was* what they called attraction. Trouble
was the surfer boys I was used to going out with always
settled for so little and were happy with that. A little
digital dexterity put them right out of their misery. You
could tell Alonso was going to be a different situation.

He moved his hand up my forearm and then over the
round of the shoulder and up to the place where the
neck muscles were all bunched up. He gently rubbed.
"You've got an athlete's frame," he said. "You ever do
any weight-lifting?"

Not exactly high romance. "No." Unbidden, the image
of Humongous Hannah, The World's Strongest Female
came to mind. She was out there somewhere, the
mule, if she was still alive. We could be passing by,
right at this very moment. I turned to look out the
window, thinking that in this frame of seeing anything
could get conjured up, but no. I wanted to see that
billboard cartoon blonde looking like she could take on
the world, no problemo.

He kissed my neck, the place where the muscle rises
up out of the shoulder, the one that sounds like trape-
zoid. Trapeze artists develop it, I guess, or maybe it
makes them look like a triangle. Whatever.

Then he kissed me on the mouth. Wow! And what
was that other hand of his up to? Magically, it slithered
up my leg. I never let boys do that.

But this was no boy.

Groggily, weakly, I tried to protest.

"Relax," he whispered in my ear. "There're lots of
things I'd like to do with you. But in the meantime,
ain't we got fun?"

CHAPTER TWENTY-FIVE

"Houston!"

Early afternoon and we were on the far edge of Texas. The night had been long or short, I forget which, and deliciously groggy. Sometime toward morning, though dreamlike snatches of rosy prairie dawn flitted through my head like bright pink bugs, my body had fallen into deep slumber. Alonso had gone away—breakfast in Austin?—but now he was back, slumped against me, lightly snoring.

"Houston," I whispered in his ear, feeling both tender and strange.

"Who cares?" he muttered, snuggling in.

Gently I extracted myself and, stiff and sticky, hobbled off the bus for a pit stop. The corners of my mouth kept turning up of their own volition; the muggy east Texas air seemed romantic and exciting, even though you knew that basically it was just more gunk coating your skin. The bathroom—even that level of grime wasn't depressing!—revealed, however, the confirmation of my hazy speculation: you can feel great but still look like dog vomit.

Grin and bear it. Spray Oh! de Love on your greasy bleached hair and wash your face like a good kid.

I bought some Snickers bars, some barbecue potato chips, a Pepsi, a Chocolate Soldier, some packets of peanuts, and three cheese sandwiches wrapped in wax paper. Halfway back to the bus, I thought: *He's gone.* But he wasn't. And from the end of the aisle where I stood watching him, it seemed like the whole Deane thing wasn't really necessary. If I could stay with Alonso . . . well, some things were better than family.

He smiled when I sat down and showed him our

provisions. "I love you," I said. "Do you love me? Where'll we go? I want to be with you forever and ever."

That woke him up. In two seconds, Alonso was upright, sunglasses over his eyes.

He hadn't said anything yet but already this sick feeling was welling up from the same place my good feeling had come from. *Okay, Pet,* I told myself—already five seconds had stretched out so that the edge was imperceptible—*you're going to remember this moment, this feeling, for the rest of your life. Don't you ever, ever, ever put yourself in this position again. Do you hear me?*

"Oh never mind," I said, glad my own sunglasses were on. "My boyfriend could never survive without me."

Alonso stroked my forearm, tense as a spring. "Sweet," he said, "I've already been married once. All you need is once."

I nodded and took a swig from the Chocolate Soldier. Maybe looking like dog vomit makes you feel like dog vomit after all.

"But I'd like to see you again, after we get to the city."

I ate a couple peanuts.

"They don't need me until day after tomorrow."

"They?" I'd never thought to ask what he was going to New Orleans for. What a kid! I guess I thought he was just there for me.

"The company that hired me. I work the oil rigs."

"Oh."

"You know how Indians are famous for not being afraid of heights." For the first time, his voice sounded bitter.

"All that experience in the pueblos."

He grinned then. "That's right!"

By tacit agreement, we held hands for a minute. Afterward, we ate the food, silently and hungrily, as the bus pulled out of Houston. The land was green now and lush, everything full of too much water.

"It does stuff to you," he said dreamily. "All that blue and green around all the time. It interferes with your imagination, but it adds to it too, like it's all one big swamp—"

"I may be a child in your eyes, but I have read Jung."

He snorted through his nose. "Get out that journal you showed me." He tilted his head back in the seat. "I have three things to say."

In a moment my pencil was poised over the page. "Ready."

"Number one. Every emotion in the world wishes to be expressed, every task desires to be done. Coincidence is the perfect texture."

"Come again?" I clapped my hand over my mouth. "Whoops."

Alonso looked at me like *get serious*.

"I mean, I get the bit about expressing emotions." My handwriting definitely didn't look one little bit like Deane's. Or whoever was writing in my journal. "And, okay with the work ethic. But 'coincidence is the perfect texture'?"

"We met, didn't we?"

I wanted to say *How's that a coincidence?* but the juju burned around my neck. Plus, there was the bit about Sammy, which was too much to think about. Basically, that was the problem here: all this stuff was too much to think about.

"You know what they say about there being no such thing as coincidence?"

"Yeah." But I didn't want to think about that either.

"Well, this is just one simple step farther along that track. That's why write it down. One day: clear as glass."

You hoped so.

"How about this," he said. "Don't write this part down, it just needs to be said. Three pains you remember all the time are the Invisible, the Ever-Present, and the Consecutive—"

"But—"

"Close your eyes. Don't *think* about what I'm telling you. See if you can't just feel it."

I closed my eyes and saw a starry field of midnight satin.

"That's better. Now, three pains: the Invisible..."

The stars faded and all there was was this midnight blue satin, on and on. It was cold, remote, beautiful, and I felt it like an icy girdle around my chest.

"The Ever-Present..."

Now the satin changed, glowed up until it was a rich
golden shimmer. Like a late autumn afternoon. But it
hurt too, in that peculiar way that makes autumn so aching.

"And the Consecutive."

This one came like a flash. It was a chain of things,
like poodles, and Deane's altar, and the spell that
Sammy gave me, and they were in these little frozen
boxes, chained together, connected like those Christmas tree chains you make out of strips of paper. Everything tied together, like an endless shave of tinsel. . . .

"Deane!" I shouted. "You know who Sammy is! Did you
ever know my sister?"

"Hush, now." His voice was so very soothing. "You
begin to see that the world moves in a slick, primal
order. But every now and then, you got to shake it up.
You got to rock it hard from top to bottom."

I opened my eyes, and the bright light and passing
green of the countryside seemed very peaceful.

"Okay," he said. "You don't need to remember that
stuff. Not word for word. That's stuff to be forgotten
most of the time. But here's the second thing you need
to write down."

The pencil readied itself.

"Sex is stronger than doors and windows."

No joke. I printed this carefully. If what happened
last night was how it could be, sex ruled the world! My
stomach felt bubbly and rich, like eggnog, and if I
shifted my eyes inward, without any attention from the
brain, there was a warm pink glow covering my forehead, oozing down from the cranium.

That kind of sex. Did Alonso speak out loud?

But I wasn't going to look up and make eye contact,
feeling he wanted me to.

"Third and last." He sighed. "Coincidence. Sex. And
the last one is ritual. Get this exactly as I say it. Rituals
align the molecules of the object with the cells of the
observer. It is the visceral way of snapping together the
attention of the *orisha.* That's o-r-i-s-h-a."

No way was I going to ask what *orisha* meant. And
then, may my heart be shattered like crystal and tossed
East of the Sun and West of the Moon, a voice spoke in

my head: Deane! *The Òrìşà, no h, are the divinities that intermediate between people and the Supreme Being.*

But how could she speak to me in my head? And her presence was there, something you sense like an aroma, before the words. Not to mention that she corrected the spelling.

"What is it?" Alonso asked.

I closed my journal.

He stared at me a moment, but I shut my mind down like a lead door. "Well," he said, "you know those three things, you know it all."

Coincidence. Sex. Ritual. (The Òrìşà.)

He did his hat-over-the-face siesta bit. "Time for a little snoozing after all that wholesome food."

In a minute, he was snoring away. But that was all right.

Deane? I called out in my head. *Deane, are you there?* Yet, what was "there" anyway?

There wasn't any answer, no big surprise. Maybe she wasn't "there" now, but she had been.

The Great Chain of Excitement, like The Great Chain of Being, began to connect itself in my mind. Tommy existed, told me that Deane existed, so I met Alonso, who told me that Sammy existed. In short, the whole enchilada looked like part of the world, not just a story kids might make up to amuse themselves. The next step, natch, was to see my own sister in the flesh—but then all kinds of stuff popped up, stuff I didn't want to worry about yet. Like, why did Sammy want Deane's book anyway? And did he double-cross me, or single-cross me, by telling me to reverse the magic spell?

And, the worst one: *Was it my fault what happened?*

My head went all tilty and I lit a cigarette, scanned out over the greeny swamp we were entering. If only you could be a tree instead of a person, think how neat that would be: out in the swamp, edging up to the deep secrets of the mysterious bayou. . . .

The sign said WELCOME TO LOUISIANA.

Mile after mile of murky swamp, cypress trees draped in crinkly gray moss, what June always called *vampire moss*. That water, it sucked you right in. The slowness, like one of those miniature Japanese gardens with the mirror embedded in clay, and with your eyes soft-focused, the mirror was real water all right.

Then I was seeing something I couldn't be seeing, but there it was. Blink your eyes and it's gone; blink again, *there*.

I saw me. I was living right there in the middle of the swamp, on a houseboat. Older. But this was the best part: my body was all muscled up and I looked like . . . Hannah!

Was this a vision? A road not taken? Or a flash-forward. Blink, there. Blink, not-there. Blink.

No doubt about it, that was me, strongly muscled and ready to go. Had any woman ever lifted a thousand pounds?

Blink.

Blink.

Blink, there still.

The bus moved on, but this other self floated over the swamp. How could she-me loom so large?

The phrase from Durrell: *Unhappiness is the enchanted potion*. That was my idea of glamour, all drugs and cigarettes and late hours and too much mascara—not this firm body so incredibly radiant with health.

The power in those biceps, the gold snake bracelets ready to burst.

CHAPTER TWENTY-SIX

"City of New Or-leans!" the driver sang out, sounding happy for the first time.

I opened my eyes to raw thrill and an aftershock of nausea. Once off the bus, I was set in motion.

Alone.

Alonso slept on next to me, his carved Indian profile shaded by his cowboy hat.

We weren't at the station yet and the window revealed exciting trashy stuff: dark-skinned women with short skirts and tight, bright tops, bits of bead and feather braided in their hair. My hair would look good like that. Men stood around in the streets, angled forward, butts pushed out, smoking cigarettes up close to their faces and nodding, nodding. A great white fat woman sat on the stoop of a rickety house, drinking from a bottle in a paper bag.

I slicked my greasy locks back of my ears and ran a Kleenex over my face to sop up some of the grease. My sunglasses covered up the raccoon bit around my eyes. Bending my head down to the opening of my shirt, my nose caught the updraft from the pit area, and it wasn't exactly good news.

All that was left was prayer. *To you,* I concentrated in my mind, so that my eyelids ached. *Whatever, Whoever. Help me.* Except a plea like that might attract help you couldn't reckon with. Amended version: *Help me to realize what will be will be.* And so forth.

Buddha.

Allah.

Jesus.

I tried to think the same thought in as many different religions as possible, so the thought itself wouldn't be limited by any particular way of reasoning, the way words restrict—the whole eskimo-seventeen-words-for-snow idea.

The bus jolted to a halt inside the dingy station, and before Alonso had a chance to wake up or tell me where to meet him or any of that jazz, I was history. My wide shoulders were always useful at effecting a rapid exit.

When I crossed through the terminal and stepped out on the street, the smell and breath of that smoggy, heavy air was pure Proust.

Bus exhaust, sweat, wisteria, hair oil, brown sugar cooking, gin, evil weed.

Whew! It added up to Eau de Sex. And the odor was right *there,* waiting in the streets or inside your body, either one.

I recognized Canal Street to my left, so that was the way to go. Even though it was getting on toward twilight, the sun was still full and wet on my head. My hand on my duffel was already sticky.

My pores sang: *This is it!*

My heart, though, felt sorry.

But my skin and the energy won over—anything goes! My sweat and body oil were oozing out like the sap of a tough young tree.

Canal was a busy street, and the openness of the boulevard, in contrast to the narrow streets that fed onto it, stood out bright. Sunglasses weren't enough against the glare, light gone crazy in the refracting heavy air. I joined the bustle of people crossing over to the other side. Over to the Quarter. Look right and there was the mighty Mississippi—you couldn't see it because of the levee, of course, but you could see the tops of the docked ships and smell the crude oil and vegetation. Not exactly the bracing breeze of the Pacific. Look left and who knew what was up that way—slums? Tenements? Mysterious alleyways where people's throats were slit in the dead of the night for obscure reasons. In bizarre patterns.

In a city like this, your mind started working that way.

I turned onto Bourbon Street, entering into the dark of the Quarter, the sunlight and open of Canal transformed instantly into dank and dim. Like some kind of yin-yang demo. This was no landscape for blondes, and the idea popped into mind to dye my hair black before I tackled the problem of Deane.

But then the voodoo shop was before me. The short intervening block of strip joints and hurricane bars had seemed so impressive when I was a child. Now it was just so much tawdriness. And there was that too-familiar building.

The nape of my neck tingled and my arms skittered as if cockroaches were running up and down.

Okay, I told myself, *here's what we'll do. We'll just peek in the old window and see if anybody's around. We won't go in yet; that's premature. We'll simply stroll up to the glass, take a casual look-see, nothing suspicious.*

And there was Deane, standing behind the counter, which was covered with gray moss and artifacts. Hand on one hip, eyes focused nowhere, she sullenly smoked a cigarette. Her hair was long and dead black. She was wearing a purple velvet shirt with a Nehru collar and her face was so made-up that you couldn't see any actual skin.

Other than being older, tougher, and more colorful, she was the spitting image of me.

Okay, now what?

You'd think a little more cunning would have been involved in tracking her down. I was so surprised that my surprise hardly left room for me to feel anything else. Actually, there was also a sense of disappointment—I'd expected to have to use shrewd acumen and clever reckoning, and the whole deal was handed to me right on a platter.

I turned on my heel and fled down the street.

My idea was a shower, a change of clothes, and some time spent looking over the new information in my dream journal. I didn't want to fare forward; I wanted to farewell.

With that in mind, I rapidly found myself back on Canal Street, in the last of the sunshine, and then I found myself a room in the Ramada Inn. There wasn't a Holiday Inn close enough.

CHAPTER TWENTY-SEVEN

I opened my eyes to body-heaviness, clean skin, mournful waves of self-pity, and jitters, the oh-boy-something's-gonna-happen kind. The ice in the Coke on my nightstand had mostly melted but I slugged it down anyway, sweet wateriness and the barest taste of caffeine. Then I just lay there a minute, head throbbing wonderfully, and the whole dilemma—alone in a hotel room in a strange city—struck me as marvelously adult. The one thing missing was the melancholy whine of a saxophone, where some forlorn musician leaned on the fire escape of his New Orleans shack and longed to give wings to the depth of his soul.

Wow!

The clock on the nightstand said ten-nineteen. My first impulse was, *Oh, it's too late to go back to the voodoo shop tonight, she's waited almost seven years so she can wait another twelve hours,* but just the same I got out of bed and put on the dress intended for the occasion: my white lace mini.

Various opening approaches ran through my mind:

"Hey, sis, long time no see!"

"The jig's up, sweetheart."

Or, simply, "Remember me?"

And then I felt what was in my heart: "Take care of me."

I sighed. It was very unlikely that Deane would want to take care of me—one glimpse of that sullen face convinced you that no way had she changed. That was not the visage of new leaves turned, not the countenance of responsibility. In other words, that was not the mug of someone who was just dying to have her kid sister land on her doorstep, unless said kid sister was carrying money or drugs, and said kid sister was out of drugs and down to her last hundred bucks.

Too bad about the drugs, though the truth was I was weird enough from the strain of the last couple days. Rimbaud on his drunken boat, Alfred Jarry on his absinthe, and Pet on her bus and cigarettes. Perhaps I wasn't quite in the same league, but still I'd had my moments. Maybe those moments would turn into a life of reasonable decadence and sin. It was the kind of thing you had to grow into, like a chinchilla coat or a necklace of baroque pearls.

I did the makeup bit—too bad they hadn't invented a light shellac you could spray on your face and keep the whole shebang intact for days. And then I was out the door, out into the night.

New Orleans! Even at night the sky was colorful,

reddish as if it reflected from somewhere else, and you could feel the music well up from the sidewalk as you got close to Bourbon Street, as if the water, which was right under the thin layer of the soil, conducted that jazzy energy.

My armpits and forehead began to blossom with sweat, but the feeling was nice: adapting.

This time I was ready for the voodoo shop. Earlier, it was all so abrupt—like Alonso said, you couldn't stroll right in the front door. You had to find another way.

My heart hurt. *Forget Alonso.*

The air was heavy with the smell of old water sitting in pools of stone, the broken fountains in the seedy courtyards on either side of the street. When I turned onto Bourbon, the smell of liquor drowned out everything else, and the swinging saxophones, and all those rowdy bodies jostling. One photo display caught my eye: the breasts on the "dancer" looked extraterrestrial. When I was a kid, I thought those big breasts were so lovely—now you could see there was some kind of bad expectation going on here, but exactly what was wrong eluded me. Something about what men expected women to do—images of Tommy flashed through my head, but he was only a pathetic old druggie, what was there to fear from him? Only fear itself, as they say.

And Sammy. Face it: hadn't Sammy had some of that same kind of weird energy? Would I see him soon? Would he remember me?

Would I ever see Alonso again?

The warmth of the amulet/gris-gris/juju between my breasts.

Goddammit! What was past was history, and you began remaking it the instant it was past! Who knew how it went, it was all imagination, who knew what had ever happened to anybody. . . .

Of course the voodoo shop was closed. Its windows were tidily shuttered down, not even a chink to peek through. And its energy felt in repose, an electric appliance unplugged for the evening.

I rapped soundly on the old wooden door. A grunt

and some scuffling ensued, an almost imperceptible altercation in the shutters, and then continuing silence.

I knocked again. This time there was that frozen, palpable silence that clues you in on the fact that someone else is inches away from you but refusing to admit it.

"Please," I said. "It's important."

Boy, that was effective, ha ha. The youthful, timorous accents of my voice didn't exactly reek of persuasive authority.

But what was the way to get me in?

While I hesitated, my hand went to the juju, burning brightly against my throat.

Just like in a Dracula movie, the voodoo door swung in on creaky hinges.

"Thanks." I spoke to the door itself since it was apparently the animate object.

The door didn't answer.

The inside of the shop was the way I remembered: herbs and dolls and trinkets and candles. And the smell—was that odor there before? The connection in my mind was with something else, gone foggy.

The curtained niche to my right was like before, except now it cost three dollars to get into the Voodoo Museum. And the fat man wasn't around.

Then I knew the smell: it was the altar; it was Deane's room; it was the wheel of fortune that pushed you right along. Deane had smelled just like this, and now this place smelled just like Deane.

"*Deane!*"

Furious footsteps and then a tall man dressed in a white robe shot through the curtain. "Who the *fuck* let you in?"

"The door." Always ready with the witty riposte, *c'est moi*.

"Then the goddamned door can see you out." He grabbed me smack on the biceps and yanked me toward the exit.

"Deane!" I bleated again, lamb to the slaughter. My heels bumped along the wooden floor as he dragged me.

"Wait." The voice was so soft, it was the whisper of wings. Bat wings.

A woman was standing right next to us. Her body was concealed in a dark robe, but her face was conspicuous in the dim light from the street: it was pocked all over lightly, like an orange.

"I am Templa Una."

And I'm the Dali Lama. Or is it *Llama?* "Where's Deane?"

There was an extended silence during which the tall man let go of my arm but remained hovering. I had the strong impression that there was no point in my saying any more; this woman knew who I was and why I was here, though with the striking family resemblance, she didn't have to be Einstein to figure it out. And the bellowed *Deane* still hung in the air like cigar smoke.

"You are bound to be disappointed," she eventually opined.

"All my life." I wanted to sound tough, one of those California detectives maybe.

"Let me extricate this child from your presence," the self-appointed bouncer suggested, his voice as glutinous as the sauce in a cheap Chinese restaurant.

"Oh no," said Una. "Disappointment is its own instructor."

That was one of those remarks that seemed profound yet rapidly turned to gibberish if you thought about it. Or it could be one of those remarks that disintegrated and then came back, say three days later, and you wake up in the middle of the night thinking *of course*.

"Now then. Who is this *Deane* and why should she be here?"

I sighed. Patience was never one of my top qualities. "I saw her working here this afternoon. And she's my sister."

Una gave me a fierce, penetrating look, which gave me the willies. It was like something they taught you in Evil School, where the stare-ee begins to feel that a fish hook is pricking the base of his neck. "I don't believe that's possible. I was the one working here this afternoon." She turned away to examine some bottles of St. John the

Conqueror. "Myself and Rondo." She inclined her palm.

At least my body was off the hook. "Deane was here too. She's got long black hair, lots of eye makeup. And she looks like, uh, me."

Una raised and dropped her shoulders. "Sorry."

Damn it to hell! They almost had me believing I'd made that up, too. "Please let me see her!"

Una turned back and smiled. "Of course, you must have mistaken her for someone else, a customer perhaps. By the way, child." She draped her arm over the top of my shoulders and then I knew what the willies *really* were. "Do you need a place to stay for the night?"

Rondo grunted in disgust.

First thing in my mind: those torture machines inside the museum. And the main part of that smell, the altar smell—fresh blood.

I was halfway out the door before I dared turn back and face her. "I'll be back in the morning. And if you don't have some information about my sister, I'm getting the police." Even to my own ears, especially to my own ears, a festival of hot air.

"The police!" Una's merriment was almost infectious. "The police in the Quarter!"

Rondo wheezed through his nose.

"If you don't want to stay here," Una said, recovering from her mirth, "you'd better run along. What you want—we don't have that."

"I'll be back tomorrow!" My voice was tiny out on the sidewalk where I'd been deposited like a bottle.

This time the door was as unresponsive as the rest of the shop.

CHAPTER TWENTY-EIGHT

Shame-faced, I instinctively headed for the river. Maybe I could jump a banana boat for Haiti, though

National Geographic once had that television special about the guys who unload bananas, and if they get bitten by a banana snake—who are apparently able to exactly impersonate bananas, if *impersonate* is the word you use when a snake makes like a piece of fruit—they have twelve seconds to lop off whatever got bitten in order to save their lives. Which is why they all carry machetes. No thanks.

Maybe a coffee barge. Or sugar cane. Or a luxury yacht bound for Bombay and needing a cabin girl. Maybe I could do what Stan and Linwood always said we would—take a slow boat to China and have a Singapore Sling in the Raffles Hotel.

Couple after smiling couple passed by. Tourist women were dressed for the evening in gauzy pastels like moths, and tourist men wore big white belts and white shoes and sweated in their ties and jackets.

Antoine's was on my left and I stopped. Through the curtains you could see the diners ending their meals with *crepes suzette* and *cherries jubilee*. Close to the window was a family of four, with two little girls, both well on the porky side. Looking at the dad, you could see how they got that way, though the mother was reed-slim and bored, the angle of her face in the dim room a sharp suggestion of Linwood, and I thought: *Maybe it's us! Maybe there's a time warp and—* But then I remembered, *I was never fat.* Was I? And anyway, they were all fussing over the youngest, it wasn't us.

You go back to a place like this, you think you can close your eyes and open them quickly, quickly, and nothing will have changed since you were there before! An act of will, why, you conjure the whole thing up—

This was working up to a big downer, so I moved on riverward, heading for Jackson Square and the Café du Monde.

It was all bustle down there, as full of happy tourists as Disneyland at high noon. "Artists" had their wares displayed around the wrought-iron-fenced square, and old men in top hats tried to get people to ride around in carts pulled by tired horses dressed up in paint, feathers, and wigs. Threading my way through the crowd, I found a little table in the café that never closed, and from the looks of the pillowy confections dusted with a heavy snowfall of powdered sugar, at least when the world kept changing, beignets hadn't.

I ordered my doughnuts and some coffee—I was all grown up now and actually preferred the stuff to hot chocolate, bully for me. Then I lit a cigarette and took the dream book, which I had never gotten around to studying earlier, out of my bag.

"Watching your step?"

As soon as the words were spoken, my right foot was raised and a loud kiss was planted on the instep.

Alonso. He'd changed into a clean white shirt with a string tie made from a scorpion frozen in amber. His freshly oiled black hair hung slick and dark down his back, stressing the prominence of the high bronze cheekbones and those dark tea-colored eyes.

"Take what's at hand," he added, sitting down at my table and grabbing my wrist. He licked my palm.

Without a shadow of a doubt, this was what they called sexual attraction. "Aren't you going to suggest I keep abreast of the situation?"

"Or," he continued, "that we get *behind* the problem."

I'd used up my quota of wit.

"Or—"

I held up my palms for mercy as the beignets and coffee arrived. Alonso charmed his way into someone else's order, so we sat there and munched.

"Have to hang around you for my daily dose of sugar," he observed after a few minutes. His lips were all covered with the stuff. Maybe I should lick it off.

"A lucky break for you."

"You're telling me?"

Clearly, we could keep this up all night. "Look," I said. "I snuck off the bus like that because—"

This time he held up his palms for mercy. "Whatever. Now you're here."

I finished my coffee. "Apparently."

"Look, honey." He leaned over and nuzzled my neck. Cooked-goose time.

"Do you want to..."

"Yes," I said, "I do."

We walked along Decatur, not the most savory of avenues, past the praline shops and the Greek groceries and then the old seamen's bars, which looked like places where Jack the Ripper would have felt right at home, and then we were in rows of funny old houses, stoop-type affairs with doors set askew on their hinges. The air smelled like sewers and fried food and cigarettes, but every now and then there was a whiff of something pungent and flowery, almost like violets, which I thought might be opium, that would be romantic. The sounds from the houses and stoops, where shadowy figures sat, were molasses-rich melancholy, and something else, which the surface could not support.

You had the sense that the surface of things, the visible dimension, was a basket, catching.

Then too, it was like the luminous fibers of my body were all caught up with Alonso's, and I wanted to be as close to him as his jugular, skin breaking skin and you got on over to the other side, where you'd never gone before. How could you know that it was there?

I knew it was there.

We filed through a side gate many blocks from the café, across a weed-filled courtyard with a chipped cupid rising in what looked like terminal depression from a stagnant fountain. A nightclub for mosquitoes. Then we climbed up some shaky stairs, and I thought: *Maybe I'll never have to climb back down.*

His hand on the small of my back.

When the door closed behind us, I remembered, *Sex is stronger than doors and windows.*

"Listen," I whispered. "I've never actually done this before."

"You think I don't know that?"
"But—"
He put his arms around me and rested his hands on
my butt. Yup, this was the ticket all right.
"You want to travel somewhere you've never been,"
he said. "Find an experienced guide . . ."

CHAPTER TWENTY-NINE

"Who's Sammy?" I asked, many hours later. It seemed
like many hours later. All you knew was that it was that
dead-dumb time of the night, what they call the Witching
Hour.

Alonso was flat on his back, smoking a cigarette with
his air of utter cool. We were both lying in a mass of
rumpled bedclothes in the middle of what appeared to
be the only room of his apartment.

"I mean, he's a real guy, right?"

Alonso performed his French exhale.

You don't love this man, I told myself sternly. But
geezo, that was one hell of a planet we visited!

"You don't want to mess with him."

"No, probably not. But listen." As quickly as I could,
I told him the whole grisly story, the whole childhood
bit, glossing lightly over the part where everybody but
me buys the farm, then on through the years with Aunt
Edith, and finally up to what happened at the voodoo
shop.

He grunted several times, held my hand during
the difficult sections, and then looked bemused at the
recent stuff. It took half a pack of cigarettes and the near-
arrival of dawn.

"Templa Una." His voice was nostalgic. "Yeah, I used
to know those people. When I saw your juju—" He
reached out and touched it, then brushed against my
breasts.

The old heat rose up, but I quelled it. "What do you know about them?"

"Like I said." He stood up and went to the sink, in a niche off the room. "Want some water? You don't want to mess with Sammy."

"Water, please." I drank gratefully, even though it was mud reclaimed from the Mississippi. "But my sister . . ."

He sighed and sat back down. "You don't know what you're up against. I can give you some protection, but there're more of them than us."

Exasperation bubbled up. "Well, what *are* they? Vampires?"

"You want to see a vampire?" He lunged for my neck.

We played vampire for a while but the truth was my body was pretty sore. That was about enough foreign travel for one night.

"They're a group of people who practice magic," he explained some time later, when dawn light began to penetrate the grimy room. "Swamp magic. And it's some nasty shit."

"Voodoo."

"There's a lot more to it than voodoo."

"And you think what happened to me really happened to me? I mean, when I was a kid."

He shook his head. "I don't know. That Sammy's Snowland stuff is pretty hard to swallow—I don't know. I only know that you think it happened to you. So what difference does it make if it really happened or not?"

That was a stumper. "But if it didn't—"

Alonso took my hand and licked the palm. "Sweet," he said. "I've been to India. I saw those ropes going straight up in the air. Not to mention some of the shit that goes down in the secret canyons of the Ancient Ones, out in the desert. Forget *truth* and *real*. You just want to find Deane, right?"

I wanted to forget *truth* and *real*. Did the Surrealists care a hoot about the "real" world? On the other hand, now that I'd met Alonso and he'd told me the voodoo people were "real," where farther could you go in the abstract? I guess I just wanted to touch Deane with my own hand. "The main thing is to find her. But I need to find Sammy, too. There's some stuff I need to know."

"You sure about that?"

"I want to know why he wanted her magic book. I want to know if he screwed me up with that spell. And I want to know if, uh, if what happened was my fault." *There!*

"You know what they say about asking questions you aren't prepared to hear the answer to."

You could guess what they said: Don't ask. "I can take it. I mean, I guess."

He looked long and deep into my eyes, and those clear whites of his were like Chinese silk. How come they weren't all bloodshot after a night of merriment?

"Here's what we could do," he said. "They have these ceremonies out in the swamp. Or at least they used to. And like I said, I don't have to report to work until tomorrow. So, suppose they have one tonight—"

"Why would they have one tonight?"

Coincidence is the perfect texture.

"You think they didn't notice you?"

My arms began to chill, so I rubbed them. "Why would they care?"

Now the full brunt of his stare made its statement. "You got that kind of attitude, you don't get back alive."

"Are we going?" But of course we were.

"We'll party crash!" When he grinned, his cheek-bones went up, like little hammers ready to strike.

"And it's dangerous."

"Oh, yes."

"But you think there'll be a chance to talk to Deane. And Sammy. To find out some of these—"

His shrug was very subtle, but it showed off his beautiful shoulders. "Hard to say. It's the only thing there is to offer. You got a better idea?"

I reached out and touched his cheek, which was smooth. That was right—Indians don't grow beards. His body too was like one smooth wash of satin skin. And he smelled like baking corn, dry gourds, verbena. "Why are you doing this for me?"

He smiled sadly. "Sweet, I'd like to say I love you."

Heart, don't hurt! You know you can take it.

"But the truth is this sounds like as good a thing to do as any."

I thought of Bread's favorite line from *Conan*. "Do you want to live forever?"

Alonso stood up and scratched his balls, the first thing he'd done that put me off. "That's not a question of choice. It's a question of how you wish to amuse yourself."

I took a little nap and showered while Alonso went scouting for information and checked me out of the Ramada Inn. By the time I emerged all pink with steam, my clean underwear, jeans, and embroidered Mexican shirt were waiting. Okay, it was baby of me to let him coddle, but it felt so good. Anyway, in twenty-four hours he'd be gone and I'd be—

Well, with Deane, presumably.

I felt a pang of nerves. I couldn't remember what day it was, but I knew it was a school day—even in New Orleans, even in this grubby little pad, where the bathroom was genuinely gross, you could feel it in the air. And I hate to admit it, but there it was: a pang that school, Darlene, Bread, and Aunt Edith were all going on without me. Had my life really been so bad? Sure, I was alienated and melancholy—*ennui is the greatest evil* and all that jazz—but, according to Linwood, I was going to feel that way as a teenager regardless, come what may.

You could see that maybe real evil was like the voodoo shop. Maybe ennui wasn't going to look like such an imposition after all.

"They're up to something all right," Alonso announced when he emerged from the shower. He had a little towel draped around him like a loincloth, and that was one good-looking guy! His long hair hung down his back like patent leather, unlike mine, which was Straw

City. "I saw a couple guys on the street, and they've got a big deal scheduled for tonight."

My stomach heaved a little. "Do they ever, uh, like kill anybody?"

He fixed those clear eyes on me. "Is that one of those questions you're prepared to hear the answer to?"

"I guess not." I closed my duffel. Everything was rolled up and packed, dirty clothes segregated from clean. "You got anything to eat around here?"

"No food!" Alonso pulled on some clean jeans, though who knew there were clean clothes in all this filth, and some kind of fringed leather shirt. He didn't look like a cowboy at all anymore. "We got to stay clean. And besides, what we're going to take has to go on an empty stomach."

My spirits lifted. "Drugs?"

He smiled. "Indian medicine."

First we lay down on the floor and did some yoga stuff. We did a lot of it, breathing and stretching and special movements to rid our bodies of all the white sugar we'd consumed the day before. In between the exercises, we drank a lot of water, and whatever it was, Alonso's voice or the strangeness of the situation or the movements themselves or the power of all that had gone on between us, I began to feel lightheaded and free, like *me* was some sort of helium balloon, only connected by the flimsiest string to the muscular shell of my body.

"Feel the breath," Alonso said. "And let it all go."

We did a lot of *letting go*.

At some points during the movements, I could see my past rolling away from me.

"Bless it," said Alonso. "And let it go."

I blessed June, Stan, and Linwood.

And let them go.

"Remember coincidence and texture," Alonso said. "Remember the strength of sex. Remember *owl flew* and The Nineteen Layers of the Soul. Remember the power of the ritual! You have to align your cells."

Or anyway, I think he said all that. It was getting kind of misty, the difference between what he said and what I heard. And, like all the Sammy stuff, what was the difference anyway? If I thought I heard it, wasn't that the same as hearing it?

And I did hear it.

"Okay," Alonso said finally. "Take this. Don't chew it or you'll gag."

He gave me some kind of plant, dried, but it had a squishy center.

Was this peyote? Or mushrooms? "God, it's disgusting."

"Just swallow."

"How long does it take to come on?"

"We've got a long drive ahead of us," he said. "By the time you get there, you'll be somewhere else."

"How do I know I can trust you?"

Alonso shrugged, his sunglasses in place. He seemed to have an extra layer hovering around the shape of his body. "You should have thought of that sooner."

CHAPTER THIRTY

We were driving across the endless flat of the swamp. The jeep, which he'd borrowed from a friend, had been a big mistake while we were on the interstate, but once we got to the small roads and then the dirt roads, it was clearly the only solution.

Twilight was lavender and pearl gray with pinky tongues backlighting gnarled old cypresses with dangling beards of dark moss. Very witchy stuff indeed.

I would go from being able to see the landscape clearly to not being able to see it at all. Those times, you could as easily be in Disneyland, only the ride was like through key moments of your life, both those that had been and those that might have been, providing that there was any difference. If De Quincey could only see me now!

For instance, sometimes I saw everybody still alive and we were all, including Deane, living out in the country in Arkansas. June had a horse. And it was okay, it might as well have been. Other times it was just me and Deane and we were traveling all over Europe together, dancing in nightclubs in Paris and London and Vienna, where the nighttime was truly black and everyone wore the finery of exotic birds.

Other times, I wasn't there at all. These were the oddest instants: I was Deane, and Deane was doing all this stuff, hard to say what, and sometimes Sammy was there, and one time—this is the only one I remember clearly—they were snaked around each other out in a weird kind of forest, and his pecan-colored skin was giving life and blood to the pale pearl luster of hers. My eyes, her eyes, were locked on those ice-blue orbits.

I wanted to say, *This is why I was born!*

Only it wasn't me, and I wasn't there. Then I'd get lucid and turn toward Alonso. "How can you drive after taking this stuff?"

"I didn't take any," he answered.

"Oh."

"You have someone you want to see. It doesn't matter what I see."

"You mean if I hadn't taken your Indian medicine, then I wouldn't—" But whatever I was going to say was lost. Instead, Sammy's hand touched Deane's bare thigh, and my body got spun off into a tunnel of pinky light. All skin and jasmine oil and wet mouths.

But if you're *there*, where's your body?

Finally, you've got to not care.

Then there was this sense of the Pure Perfect Other, only you couldn't get to it, you had to go through something, things or beings, in between—

"The *Orìṣà!*" I exclaimed. But then they were gone.

"Right," Alonso said, amused.

At that moment I knew he was amused because I was Alonso, too.

Eventually we stopped, and my mind cleared a little.

The movement on the road had made a kind of connection with the movement in my skull, and that was pleasant, and yet the very fact of that connection was keeping something else from occurring. What? You could see a glimmer of what it was out of the corner of your eye: look directly, it was gone.

Whatever it was, you needed it.

Whatever it was, it was Other.

"Now," said Alonso. His voice was low and I leaned close, almost spun off again by the warmth and smell of his body. "After we leave this jeep, I don't care what happens, you don't say a word. Not a sound, not a loud breath. You listening?"

"Aye, aye, skipper."

"Pet, listen." His impeccable cigar-store profile gleamed in the moonlight. "This is very, very serious. Probably, this is going to be the most serious moment of your life."

I thought about the car wreck, but then I wouldn't let myself.

"You don't think you're up to it, say the word. We turn around, go back to my place, fuck and eat oysters until I go out on the rig. Say the word."

I wanted to say the word. I wanted to turn around and be done with it. Same time, for sure that was not going to happen. The only way was through.

"I'm as ready as I'll ever be."

He waited a moment, as if listening to something very far away. "Okay. Now take off all your clothes."

I started to say *come again*, but then seriousness mercifully got a hold on me. Shoulders squared, with sober thoughts, I solemnly divested myself.

"The juju goes too."

No! my mind screamed. But it was like he said earlier—if I wasn't going to trust him, I should have thought of that sooner. The juju was warmer than ever, and it left a cold circle around my neck when I took it off. "But you said Sammy made this...."

"The only chance you got, babe, you go naked as the day you were born. You're not ready to play with their toys yet."

It was like the rich man in the Bible and the needle's eye.

Alonso slipped the juju into his pocket. He looked satisfied. "Now get me that book you keep, the one you wrote that stuff down in."

This required more trust, and most of me wanted to resist. Once again, my only evidence that Deane existed, or the idea of Deane, or her magic, was being threatened. "You want it, don't you?"

"Don't you think I've earned it?"

My duffel was in the backseat. I rolled up the clothes I'd just been wearing and put them on the Dirty side of the bag. I took my journal out of the Clean side. "The Nineteen Layers of the Soul," I said, forking the book over. "Maybe you can make some sense of it."

"Maybe I don't need to."

Yet it was true. He'd earned it.

"And now put this on." Alonso handed me a white garment that he pulled out of the glove compartment.

The robe was hooded and made of such a light, flimsy silk that you felt more naked with it on. "One more thing."

He waited.

"Are you one of them? Are you going to give that book to Sammy?"

Alonso's lips brushed my forehead. "I'll be right beside you all the way. Until it's time..."

CHAPTER THIRTY-ONE

We walked for miles Indian-style through the swamp, wearing the handsewn moccasins Alonso provided for the occasion. Sometimes I was *there*, feet stepping lightly in the soft damp earth, and sometimes I was *not-there*. The light of the still-full moon helped us find our way, but I had to admit that the man appeared to know what he was doing.

Sometimes a structure, like a fibrous net of Tinkertoys or a geometrical spider, clung around his back and you knew that the decision to trust him had been the right one.

Or the only one.

And then we were there.

First you heard a kind of weird, eerie chant well up through the dense shrubbery and vines. Then you could see the flickering of light from some sort of fire.

Alonso put out a hand to stop me and then directed my body to a spot behind a clump of bushes. He took off his shirt and placed it on the ground and we both sat. The fuzzy suede was surprising against my bare butt, but then it felt good. In fact, I don't think I'd ever felt quite so wonderful in my life! It was like everything I'd ever seen or done or wanted to was pushing me right against a cliff—the very edge of existence! *Whoosh*— and you were standing against a cliff and the view opened onto everything ever else, light and dark both, and you told yourself, *Now or never, baby. Jump!*

There was a ritual circle in the center of the clearing. Hooded bodies stood in ragged clumps to either side— the event itself was yet to begin.

What really got me was how weirdly familiar the look of the whole thing was. Like I'd done this many times before, and like I loved it.

The next thing that caught your eye after the circleness of the circle was that its perimeter was defined by dozens of sputtering white candles. And inside the big circle were more circles, little ones, and more candles— the candles seemed to multiply as you watched them . . .

You feel yourself being drawn into the circle.

Inside there is also an altar, facing east. It is dressed with bottles of dark rum and red wine and coconuts, honey and pieces of hard candy.

You are standing in the center of the circle, almost.

And behind the dark rum and the red wine and the

coconuts, the honey and candy, there is a miniature plain-pine coffin.

The conga drums begin.

Your identity is blown away like a leaf. You stand naked at the edge of everything.

And Sammy appears.

Sammy!

He is dressed entirely in white, a white turban with pentangles on his head and a large cigar in his mouth. Walking in a peculiar, crook-backed way, he alternately spews rum on the ground, tosses down handfuls of cornmeal, and issues forth clouds of cigar smoke.

Then I was Pet again and wanted to spring up! Sammy! But Alonso pressed a restraining hand on my forearm.

Coincidence. Sex. Ritual.

You are in the circle again and you watch him walk in this peculiar stance seven times around the magic perimeter.

Then a woman appears.

Deane!

She is dressed in full white skirts with many petticoats poofing them out. Over her white ruffled blouse hang many strings of glass beads, carved beads, seeds and seed pods. Her hair is concealed by a white bandanna with pentangles and other mysterious inscriptions.

You almost know exactly what they mean.

In fact, you have seen them before. You have seen the spider woman holding tiny dolls in the sand painting in front of her power-altar.

Now the chanting begins, weaving against the steady rhythm of the drums.

A crowd of dark-skinned people appears. They are pummeling packets of mantioc and setting them onto the fire they have built. They also hold cucumbers aloft, slit them down the middle, and use the pale green water as if it were blood.

It is blood.

It might be your blood.

Sammy crosses the line of candles. He stands inside

the circle almost touching you. He motions for the woman, Deane, to join him.

You know now why he pursued her. You know the perfect texture of their coincidence.

The woman radiates strength and power. Deane! The woman knows things that you almost know. You remember them hazily, as if you have dreamed the entire spectacle before. You want to ask her everything, but you cannot ask her anything.

You do not know if she knows you are there.

The fire licks at her heels but it doesn't hurt. Smoke billows up all around them, but her lungs breathe something other.

Dozens of naked bodies writhe outside the circle. They proliferate like mice, flimsy as tissue, shadow forms to populate all the cities of the world.

You stick your foot out into the dark, and all you receive is the silence, deep and manifold. If it had wings, it would stretch up light and cover you black, and you hold back the fungus of fear, knowing that once you admit it into the folds of your body, it festers inside—but it is cool as fresh-picked morrels, intricate as handmade lace.

How the fear can grab you.

You hear:

> Kabiyesi, Alaye!
> Ebo a fin!

And:

> May you live till old age, Oloja
> May your time be prosperous

And:

> Lizard offered two pigeons
> In order to get the woman
> But he did not offer two cocks
> Which would make the woman stay

The chanting and the drums, the writhing of the bodies. The flickering light of the candles and the fire.

There is real blood.

There is only the pale green juice of the slaughtered cucumbers.

From the folds of his pants, Sammy produces a machete. Its gleaming blade makes a statement.

He looks at Deane. "Slit my throat."

Without warning, except for the sliver of warning-pain you felt dig a line of ice in your spine, everything stops.

The group of people in the clearing are as silent as the inside of a cereal box.

"What is it?" you whisper.

"The Egúngún!"

You know exactly what is happening.

You have no idea what is happening.

Energy exits your body: you are a boat caught in the ebb tide of the Bay of Fundy.

Phosphorescence traces the outline of a veiled figure who now stands in the circle.

This is the Egúngún.

He is They who return from the spirit world to visit his children.

His feet are wrapped in a curious sort of bandage, which is layers of bandages dangling with black charms. The shape looms larger and larger. Swathed in clothing, onion skins of white on white, netting floating in a veil around his face—he is like a great, hovering, supernatural beekeeper!

You know him. He is closer to you than your jugular vein.

His hands are also wrapped in cloth. Around his wrists and hanging by the score from his neck are more black charms, red auras glittering about them.

It is blood that has turned these objects black. Blood from the centuries of loved ones gone to their early deaths.

Sacrifices of the ones you have loved. The ones who were taken from you before you were ready to let them go.

You are completely naked before him. He towers above. Your body leaks its sexual juice from every pore;

your skin is sore and red from contact with the corpore-
al world.

The Egúngún!

He stares at you, or this is the conclusion you would
make if you could see his eyes. There are no eyes, only
sockets swathed in white gauze.

He will bless you. He brings spiritual strength from
your dead. But you must make a sacrifice in respect.

"Slit my throat!" Sammy cries. "Now!"

You have forgotten Sammy was there. But where is
Deane? Only you and Sammy and the veiled Other are
standing inside the circle.

You are holding a machete in your right hand.

It feels utterly powerful.

Are you prepared for this moment? You look Sammy
in the eye; his ice-blue chips are mirrors. He is the one
who has deceived you. You understand that you have
been a pawn in his hands, trading your family and your
sister to this man.

You understand that power was all he ever cared
about.

And then you realize you are Deane. You raise the
machete and look one more time at the only person you
have ever loved. All your life, this is the only person
who has ever understood you.

This person, Sammy, wants you to save him by killing
him. As a sacrifice to the Egúngún, his journey through
the Other World is assured.

Your arm is too heavy.

Why are you failing him?

You are not strong enough. There is someone else
present whose energy intercepts your own.

She is here, your sister.

You always knew she would catch up with you. You
have always wanted her to.

But she is stronger.

The Egúngún turns to you, growing ever larger. He
raises his huge hands. Will he press on the fragile tissue
of your brain? To summon Him and not offer a sacrifice
is the greatest possible disrespect.

You no longer have the energy to kill Sammy: you are no longer the most powerful woman in the world.

But you could turn the machete on yourself.

The black charms of the sacrificed loved ones dangle from the white wrappings. . . .

"Deane!" I screamed, leaping up from the bushes, and running blindly into the circle.

PART III

*

CHAPTER THIRTY-TWO

My knees are rigid, sturdily encased in elastic bandages. I goosewalk to the squat rack. My solar plexus is shielded by the massive power belt. My muscles are aligned, at the ready like enthusiastic soldiers.

No one else is in Roy's Gym.

I grasp the bar firmly and duck my head underneath, as I've done so often before. The bar and its heavy cargo of iron rest not across my deltoids but on the fleshy mound of the upper trapezius.

Merely holding the bar in place stresses my arms. Yet, this lift is designed primarily for the legs and secondarily for the back. *Arms, forgive me, I underworked you. But don't fail me now!*

My body pressed under the load of weight, I step away from the bar.

Pause.

Then my knees bend, slowly, slowly. Sinking! And there must be total control.

This is the bottom. I am squashed down, stasis, time has stopped. In this moment my body is as alive as a body can be.

Va-va-voom!

My quadriceps belong to Paul Bunyan! I am a mythological beast! I have seen the perfect clarity of Nothing, the Tibetan temple bell pinging out in the void—and survived!

"Come on, baby, way to go!"

As I stagger back to the squat rack, someone helps me hoist the bar back into place.

I have unofficially broken the world's record.

I have lifted a thousand pounds.

CHAPTER THIRTY-THREE

"Who are you?" I ask, turning to look.

He's gorgeous, not at all what you'd expect from the cracker accent. Auburn hair wafts in gentle waves to his shoulders and his face is clean-shaven, dominated by level gray eyes. His jaw is set solid. Underneath the fresh—ironed?—sweats, a firmly muscled body asserts itself. The sleeves of his shirt are pushed up to display shapely forearms.

"The name's Barnett, ma'am," he says, total cracker. Then he extends his hand for a shake.

The jolt comes out of nowhere. You think of wild nights, speeding in a car by moonlight under the lacy black moss that dangles down from the trees and into the swamp below. You race and race: that's all there is, and whatever is trying to catch you, will catch you, but you keep racing—

Except I'm older now and deep into *health*. I pull my hand back, as if from the lip of the fire.

Barnett sits down next to me while I unwrap my knees before my legs lose all circulation.

"Look," he says, "you know what you just done?"

I nod. *One thousand pounds!*

"You just done lifted a shitload of weight." He stares at the squat rack. "Lessee. Two, three, four—plus seventy-seven and a half each side." He lets out a low whistle. "One thousand fucking pounds! No shit!"

Not very gracefully phrased, but my sentiments exactly. I wind the bandages up into two fat packages.

"You just done broke the world's record, girl!"

From *ma'am* to *girl* in less than three minutes.

"You got you a coach?"

I flex my right quadriceps and gaze admiringly at the smooth bulge of muscle. Too bad the skin is freckling up already—too many teenage summers of Southern California beaches.

"I could coach you."

When I look up to tell him to buzz off, the sight of his shiny hair, pale skin, intense gray eyes...

"You wanna compete?"

"I don't know." Once, right after moving out here, I drove over to Houston to catch a meet, but the sight of those growling women with tattoos on their biceps and hairy legs protruding from high-topped tennies—well, it wasn't my scene.

"You gotta want it bad."

"There it is—I don't." I stand up and put the bandages into my Roy's Gym bag. A few guys have come in the far end and one of them turns on the radio. Hard rock, clanging and grunting begin.

"You *got* the power. Cain't pretend you don't."

"Nice meeting you." I don't turn back but instead walk toward the exit, passing the obnoxious former marine with the potbelly. He's setting up his bench and pauses to holler, "Hey, kid, how's it going?"

I smile and nod. It took me months to get this far.

Next to the dumbbell rack stand Charlie and Phil, two college kids, who stare into the giant mirror, flexing their triceps in Zen self-absorption.

"Bye, Roy." I lean into his glass office. Dark, handsome, and morose, Roy is propping his bushy head on his arms. He's one of those veterans who left some important part of himself in Vietnam, but you don't know which part. Affable one day and sullen the next, he finds a new game plan each week—inversion boots, amino acids, megavitamins. Whatever, he suckers you in every time, because he believes.

"Take care, you hear?" Roy gestures vaguely, probably not knowing which person left.

I slip my hooded sweatshirt on before going outside. Early February, that first Louisiana false spring, the one that makes the azaleas bloom and your heart long for Mardi Gras. The air is fragrant, wisteria or honeysuckle or sweet olive. My legs and back and chest are all pumped, blood coursing through in weird giddiness,

good as drugs any day. You get this sense of the quality of
life elevated up off its feet, from pedestrians to hovercrafts.

While unlocking the jeep, I try to intuit what particular food my body is craving. No alcohol, no caffeine, no
white sugar, no salt—well, after that kind of regime,
you can practically identify and isolate each ingredient
that enters your body at the point of assimilation. Take
the grains apart in seven-grain bread.

"Hey!"

I whip around, keys aloft should the need arise to
gouge anybody's eyes out.

"It's Barnett. Hey!" This last with a yelp and a jump
backward to avoid the sudden turn and the brandished
metal.

"You shouldn't sneak up on people."

"I ain't sneaking up, and you ain't people."

Yet his eyes look so intelligent.

"*Ma'am.*"

"Look." I toss my gym bag into the backseat. "Thanks
for the attention and all that jazz, but this lifting is just
for me. Just for myself."

"I'd sure like to discuss that over dinner." His hair, in
the early twilight, glows out rose, vermillion, magenta,
coral.

"Dinner?"

"That's right, little lady, spot of your choice."

"Pet's the name." I hear the snottiness in my voice
but feel unable to control it. "Not ma'am, not girl, not
little lady."

He nods soberly, eyes alight with merriment. He's
got my number.

"And I can't go anywhere dressed like this, unless it's
McDonald's."

"Well, uh, *Pet*, why don't you go on home and
change. I could follow you—"

He sees my expression.

"You don't like that, meet you there. This ain't what
I have a mind to wear neither."

"I live out in Whiskey Bay."

He whistles. "That's some dangerous waters."

"Yes, and it's also far away. By the time I got

home, changed, came back—so thanks but no thanks."

"I'll buy you a new dress, shoes, whatever, just for tonight." He holds up his palms. "No strings attached!"

"I don't think—" His gray eyes stop you—they're like nothing you've ever seen before! Inside them is kindliness, goodness, elegance, grace. Something niggles my memory—gray eyes that hypnotize you.

Barnett has taken my hand and pried open the fingers. He inserts several bills. "Honey," he says, "I got an expense account. You take yourself on down to the mall and buy you something special."

Robotic, my head nods.

"Right now, it's near six. Let's say we meet up about eight. You with me?"

Head nods again.

He reaches out and touches the hollow in my throat, very intimate. "You ought to have you some kind of magic charm to hang there."

I shift away from his touch.

"Lifters." He turns away. "They're a superstitious bunch."

"Oh, Diamond Jim?"

He turns back. "Yes?"

"You didn't say where."

"Neither did you." He wiggles his eyebrows comically over the level pools of his eyes. "Jacob's? It's over—"

"I know where it is." I hop in the jeep without a backward glance, stuffing the bills in my sweatsuit. Maybe he just lost some good money. Adolescently, I punch in my cassette, turn it up, and "Sweet Dreams Are Made of This" blares out as the car squeals out of the parking lot.

CHAPTER THIRTY-FOUR

After fifteen minutes of winding through the sleepy town of Lafayette, Louisiana, I pull into the mall. This

is the place to go when you're feeling homesick for
California. The rest of the world likes old buildings,
constructs with "character," but Californians like everything spanking new, clean as an unopened package of
plastic spoons. Rather than try to defend a position
morally repugnant to my few friends out here—immediacy
and stylishness over quality—I simply repair to the mall
for uniformity, freshness, safety. Also happy-making are
the arrival of fast-food chains, Taco Bell and Wendy's,
insinuating themselves into the South, the old roads
repaved into broad fanfares to accommodate the traffic.

You'd think I would have moved here to avoid such
an invasion, but that's the human heart for you—whatever
you flee, that's the thing you are longing for.

I climb out of the jeep and head for Goudchaux's
Department Store. In the short walk through the increasingly chilly evening, I attempt a strategy to deal
with this male, this *Barnett*. He should have had the
bills thrown back in his face.

Speaking of which, my hand pulls them out of the
pocket.

Five hundred dollars.

The thrill goes both ways: horror that he would throw
this much money away, delight that it will purchase
such a nice dress. Clearly, my intention is to spend the
money—I acknowledge that fact with half-shame. And,
in that case, you might as well enjoy the experience
instead of chastizing yourself with a lot of unproductive
guilt, since you have no intention of changing your mind.

Back to the strategy. Pressing open the glass doors of
the store, I am assaulted by jumbles of bright merchandise, the smell of fabric dye and rubber and stale
chocolate, the chatter of shoppers and the ping-ping-
ping of the paging device.

One of my natural habitats, and my body relaxes.

Systematically, I circle the ground floor and stare at
mannequins. The first one is attired in a spring safari
look: khaki jodhpurs, pith helmet, and a coy spray of
veiling over the eyes. Interesting but too comical—you
don't want your opponent to have the advantage of
mockery.

The next models what you can only describe as Preppie Pastel—what else is there to say except that perhaps one does not wish to look like a child's dessert.

The third mannequin is Audrey Hepburn retro, the black silk cocktail dress, the audacious big-brimmed hat, the elbow-length gloves, and the pelvic slouch. Here is problem number one (Don't look like a fool) combined with the additional problem of having a physique too athletic for svelte.

You are not fat! I insist to myself and check the convenient mirror to be sure. At five-feet-five, 120 pounds, this body is *almost entirely muscle*. Skin-fat calipers cannot lie, nor can the dreaded test-by-immersion. Many professional people have registered my near-total lack of porkiness. What I see in my reflection is the dieted-down, bodybuilder look.

But it isn't the same as simply being thin. *Fatso,* I can almost hear June whisper in my ear. *Tub of lard!*

Implementing a policy decision, my feet propel me out of Godchaux's and out into the mall, proper. Without any significant thought at all, I buy a Diet Coke and a pack of Camel Lights. There's a nice spot on one of those prolonged benches next to the plants, where you can sit and watch and give the twenty-second critique to everybody who saunters by, seemingly unconcerned with their bodies. As always in Louisiana, there is a constant and shameless display of girth.

The Coke and cigarette taste good, dizzy-making. So much for maintaining the temple of purity.

And, unfortunately for my karma, the sight of all these Genuine Fat People cheers me right up. Quick calculation assures me of my ongoing theory: two out of every three people who stroll by in the mall, and that includes kids, are conspicuously overweight. Not only are they corpulent and seemingly unashamed, they are also *eating fattening foods in public!*

Ah, the temptations of malldom. A family of chubbies passes by, the father eating Karmelkorn, the mother eating those really gooey chocolate chocolate-chip cookies, the boy and girl slurping up ice cream cones covered with tiny candies. And they all have visibly convex tummies.

People who look like this, people who are not obsessed with the constant maintenance of an impossible perfect shape, are illegal in Southern California.

In a way, these merry beefers are a sort of natural resource. With so many thin people in California, nobody looks thin. No contrast, and so the eye insists that there be one, and even the most elegant bod reveals the minute pockets of surplus. What they ought to do is send these people out west for the summer, to sit on the beach next to thin people, to make the thin people look thinner.

Rent-a-Fatty.

Covertly, I pinch my midsection, half-convinced that these uncharitable thoughts, and the sodium in the diet drink, have already begun their evil work on my washboard abs. But no, the flesh is tight as ever.

And of course this nasty speculation is getting me no nearer to my dream dress, not that I deserve it. I stub out the cigarette and wonder at this welling up of self-loathing. You'd think that after lifting a thousand pounds and all, I could take a day or two and rest on my laurels.

No way.

Tomorrow my body must recuperate from the weights, but there's no rest for the weary. Tomorrow is fifteen miles, and not a slow jog, either.

Okay, Pet: it sure is hard being you. Feel better?

I fare forward, passing a cluster of shoe stores, and House of Cards, and that organ store where someone is always playing "The Shadow of Your Smile" with some kind of weird electric mariachi accompaniment. Away from the food concessions, the traffic clears out—it is dinnertime, after all, and only regulars like myself prefer this twilight hour, when the simple and quiet abundance of worldly goods can soothe you into believing that with new clothes, new jewelry, and new make-up, you will discover the other, more attractive person who has always been there, just below the surface of your skin.

Remaining outside the range of the store's electronic sticky-fingers catcher, on principle, I peruse the interior of Contempo Casuals. Two teenage girls are smearing black lipstick on their mouths. An older woman with stiff blond curls is rifling through the party dresses.

Nothing calls out.

Next door is Suzy's Sophisticates. But this is hallucination! Two identical girls are coating their lips, the identical blonde fingering shoddy satin.

If I still had my lost juju, my gris-gris, my magic amulet, I might touch it now. Now there might be comfort in its warm and demanding presence over my collarbone.

A new wing of the mall has been added. My heart leaps a little—it's finally open! Perhaps the dress store of my dreams will be waiting.

The new wing is darker than the rest of the mall. Perhaps the full battalion of fluorescent lights has yet to be installed. The corridor winds a little, narrowing in dimness.

Perhaps it would be better to return to the main thoroughfare. No other shoppers are present and probably the new wing is not open after all—possibly the workmen have simply failed to rope it off as usual.

But then the lights in one shop are on after all: it's called Clothes for a Spur-of-the-Moment Date When You Want Him to Think You're Fabulous But You're Not Sure What You Think of Him.

Hmmm.

In the window are several shimmering frocks. The flowered one looks uncannily like a dress I once saw in San Francisco. And the nubbled saffron linen—isn't that the same dress as the one in New York, when the shop had just closed and there was a plane to catch that night?

Inside the store, elegance and haute, very haute, chic are rife. The walls are midnight blue, the carpet is cream-colored and as thick as a carton of cottage cheese, and the ceiling is decorated with phosphorescent moons and stars. Peculiarly, sprinkled about among the clusters of fancy garments are cages filled with live, small animals: canaries, lemurs, long-haired guinea pigs dyed like carnations.

Is this what happens when you lift a thousand pounds? Life decides to be amusing?

And I haven't taken drugs for years.

To my left is a gunmetal vintage forties' jacket with bugle-beaded shoulders—but surely it costs five hundred all by itself, and what about a skirt, never mind shoes and panties and stockings?

"May I help you?"

Standing behind is a guy who looks like an extra from *Stormy Weather:* cinnamon skin, zoot suit, and snappy fedora. Opaque shades hide his eyes and most of his personality.

"How much is this incredible jacket?" My voice is unable to do anything other than gush in the presence of so many beautiful clothes. "What a fabulous store!"

"For you," he says, "ninety dollars."

My body starts to hyperventilate. Damn that cigarette, and that lousy caffeine. "What about that Romanian blouse?" Next to us is this transparent garment, light as a promise, red, yellow, and green flowers obviously embroidered by fairy fingers.

"Fifty-five."

My stomach queases up. The only thing more stressful than finding what you want is finding what you want for very little money. Wildly, I scan the store—Jean Harlow white satin sheaths, Balenciaga suits, lizard and snakeskin and alligator pumps.

"Nothing in the store is over a hundred dollars." With unerring cool, he lights a long tan cigarette. "Otherwise we could not sustain ourselves in this 'mall.'"

Sitting down in a peach velvet chair, I attempt to conquer my nausea and exhilaration. You go on for years and nothing happens to you. Then everything happens at once. Obviously, that's the story of my life. If only you knew during the dull time that the wild time was coming...

Thoughtfully, the gentleman hands me a glass of iced Perrier.

The ice water restores some sense of order. If you

knew what was coming, then it wouldn't be life, would it?

"Would madam care for me to select precisely what would enhance her exquisite figure and small oval face? Her delicate coloring?" His voice is wonderfully free of sarcasm.

My eyes widen over the brim of the glass and my head nods.

He disappears for a moment and then returns with an item so magnificent you can hardly dare look at it. Vintage twenties, it is a lavender silk evening dress, sleeveless and low-slung. The material is so thin that you could bunch the entire garment in your fist, except for the crystal and indigo beadwork and embroidery, which consist of paisleys and curlicues worked into the subtle, lively pattern of an ancient Persian rug.

"To go with these." He lays out the entire ensemble: lacy lavender brassiere, silk lavender panties, silk and lace lavender garter belt with, obviously, genuine silk lavender stockings. For my feet, indigo snakeskin pumps, with a very low vamp for extensive toe cleavage. The matching bag has pink stones set in the fastening. Fingerless indigo gloves and a mink capelet in mauve and periwinkle complete the vision.

"How much?" I am unable to remove my eyes from the goods. "How much for the whole enchilada?"

Carefully he cuts a piece of cheese from the hors d'oeuvre table and feeds it to the chartreuse rat in the golden cage. The rat stands on his hind legs and nibbles delicately. "How much do you have?"

CHAPTER THIRTY-FIVE

I pull up in front of Jacob's exactly on time. Either the world has changed in a major way, or I have.

And I don't even know which is easier to believe.

"Miss Pet?" the maître d' inquires as my snakeskin pumps step inside. "Your table is right this way."

Across the gloomy red and gold restaurant, Barnett is natty in robin's-egg linen. The half-crocked expression on his face would seem to testify that he's been here awhile.

"Lay-dee!" He wolf whistles to excess, then hops up to pull out my chair.

In the baroque mirror, I sneak a look at my reflection. When I took my loot over to Julie's, she braided and pinned my long brown hair. In addition, she cosmetically treated my wide-set green eyes, big mouth, and tiny nose in what she claimed was a necessary makeup update. I don't still put white circles around my eyes since nobody in Louisiana has a tan anyway, but the eyeliner was pretty dated.

Okay, it's true: I look terrific. And the feeling is good too—it is sinking in, a thousand pounds.

"About that money..." The five hundred can come out of my savings, well worth it.

Barnett throws up his hands in the gesture of denial. His red hair dances in the candlelight. "History!"

"But—"

"A business expense," he drawls. "I can deduct."

For no particular reason, the remark hurts my feelings.

"What's your pleasure?" He holds up his own glass, half-full of pale brown liquor. The smell, poignant as childhood, is bourbon.

"Perrier."

His eyes crinkle with mirth. The waiter materializes and takes our order.

Now that my entrance has been made, now what? This feels like a mistake, the rosy glow of seconds before already on the fade. I could be back on the swamp in my houseboat, feeding the cats, sipping apricot nectar while hearing the evening song of heron and loon, whose words you begin to understand, the sweet melancholy they share with each other.

"November one," Barnett says with conviction.

"I beg your pardon?"

Again with the crinkly eyes. Apparently, my comments are a never-ending source of hilarity.

Inside the beaded dress my spine is stiffening with fatigue. Back and legs are beginning to throb as well, from the massive exertion, but the feeling is not unpleasant.

"November one," he repeats. "Southeast Regional Women's Powerlifting. Out to New Or-leans."

"Oh." Again with the disappointment. Did I think the whole coaching bit was a ruse—and for what? Animal reaction to my deadly sex appeal?

"That's near nine months away. We gonna make you a star, girl!" Grinning, he tips his glass and slugs down the booze. "After tonight, no more wild living. You're in training."

"But I've already broken the world's record!"

He shakes his rosy curls. "Yeah, in the gym, sure. But you gotta do the right form, hold the bar just so. Plus, maybe you crumble under pressure?"

"In that case, please order me a vodka gimlet." No alcohol in five years, but this is what they drink in Raymond Chandler novels.

He just looks at me. And in that look, there's a spiritual purity so intense and innocent that you can only feel naked and ashamed.

"One vodka gimlet," Barnett tells the waiter after signaling him. "Stoli, stirred, and straight up."

My discomfort increases, so I excuse myself and repair to the women's room. It is also dull red velvet and tarnished gilt. Privacy is necessary so I install myself in one of the stalls, padding the seat with a good inch of tissue covers before settling down my vintage-clad rump and opening up the indigo bag.

From their black satin case I extract my thirteen precious stones. Yet another talisman I have made up in order to read the weather in the Other World. They sit in my palm like a still pond, and then they seem to glow softly, an electric appliance warming up. The rose quartz brightens first.

The Apache tear is next.

What do they mean? You can never know for sure,

but this is a new sequence for me. The stones, like so much else in your life, are a language half-remembered from childhood, lost to the adult mind yet yearning in the heart.

The Apache tear, of course, is to remember Alonso.

The third stone to go bright is pale green, picked up from Jade Beach near Big Sur. It is transparent as lettuce.

Pink. Black. Green. Whatever— I return them to their satin bag. As I leave the restroom, something catches the corner of my eye: a tiny goblin, hovering in another dimension of the air? But when you look directly, natch, you come up with one big goose egg.

Barnett is busily snarfing down the bourbon. Who knows how many drinks can have passed?

"I got me some cheese comin, and some of that Frog stuff, pat-tay? What you want, darlin?"

"A crab cocktail please." The gimlet, the shade of celadon and also the third stone, sits before me.

"Gotcha." Barnett effects the order.

The first sip is for courage, and the sweet lime with its poisonous vodka tastes pretty good. I lean close to Barnett, seeing my own earnestness reflected in his even gray eyes. "What do you really want?"

He leans back, pleased.

I lean back, expectant.

"Let me tell you a story," he says, making a steeple of his fingers. The red hair shines like earthly gold in the candlelight.

Our waiter plops down a plate of Brie and pâté for Barnett and a luscious mound of snow-white crab for me. It sits in a crystal goblet, surrounded by shaved ice. The first bite is tender as butter.

"Two boys grew up out in the swamp. I mean, *swamp*. And I mean way way out, where you never been."

"How do you know that—"

"Honey, you ain't."

That voice convinces you.

He dips his knife into the soft cheese, its sweet and slightly ammoniac smell. "We're talking thirty, forty years ago. No school, cuz them schools didn't even know these boys *existed*. Lotsa kids like that still. Ain't nobody can navigate them swamps less they was born to it. Out to Whiskey Bay—" He stops, mischievous. "Why, your people musta been from there."

"I'm from California." At least the crab is delicious.

"Anyways. Them kids grew up a-ridin they boats through the bayous, a-rasslin with they gators...."

"Look." I put down the tiny fork. "Do you think you could tone it down a bit?"

"Avec plaisir, mademoiselle." The accent is impeccable, and for an instant, in the hook of his smile, you would swear we understood each other. Precisely.

And then the feeling fades.

"What they discovered is this: they discovered a place in the swamp, kind of a doorway, where you could get through to someplace else."

"What do you mean, *someplace else*?" More gimlet is in order.

"I mean, like a different world."

Well, it would be hypocritical of me to be surprised. Here we go again. The only surprising part, perhaps, is that you get results this quickly. This afternoon I lifted a thousand pounds; for the third time in my life, I am being offered another way. This time, I am ready.

On that note, we both polish off our appetizers in silence. When the waiter removes our plates, we order more drinks and our entrées: veal with artichokes for me and duck in a raisin glaze with candied yams for Barnett.

Even though this red meat isn't technically red, it's my first in years. If you are going to pollute the temple, why, then, just do it.

"A world peopled with different creatures," he continues when we are alone again. "But it's transparent. You can look right on over to this world the same way you'd watch fish in an aquarium."

Suddenly I glance to my left, where moments before there was a wall. The wall is still there, of course, but it shimmers oddly, less than a wall. Then it seems something is about to happen, happen—and then nothing does.

The wall is a wall.

Nicotine, caffeine, alcohol. Coming up: red meat and sugar.

"So every day they could, these two boys would paddle their pirogue—I done forgot to tell you about the pirogue!"

Slipping back into cracker.

"Well, they built themselves a dugout, just like the ones them Asmat Indians use to visit their ancestors. I don't mean one of them 'soul ships'—the kind's got no bottom? With them carved figures and the tortoise in the center?"

Wait just one minute. Are we in a dream now? Here is stoptime déjà vu, the effect they claim is merely caused by an overeager brain, even though it makes the world go wrinkley and then smooth, as though someone were shaking out a huge bolt of gray shot-silk. Does anyone in the world believe the scientific explanation?

"Anyways, those boys had an Asmat pirogue and they wore them masks. The ones that cover the body entirely, kind of a hood? They got a feathered rod protruding from the head and wooden eyepieces. The heads was huge black whatjacallits? Cockatoos."

Irrevocably, he's sucked me in, into the mystery of the swamp, the story of a carved canoe decked out in twine and feathers. "This was in Louisiana," I point out. "How did these boys, who never went to school, know anything about headhunters in New Guinea?"

Barnett looks triumphant. "I didn't say they didn't have no books!" He snaps his fingers for the waiter and orders a white Bordeaux, once again employing his exquisite French.

I chug the last sip of my second gimlet.

"So off they'd go," he continues. "And one of the best parts is how they could stay in this other world, oh, days, but when they got back to this world, why, nothing had changed."

He wipes his mouth and leaves the napkin in a crumple on the table.

"'Scuse me," he says. "Be right back."

Obviously, he's gone to the men's room, all that bourbon. I think about lighting a cigarette but then he's already back.

He hands me a two-foot wooden item. Very heavy. Then he sits back down.

The object is made of dark wood, its center section a lozenge-shaped openwork. At either end of the lozenge is a head, carved in peculiarly intricate detail. You don't need much imagination to see that one of the heads is Barnett's and the other one is mine.

He points a delicate finger at the geometric lattice. "This is a stylization of the intricate root pattern of the holy banyan tree." Sounding for all the world like an effete anthropologist.

"But the heads—"

"You and me."

I stare at the wooden carving, which is warm to the touch.

"I went on over there and told them what we wanted. Then there was a wait while they carved it, of course. Since it's ironwood, it took them a couple days. But I ate well and rested a lot."

"You went on over *where?*"

"To the other world, of course."

"Oh, of course."

"Never mind." His gray eyes are kind. He takes his napkin and dips it in ice water, placing the cold compress on my forehead. He smells like suntan oil. "Just lean your head down now."

"I'm not used to alcohol. I guess—"

The cool napkin, the reassuring hands. "Feel better?"

"Yes, thanks." I sit up again and the room has cleared a bit, the air not red and ugly, as it was threatening to go.

The statue is still on the table, plain as day. Part of me says, *He must have gotten someone to carve it before he met me for dinner. He's been watching me for weeks*. But the other part, the better part, of me Believes.

"Let's have some wine." He holds up the freshly delivered, uncorked bottle.

"Perhaps not for me."

He spins the bottle on his finger like a basketball; it vanishes into thin air.

"Oh!"

Barnett swivels in his chair, revealing the bottle concealed beneath. He takes the bottle out and puts the wooden carving where it was, out of sight. "Some things are only tricks," he opines, pouring us each a glass.

We clink a toast.

"To the life of the imagination."

I'll drink to that.

Gathering my forces, flexing my quadriceps, my pecs, and my traps under the silky, beaded dress, I jump in. "Suppose, just suppose all that stuff were true, about the way to the other world. Why are you telling me?"

"Why am I telling you if it's true? Or why am I telling you the story either way."

"Either way."

"Because today's the day we met. When else?"

"Why did we meet today?" The wine seems to go straight to my lower abdomen and thighs.

He smiles but not really. I've seen faces like this before. Sammy. Alonso. And now Barnett. This is the third and last time to try and figure out my life, or Life Itself. It's all got to do with the thousand pounds.

Coincidence is the perfect texture.

He shrugs. "This was the first time I've been to Roy's."

And let's not forget *Sex is stronger than doors and windows*.

"Why?"

"Because I usually train at Red's."

Another sip of wine. "So why did you go to Roy's today?"

Now the smile is genuine. "Because I didn't go to Red's!"

My eyes narrow, lupine. Remember, this body is the strongest woman's body in the world.

"Look here." His eyes are serious now, and so are the slices of cheekbone, the slender pale lips, the thin nose. "Perhaps there ain't no such thing as coincidence. But that don't always mean you can have your reasons lined up before you, like a row of empty bottles."

Defensively, I raise my palms and hold them up before me.

"You no want zee veal?" The waiter mistakes my gesture.

"Yes, of course." The aroma is tantalizing.

"I take eet back! I get you zumthin else!"

"No, no!" I cut off a bite and savor it. "Fabulous!"

"Hmph." The waiter huffs off.

"This duck is great, hun. You wanna try a bite?"

"Plenty here, thanks." The presence of redolent calories distracts me, fogs up the issues of importance. After such a heavy lift, this body needs sustenance, not alcohol abuse.

Silently, comfortably, single-mindedly, we consume our dinners. My whooziness departs; no damage has been done, after all.

"Personal power," Barnett announces over his cappuccino and my herbal tea. "The getting of it and the keeping of it."

With the tea, my precious little system is surely back on track. "And what, pray tell, has that got to do with the other realm and the boys with the canoe and the Asmat Indians and all that jazz?"

"Oh yes!" He laughs melodically, artificially. "Why, babe, that was just a story. A little tale to amuse yourself. You know how we country folk, jes' good country people, like to tell us some tall tales. Don't you bother about that."

I sigh and sip my tea.

"But never mind all that! Let's us talk serious now. We gotta talk about personal power. About your *career*."

"Don't farewell," I muse aloud. "Fare forward."

"You lift something heavy," he offers, gray eyes getting me again. "That act don't go away when the iron's back on the ground. It gets stored in you, just like money in the bank."

Is that what I represent to him: money in the bank?

"You want to know how to get at what you got stored up in you?" The voice is sweet now, lyrical.

I nod, hooked. *Admit it*.

"Ain't easy, but there's a way. Lotsa people—" Barnett motions at the other diners, virtually invisible to me by the sheer predictability of their appearances. But they're ciphers, mysteries, all the more difficult because of their imagined accessibility. "Lotsa people know how to put it in. Only a couple know how to take it out."

After paying the check, Barnett leads me outside, into the cool moonlight. My body is keen to the dress, the whisper-silk of the lingerie.

At the door to my jeep, he kisses me chastely on my forehead. "Night, babe. Roy's tomorrow, same time?"

"Wait." I touch his sleeve. "That stuff with the boys. Do you think it really happened?"

Oh, moonlight. Moonlight. His face is all shadow. "Babe, if they think it happened, what difference does it really make?"

The difference between *truth* and *real*. I keep holding on to his sleeve. "Those two boys," I insist. "That's you and your brother, isn't it?"

"I don't have a brother anymore." And then he slips away into the night, like a trained assassin.

When I unlock my car and climb in, the carved wooden lozenge with the two heads is sitting next to me on the seat.

CHAPTER THIRTY-SIX

The drive through the swamp is scary tonight. Tonight the illusion is broken that I'm immune to the

eerie hoot of the owl or the splash the alligator makes as
he slips into saliva-warm water.

The carved figure has not improved my frame of
mind. The ironwood seems to give off heat. Plus, even
though my eyes are fixed on the road ahead, out of the
corner of my eye I keep seeing the thing *writhe*.

Everything has a life of its own. Especially the road,
which ripples and rolls like the back of a sea serpent.

And the drive is taking forever! Departing Jacob's,
the clock in the jeep said nearly midnight. In half an
hour, I was at my exit. Then, there's the stretch of
about ten miles, where the road is as direct and flat as if
it had been pressed by an enormous iron. Even in this
vehicle, that section only takes about fifteen minutes,
providing you don't need to brake for small animals,
waddling packages of fur and quills wending their low-
bellied ways. The point is: so far I've been on these
same ten miles for half an hour—the clock reads one.

And the road continues, instead of ending like it
usually does, straight as the edge of a blade. On either
side the landscape is primordial, the great oaks tufted
and swathed in lacy moss, vampire moss, their limbs
humanoid, trunks extending down into the muddy loam.
Every now and then there's a break in the trees and
you can see moonlight shining on pools of water, quick-
sand, white egrets ghostly and proprietary in the shadowy swamp.

Forty minutes have passed since I exited the interstate.

Hoping to break the mood, my conviction that this is
a time warp, I pluck a random tape from the shoebox
and pop it in.

David Bowie begins to intone, chill and sepulchral,
about the coldness of the sun.

Then he shrieks! I've always been a washout at
hearing the lyrics intact (I thought the song "Bad Moon
on the Rise" was "Bathroom on the Right") but this is
the part about putting out fire with gasoline.

The shriek and the intensity get to me: I scream a
little too, my nerves are so on edge. I've been wanting
another chance to reenter the mysterious realm and

now I have it—few things are as upsetting as getting what you want.

I stop the jeep. Forty-five minutes for a fifteen-minute drive is ridiculous.

As soon as the jeep is turned off, the headlights gone, and David Bowie silenced, the real noises of the night rise up to greet you. Animals swish and rivet and cry out, as if in pain but really to tease. Evil melancholy. Insect life, teeming and humming, is the parallel world.

Where on the road is this exactly? Twice a day almost every day, you should know every ripple and ridge.

But in the dark—well, nothing is quite certain. It seems to me, from what my senses perceive, that this spot is halfway along, which would have taken ten minutes at the most, not nearly an hour.

Slipping off the snakeskin pumps and the silk stockings, I step out of the jeep into the night air, simultaneously sweet and foul. Swamp air isn't fresh: it's rich. At any given moment, some animals are feeding on other animals, death occurring every second, constant slithering and tension; since the land is neither earth nor water, all life is amphibious, peculiarly adapted in the way that creatures from two different worlds must learn in order to survive.

I decide to get back in the jeep. The wind is cold and my feet aren't too crazy about the slimy pavement.

But what is that thing over there?

My heart twitches a little bit, beating down the fear. Something discordant is cradled in the curve of a cypress root. In the moonlight your eye can see that this something is out of place because it was made by human hands; the light strikes this object differently.

I walk over, thinking *tough*, and lean over to see what the three-foot item is.

It's a kind of a boat, fashioned from palm fronds, and my first reaction is familiarity, yet I can't say that I've ever seen anything like this before. Inside is a jumble of stuff, unarticulated in the dim light, so I rush back to the jeep and retrieve my lighter.

The first thing my hand touches is a white silk scarf

with something squishy inside. Flick of the Bic: inside the white scarf is the head of a chicken.

Gross!

But my curiosity won't let it alone, so after a moment to regain composure and stomach, the Bic flicks on again.

The scarf with the chicken head is tied to a small white pole with another white scarf. Also inside the boat are shells, mostly broken, and rotten fruit with God-knows-what grisly insects snacking away. There are also many pieces of colored string arranged in deliberate patterns and several small mud figures.

You might think this was a child's toy. But you'd be a fool to assume that.

Being extra careful not to disturb anything, I try to get a closer look at the tiny mud statues. Their minute features are meticulous: two men and two women. Oh, and a little bird—tiny, it has slipped slightly behind a molding orange, fragrant and revolting.

With a little imagination, you could say that one of the women was me and one of the men Barnett. But the other woman is very bizarre. Old and shabby and tired, the mud figure is holding miniature shopping bags, no bigger than raisins. Thick ankles swell over shabby tennis shoes. Her hair is a mass of wire designed to resemble diminutive dreadlocks.

The other man has no face at all.

Is this what has become of Deane?

Or is this what will become of me.

Obscurely annoyed, I leave the scene of the crime and get back into the safety of the jeep. The edge of some realization is there, but it recedes automatically like the tide. *Personal power, the getting of it and the keeping of it.*

I gun the motor and away we go. Within five minutes, the road takes me to the curving stretch of crushed shells. Soon the drive to my houseboat will appear.

Reality is only the taut feel of your muscles after a strenuous workout.

CHAPTER THIRTY-SEVEN

I slip the jeep into its lean-to and grab my bag of sweaty gym clothes. The houseboat sways at the touch of my foot.

Dominique is the first to yowl at the sound of arrival, shortly followed by Clive, Mud, Norman, and Wendy. No doubt the rest will be along momentarily, leaping up on the galley table, weaving frantically in and out between my legs as I try to navigate the distance from cat food cans to can opener.

After lighting the galley lantern, I prepare the cat trough. And the kitties fall into their rigidly observed pecking order, now that they have stopped harassing me. Wendy, the oldest female, is at the head of the line, with the youngest male, Norman, bringing up the rear.

Once their food is set, they lose interest in me. Eventually, gorged from their repast, they will come lap-seeking, desiring the scratch on the ear and chin and the smoothing of their glossy coats. But for the moment they are scant comfort.

I pour myself a glass of half rose-hip tea, half unfiltered grape juice and flip on the cassette player: one of Franck's piano and violin duets, sad as this time of night, fills the air. Unzipping my dress, padding across the floor with tired feet, the music surrounding you in a protective bubble, and the barbaric sounds of cats wolfing down tuna—well, it's home.

I sink into my favorite chair and stare at what lies directly across from it: the Power Altar.

The altar is the center of the houseboat, spiritually and physically.

Each one attired in his or her favorite costume, beaded collar and monogrammed bag filled with toys

and matching pillow, the poodles are regally displayed
on the highest tier. Mine are on the right and June's
are on the left. Separating the two clusters of battered plush
dogs (how clean and fresh childhood toys remain in
your mind when you have lost them; how tiny and dirty
they seem when you have saved them, especially if, like
mine, they've survived a car wreck) is a large black urn,
for storing various votive candles and herbs. Guarding
the urn are a pair of Chinese Fu dogs, guaranteed to
scare away evil spirits.

On the next lower tier are African statues, proudly
carved and noble. The panther is upright and lean, the
warrior man is alert but kindly, and the woman, sturdy
and muscular, is purely strong. Other figures mingle in
with the Africans: Hawaiian wahines, ceramic rumba
dancers, tiny rag dolls.

The next shelf down houses a collection of feathers
and bird nests and bones and swamp moss, everything
discovered outside. This layer also contains a flat wooden
tray with various nostalgia pieces: the silver badge
Gaylin sent me from Carlsbad Caverns—HI PET LOVE
GAYLIN—the mysterious piece of brick with the single
letter P, found one recess on the playground. My beloved cat Marmalade's torn leather collar.

The bottom shelf holds only one object: a sculpture
commissioned from a mediocre artist. A sort of cartoon
goddess flexes her biceps, decorated with golden bracelets. Although she has a mane of platinum hair and
sports a pink and green polka-dot bikini, she is not
entirely humorous. Here is a woman, you tell yourself,
who could lift a thousand pounds.

I tip my glass toward Hannah and drink.

After a few minutes I begin to feel peaceful and so
get up and light a couple votive candles, for all my
loved ones gone from me. After finishing my juice and
checking to make sure the cats have enough food—
they've nearly worked to the bottom ranks, sated cats
lolling on their sides like beached whales, and washing
themselves—I wander out onto the deck.

In the cool night swamp, strains of poignant Franck
violin wafting out, you can watch birds float white on

the water, hear the plopping of fish and the random paddling of some beast projecting himself across the murk.

To buy this feeling of isolation and quiet, this luxurious indulgence of my solitude, I used my meager inheritance, which I had shrewdly allowed Aunt Edith to allow a friend to invest. Nothing could be touched until I turned thirty, at which point travel and education were taken care of.

Turn thirty and repair to the bayou. There's something to be said for that. And now that my goal has been reached, now that the houseboat and the strength are all mine, now what?

Time to farewell?

And where would *forward* be?

Seems like it's always just a step ahead of your eyes.

I lean on the railing and stare out over the water. In the distance, walking toward me over the shiny liquid surface, is some sort of glowing shape.

Blink and it's gone.

Blink: Greenish, luminous, the phosphorescent body appears to be a slender man with bright, shoulder-length hair. He walks carefully, as though cautious about his ectoplasmic feet.

Blink.

Blink: As he approaches, his resemblance to Barnett is pronounced.

Blink.

Blink: You can see right through him, of course, the moonlight behind.

Blink.

Blink: He puts his arms around you, he kisses you, he promises to guide you through not only this world . . .

CHAPTER THIRTY-EIGHT

I open my eyes and it's morning and I'm in bed, naked. Although there's no trace of sweet stickiness between my thighs, my first impression is last night was hot stuff—but dreams can take you to that same place and leave no evidence.

My eyes close and my body sinks back into pillow—

Bam! Bam! Bam! at the front door.

Refusing to believe that anyone's out there, or that this is what must have made me open my eyes, I nestle back into my big plump nest.

"Open up, Hulk! I know you're in there!"

Julie.

Bam! Bam! Bam!

"Okay, okay, hang on to your hat!" I grab an old pink satin bed jacket and a pair of cut-offs, unfortunately catching my pubic hair in the zipper.

Julie's baby-chicken fuzz hair is plastered to her head, sweat rolling down her athlete's body. "About time! What's wrong, you got company?"

"I wish."

We walk into the galley, where several cats jump up in annoyance, several mew with delight.

Julie opens the fridge and guzzles orange juice straight from the glass container. Her brief blue shorts and T-shirt are drenched, and her lean legs, twitching like a horse's, run rivers.

"You want a towel?"

She nods, putting the juice back and wiping her mouth with the back of her hand. "Two hours, three minutes, fifteen seconds." She drapes the terrycloth around her neck.

"That's great!" I pour myself a Perrier and shoo some cats away to sit down. "Still feel like running with me?"

"You know what I feel like doing?"

"No."

"Going to New Orleans and getting into trouble!"

This is very tempting. I had planned on running today, and then foolishly agreed to meet Barnett at Roy's, without stopping to think that there must not be any lifting today. My quadriceps and lats are about as sore as body parts get without bleeding. "I'm supposed to meet this guy at Roy's around four."

Julie snorts, sitting down across from me with a

package of brown rice cakes and some kefir cheese. "Did he kiss you? Or should I guess rape, considering how you looked."

"Oh, come on. He wants to be my manager. That's it."

She cocks an eyebrow while slathering on the creamy cheese.

"There's something you could give me your opinion on." I walk out to the jeep, into the warm midday with a misty layer over the olive-colored trees. The bizarre wooden object is even more peculiar in real light.

And warm, not sun-warm, to the touch.

"What do you think?" The item is so heavy that it makes a very loud sound on the table top.

"Hey!" Julie says, mid-bite. Her fuzzy hair is beginning to dry, swirling into punky stiffness. Beneath the spiky hair, her face is round and cherubic, lips like a kewpie doll's. Never mind her panther-sleek body: the bee-stung mouth and arched brows tend to flapperize her.

"Well?"

"Well what?" Julie picks the thing up. "Heavy sucker, isn't it?"

"Don't you notice something odd about the faces?"

She studies them. "No. What?"

"You don't think one of them looks like me?"

She squints at the statue, squints at me, squints back at the statue. "Okay, so one of them looks a little like you. So?"

This is how you get to feel like an idiot. "Okay. Never mind." I take the statue and walk into the next room. There's only one place to put it, on the bottom level of the altar, next to Hannah. Either there or in the trash, that is.

"So what do you say to New Orleans?" Julie is tucking into the raw cashews.

"Well . . ."

"Come on, Pet! You lifted a thousand pounds. Let me take you out on the town and celebrate!"

"Give me a minute to think about it."

"You think. I'm going to shower." Julie exits the galley.

Idly, I peruse the magazines on the table. *Cosmopolitan* is full of career tips and articles like this one, "I Was a White Slave for a Chain Gang." *Vogue* is slick and smug. There are several photographs in the "View" section about an architect with real fashion flair. She is shown strolling the streets of New York City, looking whimsical: a gray flannel suit and a Mickey Mouse T-shirt, for instance. *I'll just wear something whimsical,* she confides to the interviewer, *for color, you know. For texture.* In another picture she is holding hands with her husband and smiling; he is young and handsome and they are standing in front of the ubiquitous New York fruit-and-flower stand.

What about my life: isn't it full of *texture*? The galley walls are covered with photos of Kay Baxter, Rachel McLish, Pillow, and other female bodybuilders. In addition, there are many bright scarves and plastic knick-knacks from the fifties and miniature watercolors and handmade potholders and, especially, local "primitive" paintings by Louisiana women artists: lovely garish oils of revivals, baptisms, and hog butcherings.

The sound of running shower water and a nasty rendition of "Every Breath You Take" wafts into the kitchen.

Once Julie gets into the shower, and singing, she's likely to stay for half an hour. I get up from the table and walk back into the living room and stare at the altar. Then my feet tap the floor until you can hear where the loose board and the hollow are. Inside the hollow is a series of objects wrapped in velvet. The colors are so pretty and bright that you'd think you'd discovered a nest of flowers. My hands reach for the item swathed in lavender.

I remove it, replace the floorboard, and, after lighting a candle and whispering a brief prayer, sit crosslegged before my power objects and unwrap the flat, square parcel.

Neatly framed by a gold-leaf rim and revealed behind reflection-proof glass is a photograph: the quintessential American Family. The Dad stands in back, handsome and healthy, somewhere in his early forties. Proudly he surveys the bevy of girls before him.

In the front row sit the Mother and the three Daughters, sweet little stairsteps. The Mother is deep-chested and robust; she wears a neatly pressed shirtwaist dress and her arms are spread protectively around the Daughters.

The oldest Daughter is a real charmer, curly brown hair, long lashes, hint of a Bardot pout. Perhaps if you knew that she would turn out to be the "bad" child, you would look more closely at the way she stares straight into the camera, knowing that she will always be the star of the show.

Not so the middle Daughter. This one cannot enjoy herself and you see why: the Baby is sitting on the Mother's lap. Worse, Baby has been given a toy telephone to play with and she, the middle Daughter, has nothing. Her round face and intense, jealous gaze are so intent on the telephone and the lap of comfort that she does not realize the picture has already been taken.

And the Baby? Why, she nestles into the warm breasts of the Mother, and she tinkers with her toy. Not a care in the world! Isn't she protected, safe and cuddly, isn't she the precious darling, the adorable pet?

"Hey, Porko, I'm talking to you!"

For a minute I am confused, convinced that June has come back to life, speaking from the confines of her printed image. But then the voice is only Julie's. She stands in the doorway wrapped in a towel.

"When was the last time you got laid?"

A bit of a stumper. There was a guy in New York. But in the several months I've been here—

"Not lately, right?"

"Right." I wrap the picture back in its lavender velvet.

"New Orleans is the answer. Take an evening off from training." Julie turns back to the bathroom, satisfied we're in accord.

I put the item back, wondering at the constant, never-ending disparity between what *appears* and what *is,* between what you remember and the evidence that refutes it.

When my hand reaches into the cache under the hollow board, it touches something warm, waiting.

Wrapped in paprika velvet is a white silk hooded robe, so flimsy that when you're wearing it, you're more naked than you are without any clothes at all.

Suppose you wake up in the middle of the swamp, in the remains of what must have been one hell of a wild party. You cannot remember anything at all after you ran pell-mell into the circle, convinced you had been watching the imminent death of your only living sister.

No sister now. No anybody: just empty wine bottles, squashed fruit, unidentified splashes of blood.

Let's say the person who brought you here has vanished as well. You go back to the place (slowly because everything on your body aches: the sun is nauseating and your skin is bruised, your thighs throbbing as if they had been engaged many times during the night) where you left the car and there is your duffel bag and a one-way bus ticket to San Diego.

Let's say you've had it.

Let's say you take off the white silk robe and put on your jeans, walk until you hitch a ride, ride until you get to the bus station.

You are not concerned with the voodoo shop anymore, whether or not it is still there, whether or not it ever was there.

Your body and your soul have been battered.

What you want is to go back to your old simple life as a teenager. Ennui is not the greatest evil.

Not by a long shot.

Now you have half a dozen things you can name that are far worse.

What is this sickness of soul, for instance?

What you want now, what you will dedicate your life to, is being too strong to let anything get you again.

Personal power: the getting of it and the keeping of it.

"Well, Fatso, let's move it!"

When Julie goes into the galley, I return the robe to its spot beneath the board. It waits there for a reason.

"I'm not fat," I remind her quietly.

She flexes a bony arm. Her puny biceps amuse me. "Next to me you are."

Summoning my muscles like so many well-trained animals, my body snaps into the ever-impressive Crab.

"Wow!" she says.

"Next to me," I brag, "the world is fragile like an egg."

CHAPTER THIRTY-NINE

The late afternoon sky broods down on us as we head east, gray February. I called Roy's with the message for Barnett to meet me the following day; I feel guilty for not feeling guilty.

What possible difference can one day make in the great scheme of things?

Julie is resplendent in black lurex pants and a red satin halter, gold Christmas ornaments for earrings. I am no slouch either in my shiny blue zebra mini, hair puffed out in a thousand lacquered ringlets, and two-inch false eyelashes. We both wear spike heels so sharp you could pick up trash from the sidewalks.

This close to Mardi Gras, there's a lot of trash.

We snap our fingers to rock music, loud and brash, but the falling of evening and the length of the drive—you really have to work hard to sustain your energy, your sense of the prowl.

Finally New Orleans slides into view, a few towers of twinkly lights, the huge UFO they call the Superdome, the slow slug of the Mississippi out there.

Julie exits on Esplanade, to enter the Quarter from behind.

My stomach kinks up and I roll down the window, to inhale the sweet fetid air of the city.

It's been a very long time.

You can hear the distant reverberations of parades; Canal and Saint Charles will be impossible to cross. People press in on one another, jostling and bruising to catch the odd plastic bead or aluminum doubloon. The bands beat drums, sound horns. The air, though chilly, has that weird frantic edge.

"So where's a good bar?" Julie asks.

"Hey, you're the native. I don't know the first thing about New Orleans."

She frowns, hesitating at the turn to Saint Phillips. "But didn't you say you'd been here before?"

"Not lately."

We cruise for a parking space, weaving around choked traffic and past the rundown buildings with their lacy iron balconies, winos sleeping on stoops, plump tourists with their tumblers of potent red drink.

"What about herpes?" Julie says.

"I vote against any bar named Herpes."

"No, Dodo! I mean, how do you pick up a guy and not get herpes?"

"Ask the gentleman to kindly wear a rubber." You feel something very strongly in this city, irresistible—but what?

Julie snorts. "Ha ha."

"Look." My hands smooth down the slippery fabric of my dress. "No tips on bars, no tips on men. Basically, I'm a washout. We compulsive athletes rarely get to see the jazzy side of life."

"Ain't it the truth," Julie says. "Whose idea was this anyway?"

"We could go to the movies."

"The movies."

"Sure. We could—"

"Hey! All ri-i-ight!" Julie steers her car into a genu-ine parking space.

Suddenly, when we exit the car, the air is very quiet. We seem to be on the far edge of the Quarter, the few streetlights peculiarly bright.

"Where are we?" I point to dark old trees dripping heavy moss; the raised tombs and gravestones are white as teeth in the night.

"Saint Louis Cemetery." Julie checks the doors to make sure they're locked.

"Do they still bury people there?"

"I don't think so. Come on." She pulls my arm.

"Then what's all that?"

There is a small crowd inside the graveyard. People dressed in white from headcloth to sandals are sitting in a circle lighting candles.

Déjà vu.

Low chanting begins.

"That's where Marie Laveau is supposed to be buried. Now, come on!"

Is this where the strange sense of excitement is coming from?

"Pet!" Julie whispers urgently. "Come on, they won't want us gawking at them. And it's no big deal. People leave flowers and fruit and shit there—it happens all the time!"

At her insistence, I allow myself to be pulled away. But now the evening has irrevocably changed. My last glance over my shoulder shows the crowd of worshippers beginning to sway. The chanting grows louder. In the center of their circle, you can almost see ectoplasmic forms dancing in the air.

"You go for that mumbo-jumbo crap," Julie opines when we turn the corner.

No point answering.

"But just forget it for tonight, okay? I don't want to deal with *anything* like that! Tonight we're supposed to have fun."

Our night on the town, hot to trot, looking for trouble. Set foot in the Quarter, and you are surrounded by this heady essence, this sense of pleasure that is supposed to cut you loose from the regular rules. Forget diet. Forget exercise. Forget any notion you might treasure of "the healthy life."

"These heels are killing me!"

Remember that in every city in the world, people in

perfect health are being stabbed by strangers hiding in the alleyways.

We turn onto Bourbon.

"Whew!" A fine sweat breaks out on my forehead, under my arms, and between my legs. You get swept by *want* but not for anything in particular.

Here is the world of dancing boys in the streets, tapping their toes for nickels in a hat. And bars with naked women, and naked men pretending to be naked women. Don't you want to find out what goes on behind those swinging doors, the depth of the sleaze, what happens upstairs in the old, leaky rooms, body smell so strong that you're high by osmosis?

"I'm cold," Julie says. "Let's try the Napolean House."

We walk up a couple blocks from Bourbon—was this where the voodoo shop once was, these endless stores full of Mardi Gras masks and porcelain clowns and T-shirts that say I CHOKED LINDA LOVELACE? Hard for me to say. Everything seems exactly as it was, except that the whole world is different.

Now my body feels through the senses, the muscles, and what is out there becomes strangely literal.

"Ever stayed there?" Julie points to the Royal Orleans as we pass.

"When I was a child." The old hotel is all agleam with its white marble stairs and its grand piano, the well-dressed patrons listening as they sip their mint juleps. This world at least is inviolate and unimpressed by the passage of time.

By way of contrast in mood, the Napolean bar is dark and artfully sinister, sawdust on the floor, walls so old that they perpetually ooze. It was either an auction block for slaves or a hangout for pirates. Or both.

Several heads turn as we enter. Couples in various stages of seduction nestle at remote tables. The jukebox is playing Bobby Bland.

We insert ourselves at a model spot: far enough toward the back to scan the clientele, close enough to the light so we can be seen.

"You want a drink?" Julie looks happy. "I'm going up to the bar."

"A vodka gimlet."

"Whoa! Actual hard liquor!" She sashays off with excess wiggling of hips—not that she has any hips to wiggle. In case any of the inscrutable hairy men around us should happen to notice.

Covertly, I check out my neighbors, but the sight is not terribly promising. Level gray eyes and a fluffy dahlia of crimson hair are a tough act to follow.

My heart pangs a little—by now we would have finished lifting and then what would have happened?

Well, if anything would have happened, it can wait until tomorrow.

"To sex!" Julie toasts a little loudly, returning with the drinks.

"What do you have?"

"A rum and Tab."

"Oh."

"Dynamite pair of chicks," observes a chubby man, straddling a chair at our table. He sports a neo-punk haircut and a cut-off LOOSE AS A MOOSE T-shirt.

"Suck dick and choke on it," says Julie.

The creep makes tracks.

"Subtle but effective." The first taste of gimlet is my madeleine, reminding me of last night.

"I've lost the knack. And they've lost their looks."

Right on cue, two pencil-necked geeks from across the room walk over and offer cigarettes.

Julie uses her third finger to press her nose upward into a pig snout.

When Julie rebuffs our third visitor, a charmer in navy double-knit, my patience grows thin. "Look. Is your heart really in this?"

Julie shifts in her seat and drains her drink. Tufts of corn-colored hair stand at attention over that madcap face. "Why are they all so disgusting?"

"You think attractive, interesting, and sincere guys are going to hang around the Quarter trying to pick up women? Didn't you say you just wanted to get laid?"

"Let's try a different bar."

"Whatever." The whole episode is becoming wearisome to me. The more I see of other men, the clearer it is that Barnett is special. It was foolish of me to stand him up.

Several bars and many rude remarks from Julie later, we stand in front of Jackson Square, tired and disappointed.

"Let's just get some coffee and beignets and call it a night," is my argument.

"How can we give up now?" is Julie's rebuttal.

"Maybe there are some cute guys at Café du Monde. Or strolling the levee."

"Pet, do you realize how many calories there are in a beignet? I figure two hundred. Plus, you gotta eat two or three or why bother?"

She's got a point. "Then what do you suggest?"

She snaps her fingers. "Wait a minute! I can't believe I forgot this—there's the neatest little bar way up on Decatur. I only went there once, it's real far out, but I bet we can find it again."

"What's so great about this bar?"

"The clientele."

Something about the idea of going up Decatur begins to nag at me, particularly as we fend our way upstream through the crowds. As the jolly tourists snacking down pralines and quaffing tropical drinks begin to thin out, and the real bars, full of sordid types and horny seamen, begin to assert themselves, I remember, as if it were possible to forget, Alonso.

Our night winding around the labyrinth of these narrow alleyways, which seem not to have changed at all in the intervening years.

"Let's turn back." But I don't really want to.

"Don't be ridiculous." Julie grabs my arm. "Nothing can happen as long as we stick together. Besides, it can't be too much farther."

Where are all the streetlights? You can't exactly see, even under the barely waning full moon, who is sitting on the stoops. Or what.

A burst of laughter erupts like spontaneous combustion.

"Turn here," Julie says suddenly, as if we're driving a car.

We duck into an especially unsavory alleyway, the smell of rancid oil and far worse assaulting the old nostrils.

"Do you have to throw up?"

"No, no!" She points her finger. "There!"

Then I see the neon sign, way at the end of the alley. A pink champagne glass, tilted on an angle, emits golden bubbles, rising and popping.

The vibration is very strong. I want to hold back, just wait a minute and think, but before the words get uttered, Julie has disappeared down the dark passageway and into the bar.

I hesitate, knowing I'm about to plunge back into *something*. First Barnett, now whatever. This is what I've been striving for: to go back into the other realm, but this time be in control.

What else do you expect to gain from accruing power, except the chance to exert it? Once, when I was studying karate, Aunt Edith pointed out: *Prepare yourself to defend yourself and you will find yourself in a position that needs defending.*

If you make yourself strong, doesn't that mean you'll have a heavy load to carry?

At the doorway, my eyes blink: the bistro is very dark inside. The only light comes from a few scattered neon signs and objects on platforms. They look like . . . well, they are, in fact, holograms.

The nearest one is entrancing. Inside a lucite rectangle is a plaster arm, attired in romantic-heroine fashion: velvet sleeve and trailing lace cuff. The hand presents a candle recently blown out—the wick is black. But the arm is positioned in front of a mirror covering the back wall of lucite. The mirror reflects the arm, the sleeve, the upright candle, and the dancing flame of the hologram. In the mirror, the lively laser mirage is merrily burning.

"Take a load off," Julie suggests.

Her voice startles me, so intense is the experience of the fantastical candle.

"Fresh gimlet waiting." She's seated at a cozy table right next to the bar.

"Give me a minute. I need to walk around and take a look at these *things*."

But the other dozen or so holograms are disappointing. Animals cavort in the jungle or naked bodies writhe, but it is the movement of the viewer, like a wiggle picture, that creates the surprising effect. The candle in the mirror will waver even when you are standing perfectly still because it is affected by your breathing: the merest vibration in your lungs gives the flame the illusion of life.

Not so the naked dancers, who seem, if you stand too still, like Keats's urn: sadly frozen in the act of chase.

Tucked away in the farthest corner is the last hologram in the room: a man's head. I lean over and his lips seem to be moving to the song playing on the jukebox—

Every breath you take . . . I'll be watching you!

Cheekbones like slabs, straight black hair, and those clear clear brown eyes—

The face is Alonso's.

CHAPTER FORTY

"Julie, let's go."

"No way, José! We caught us some live mountain bass!"

Before there's another chance to protest, two men hover over our table. Both are tidily dressed, chinos and pressed flannel shirts. The blond has a rather splendid mustache and the brunet has a neatly trimmed beard and a gold ring, very discreet, in one ear.

"Y'all aren't local girls," Blondie observes in a soft southern accent with a predatory undertone.

"Not girls, *women*!" Brownie admonishes.

"We're from Lafayette." Everything about Julie's voice sounds like trouble.

"Not *you!*" Brownie protests in my direction.

"Yes, me." A giant gulp of gimlet for protection.

"Not *born* there."

"Okay, have it your way. Not born there."

"I can always tell." He smiles smugly.

"Bully for you."

"Back, Hulko!" Julie commands. "Be nice."

"Look who's talking," says Blondie.

"Hulko?" asks Brownie.

I look from one face to another, all the cute little games and whatnot, and here's my thought: *I do not want to be here!*

On and on in my head:

I DO NOT WANT TO BE HERE!

I DO NOT WANT TO BE HERE!

I DO NOT WANT TO BE HERE!

I WANT TO BE *THERE!*

Then be there! A familiar voice seems to whisper in my ear.

The strangest thing happens: time simply stops. My companions are frozen before me like fish under glass. Yet my own body is capable of movement.

The music sustains itself on one note, indicative.

The entire bar has become a wax museum, atmosphere of the embalmed. Only the holograms undulate, as if the stasis of the room provides them with sudden life, sets them free.

A figure walks toward me, a man, stalking over the air as if it were water.

Alonso. Natch!

"What do you want?"

He stares at me, his eyes so clear you could see all the way to the Rio Grande.

"Why are you here?"

Again, the eyes, the expanding eyes big as Ferris wheels. They come to swallow you up.

"Can you help me?"

At that, he extends his palm, but it is as if his arm were a kind of accordion, the way it magically lengthens itself, then retracts, the body not having budged an inch.

My own palm opens up and this is what it holds: my long-lost juju.

I want to follow him. I want to ask him a thousand questions. I want to be with him forever, but already he is thinning out, turning into air, into memory, and even with all of my muscles pulling for power, I know that I will never, ever see him again.

Not in this world.

CHAPTER FORTY-ONE

"What've you got there in your hand?"

The world cranks on again, the slow whine accelerating to normal noise, like a vacuum cleaner that's been unplugged with the switch on, replugged.

My palm closes up quick. "Nothing."

"Then why did you pick it up off the floor?"

Three pairs of eyes watch me curiously. "Pick it up off the floor?"

Julie sighs. "Yes! What's wrong, you going sieve-brain on me? You leaned over, picked up something under the table, stared at it like it held your future, and now you tell me 'nothing.'"

"Can we go to the women's room?"

"I don't have to go."

"Julie!"

"Okay, okay. Isa comin, Massah." She shuffles along behind me, hamming it up for the two guys now seated at our table.

We weave our way through the suddenly crowded bistro, and indeed it is an interesting clientele. The plaster hand and its hallucinated flame wink, imaginary as the unperceived-to-the-eye daily rotation of the earth.

The women's room is maybe three square feet, and a

staggering number of women, clowns piling out of Volkswagens, are crammed inside, slicking down their hair, spitting in their cake mascara, poofing talcum powder between their legs.

"You don't want the brunet, you can have the blond."

"I don't want either one."

"What was that on the floor, Mel Gibson's telephone number?"

"There's nothing wrong with those guys—"

"You can say that again!"

"Scuse me!" A fluffy redhead elbows me away from the sink.

"—But this isn't me, not at all. Maybe you could stay and I could take a bus back. Or . . ."

"Look, what is it?" My friend gives me a look of sympathy. "If you're this upset—"

"I am."

"Then let's split. No use ruining our lungs in here."

Several women are utilizing aerosol cans, spraying away God-knows-what.

By tacit agreement, we duck out the back way, leaving our boys all alone at the table. But never mind—several women eye them happily, freshly concocted desserts.

Outside, the world is quiet and cool and calm. The raucous beat from the jukebox is softened by distance, and already by time. The sound evokes the sweet sadness of other people's parties, when you pass by in the evening. The guests are dressed in pastel clothing; you hear the melodic tinkling of glasses filled with ice cubes.

"Oh well." Julie's voice is resigned. "The best part is over anyway. We could have gotten laid if we wanted to. Now you don't have to think about herpes."

Perhaps this departure is too selfish. My hand clutches the juju, which glows with its old familiar heat.

"Besides, they didn't look very athletic."

"I'm sorry," I say as we emerge from the remote part of Decatur. It takes much less time to come back than it did to go in. "I guess I'm just not much of a party girl. You would have had a much better time without me."

"It isn't my specialty either."

"Well, then you're a better fake."

We both laugh at this as we order café au lait to go from the Café du Monde, then head away from Jackson Square to the place where the car is parked. Even though it is well after midnight, the Quarter feels like an enchanted, timeless zone in which nothing ever closes, the night is never over, people never go home.

"These people know how to *party*."

I shrug. "What does that mean anyway, *to party*? It always sounds like so much fun, but all it ever turns out to be is people getting together and drinking a lot."

"Ain't that the truth."

"For instance, we could say that tonight, we *partied*."

"We did." Julie points to the street we turn on.

And yet the other people are the ones, always, who seem to have fun.

"What's the most fun you've ever had?"

We pass the happy drunks on Bourbon Street, badly dressed, overweight, and having the time of their lives.

"When I ran my first marathon."

"There you are!" I sound triumphant even if the feeling isn't there. "Special people, special ideas of what a good time is."

"Right."

We turn down the street toward Saint Louis Cemetery and all the old eerie feelings come back: cloudy night, distant chanting, whiffs of peculiar and pungent scents.

"Do you think those people are still there?"

"Pet, it's none of your business!"

But as she opens the car, I can't resist first looking, then moving through the old black trees and dangling moss. Before the thought is conscious or intentional, my feet are standing at the outer edge of the circle.

The same white-garbed worshippers chant and light candles and smoke dubious herbs. In whatever kind of altered state, they remain seemingly oblivious to my presence.

Yet this is the important part: the power of the circle is mine. They generate a clumsy, strong energy, and that energy becomes me.

"Pet!"

A couple of people look vaguely in the direction of Julie's voice, but I remain invisible.

It's like sucking the life right out of their veins.

"Pet!"

No danger, no evil. Only a clean muscular pull.

"Pet, this is it!"

And no damage has been done. That's the beauty, feeling it for the first time, accruing genuine power.

When the car starts up, I trip back through the gravestones, seeing in the corners of my eyes the ectoplasmic shapes that hover and embrace.

CHAPTER FORTY-TWO

I arrive at Roy's Gym an hour earlier than usual. My stomach feels like a cement mixer, one that has been turned off and the hardened ball of concrete just sits there in the middle.

Inside the gym, no sign of Barnett. The usual grisly collection of males are pumping up, sweating it out, flexing and crunching, burning and ripping.

My muscles automatically feel warm, and so does the juju around my neck.

The huge room is chock-full of row upon row of weight plates, aligned with military precision. They reek of that mysterious lubricating oil that men love to spray on anything metal.

"Hey there!" Roy calls by as I pass his office.

"How are you?"

"Got another personal." His face is handsome and kindly, with classic macho-man dark looks: mustache, massive but trim body in cute red short shorts, deep tan—yet his skin is entirely, excepting subdued afro and mustache—hairless. He shaves every day from top to bottom. "Six-seventy on the bench."

"That's great, Roy! Listen, did that guy I called you about yesterday ever show up?"

Roy squints, as if to recollect. "No," he says. "I don't believe he did." His voice is sad, but that's normal. Sometimes the other lifters tell stories about Roy, about the time he worked out for forty-eight hours without stopping, or about how he used to drink six gallons of milk a day, a pint between each set. Right now, though, he seems like a regular guy. Only sadder.

"Oh. Well, thanks."

"Deadlift?" he asks hopefully. He likes to spot me on deadlift because my spirit rises up strong and inspires him.

"Chest."

His face reveals his loss of interest. Women are dismal on the bench. And besides, the telephone is ringing.

I'm disappointed that he won't coach me today—it's always an iffy business, depending on his mood and attitude and how crowded the gym is. This is Friday, the busiest day, and perhaps Roy doesn't enjoy the other guys seeing him help a girl, though my strength is special.

Because I am a girl, my strength remains largely invisible. Of all the men who have seen me lift—though the empty times are my preference—only Roy understands.

And Barnett.

Weaving my way between machines and bodies, I find "my" corner, as usual, unoccupied. After the bag is placed on the bench, the strict ritual begins. *Ritual*.

First you pose in front of the mirror, feeling the heavy beat of the rock music, waking up your muscles, the banging and clanging of the other athletes. Your chest and arms pump up rosy in the glow of near-exertion. *Chest:* you regard your torso in the black-on-white suspender leotard and imagine your perfect physique. A ghostly image of perfection hovers before you, the model and inspiration.

You look hard enough, or quick enough, and it's *there*.

After the posing and the visualization, I lay out the book and pen to keep track of reps and sets and time. Also, it is useful to comment on the degree of soreness, which is special today from the other day's thousand pounds.

A thousand pounds!

The rock radio insists: "You don't have to live like a re-fu-gee-ee-ee."

After duly inscribing all necessary data, I utilize the "Joe Weider Instinctive Principle," which is simply Weider-jargon for doing what you want to do. Which is flat bench first—the literal feeling of "a weight off your chest." Then some incline dumbbells. Then incline flyes. Then flat flyes, pullovers, triceps extension prone, and perhaps a few sets of wrist curls.

The whole pattern strings out in the air before me, a mystical pathway to whatever. It could be drugs, it could be poetry, but here and now it is the body, pure and simple.

The Body becomes all and then there is no Other.

Because the truly great thing about lifting is that you cannot think while you are doing it. Stuff in the mind interferes with the power load to the muscle, primal and direct.

I lie on the bench and begin.

Zen nothingness.

Sufi dance.

Arms bend and straighten, muscles burn, you call out:

"Aurgh!"

And the weight goes up.

In between sets you stand there, as if listening to the music of the spheres, or the sound the electrons and protons make, whirring around the nuclei of the atoms.

"Night, Roy." Two hours later I exit the gym. The place is packed, all the slight misfits in the town consoling themselves for not having dates tonight or, worse, for having people they dread waiting at home. You come here to bang the iron around and try to

connect with a few people who might speak the same
language you do.

"You too," Roy replies vaguely from his glass cubicle,
where he is concocting some sort of mysterious bever-
age in a blender. No doubt next week I will be purchas-
ing the ingredients.

The early evening air is cool and clear. Every pore in
my body breathes deeply. As my hand fits the key into
the door of the jeep, I envision dinner: fresh salmon,
Cajun tomatoes, heaps of snow peas.

A hand clamps down on my shoulder and my body
whirls around, keys at the ready.

Barnett!

"I see you got yourself a magic charm," he says,
pointing at the juju hanging from a string around my
neck.

My hand lowers the keys; the sight of his level gray
eyes and whirling mass of red hair subdues me like a
lullaby. "Look, about yesterday—"

He waves away my apology like a gnat. "You needed
a day off and that's the truth. I knew where to find
you."

No doubt he means Roy's, but my mind flicks back to
the ghostly figure crossing the swamp at night. . . .

"But where'd you get this sucker? I haven't seen one
of them things in years!"

"You've seen one before?"

"Oh, hell, yes. They used to be all over the Quarter,
like pralines or pickaninny dolls."

"They did?"

Under the pretext of examining the juju, he strokes
my throat. "Made them at some sort of tourist trap
voodoo store. They closed that thing down after all the
trouble they got in—must of been near fifteen years
ago."

The cool night air is now cold night air. "What
trouble?"

His face doesn't look happy. "They had these torture
machines in there? Part of the so-called museum? Come
to find out they was still using 'em. They'd collect street

people, murder them as part of their ceremony, or whatever they called it."

"What happened to the people that worked there?" All of this is horrible, but none of it is really a surprise.

"The head guy—"

"Sammy?"

Barnett looks at me oddly. "I dunno what his name was."

"I'm sorry, go on."

He steps back and looks off toward the lavender remainder of sunset. "Whoever the head guy was, they never could find him. Seems like everybody else, all the women, went to jail."

Has Deane been sitting in prison all these years, provided I ever saw her, that she was ever there, that they ever caught her . . . endless unraveling carpets, and whatever matters anymore?

"Do you remember any of the names—"

Barnett holds up his hands. "It was in all the papers is how I know. But, honey, I don't think they ever named names. Only a couple paragraphs—the rest was word of mouth. You know how that kinda stuff goes down."

I nod, seeing wild goose chases, corridors running into corridors, mementos that turn to dust and surprise you over time. In the partial light of twilight, I take a good long look at the thing hanging around my neck. "Listen—"

He is.

"Want to come to my houseboat for dinner? We could—"

"Fine."

CHAPTER FORTY-THREE

We take our fresh raspberries out on deck and sit in the canvas chairs. The evening is so lovely, it is like an advertisement for giving up real life and moving into the swamp.

"This is the third night in a row that the moon looks full," I opine.

Barnett nods. "Maybe this is the third night in a row that it *is* full. Think of that?"

"But that's not possible."

"Oh really?" He tilts back in his chair, one of those overly confident men who will never tilt too far and bruise his butt. "What the hell is a full moon anyway?"

My fourth grade science is rough. After all, that was the year my family tramped around the country. "Well, it's the night that you can see the whole moon. I mean the whole *half* of the moon."

"Now, does that moon up there really change?"

"No." I sigh. "It just looks like it's changed because of where we're standing."

He grins, his full lips resembling mine in a pout. "Alright! So, if the moon looks full for three nights, why then it *is* full for three nights."

"'Appearances are evil,'" I mutter. "'But they are everything.'"

"Come again?"

I smile, thinking of Alonso and his double entendres. "That was just something Jean-Paul Sartre said. 'Appearances are evil, but they are everything.'"

He snorts. "Them Frogs and their ideas."

The silence, if you can call it that, continues. And all around us, the bayou continues its eat-and-be-eaten agenda.

"Third full moon in a row," he muses. "That's the night to do what you've been afraid to. Never can tell when you've missed your last chance."

My arms goosepimple up. "Okay," I say forcefully. "This is it. Now or never. What the hell do you want with me?"

He doesn't miss a beat. "Honey, the question is the other way around. You called out to me, I came. Here I is. Now then, what do *you* want?"

"I want you to take me in your pirogue to the place where the boys went into the other world."

"You sure about this?"

"Absolutely. And I know where that place is going to be."

"How come?"

"Well, remember the voodoo group we were talking about? Before the shop closed down, I had this sister, and she . . ."

You've already heard the story.

CHAPTER FORTY-FOUR

We drive and drive through the back muddy roads of the swamp, me at the wheel and Barnett directing us. After the first fifteen minutes I lose all track of space and then, after however long, all track of time.

"Pull over here," he'll say, then hop out for a minute, to study a tree or a bog or the angle of the moon.

A couple of times he lights candles at the roadside, which he pulls from his jacket pocket.

"What are those for?"

He smiles. "Offerings for the ancestors."

Eventually my back and shoulders get tired, my lats and my delts and my pecs are throbbing from the workout. "Are we going anywhere for real, or are you just torturing me?"

"Patience, babe."

And silence.

Once he asks, "Honey, would you say that the individual was more important, or that the principle was?"

Think a minute. "Depends on the principle. And the individual."

"Let's try a for-instance. For instance, would you die for something you believed in or someone you loved?"

"What are you getting at?" *Ah, well, all that is left is forward.*

"Just answer."

I try to think about the "thing" I believe in. And who in the world I love. Aunt Edith, Bread. Julie? Die for them? Die for "good"? And what about the cats. "Yes. Who wants to live forever?"

Out the window, the moon grows ever rounder, ever oranger. It is too large to be innocent.

"Would you die for me?"

My mouth opens with an indignant response, but freezes open. Out of the corner of my eye, Barnett's body seems to glow. His hair acquires a life of its own, snaky red and pink and fuchsia and mauve and rose and vermillion and crimson and scarlet and flamingo and coral. His gray eyes are like two beams of the search-light. *Is he human?*

But of course he is. Only my eyes are tired.

And then, however much time later, he says, "Okay. Here we are."

We climb out of the jeep and I'd swear this was the same place Alonso and I parked.

And the whole of the swamp is exactly itself, the separate places indistinguishable.

"The boat's thisaway."

"Wait a minute. Do we need special clothes? Clothes at all? What about this charm around my neck?"

He laughs softly. "Honey, it don't matter what you wear. What you think, who you thinking about. At this point, either you got it or you ain't."

This is the most sobering thought of all.

And my mind goes completely clear.

Here and now.

Either you are here, here and now.

Or you aren't.

"Okey-dokey," he calls. "Climb on in."

We paddle soundlessly through the thick, dark water. In the moonlight, leaves are glossy, moss is dense as memory. The other denizens of the waterways, the alligators and the shockingly large snakes, ignore us—disguised as a tree trunk, we are part of them. And It.

You think of the Asmat Indians and their Soul Ships. Traveling to visit their ancestors in damp little boats with magnificent carvings.

Our boat is plain but at least it has a bottom.

"Where we're going," Barnett says. "Maybe this ain't what you have in mind."

"Oh yes it is."

And we paddle on in the night.

And then I hear it. A low rumble fans out over the bayou. The rumble turns into a chant. And when the chant is clearly audible, the shimmer of fire is there, yards away, right through the trees and the vines.

Dozens of figures clothed in white sway and chant, gathered around a circle enclosed by flickering candles. Inside the circle is an altar, facing east. It is dressed with bottles of dark rum and red wine and coconuts, honey and pieces of hard candy. Behind the altar is a plain pine coffin.

"Is this what you had in mind?" he whispers.

"Yes."

Conga drums begin. Sammy appears, dressed entirely in white, a white turban decorated with pentangles on his head and a large cigar in his mouth. Walking in a funny, crook-backed way, he alternately spews rum, tosses handfuls of cornmeal into the fire, and issues clouds of cigar smoke.

He is joined by a woman dressed in a full white skirt with many petticoats, a white ruffled overblouse, and many strings of glass beads, carved beads, seeds and seed pods. Her hair is tucked under a white bandanna covered with signs and symbols.

Her energy is down. Even with all the things that ornament her, she appears less a priestess and more a transient in the world of the spirit.

And the face?

Bruised, sickly, and oh so weary.

Deane.

My sister Deane stands in the center of the circle.

As if it were possible to walk over water, and no doubt it is, my body makes to climb out of the pirogue. But Barnett's hand like a circle of iron clasps my wrist.

"Don't."

"Are they really there?"

The moonlight. The water. The lacy trees—

And the way you can see the trees on the other side of these people. I mean, right *through* them.

"Are they ghosts?"

"Just watch."

The chanting grows louder and louder. A crowd of Africans pummels packets of mantioc and sets them on fire. They also hold cucumbers aloft, slit down the middle, and use the pale green juice as if it were blood.

> Kabiyesi, Alaye!
> Ebo a fin!

And:

> May you live till old age, Oloja
> May your time be prosperous

And:

> Lizard offered two pigeons
> In order to get the woman
> But he did not offer two cocks
> Which would make the woman stay

From the folds of his pants, Sammy produces a machete. Its gleaming blade makes a statement.

"The Egúngún!"

A veiled figure stands in the circle between Sammy and Deane. It is entirely bandaged: hands, feet, and face. Phosphorescently it sways, blood-black charms dangling from its limbs, red auras glittering out. He is the soul of our Beloved Dead.

"*Now!*" Barnett shouts, pushing me forward.

Do I walk over water? Do I fly? Am I really in my bed at home in the houseboat? Am I in my bed at the beach in California? Am I back in my childhood bed in the house I grew up in, Pole nestled against me for company, the poodles and my beloved doll Roberta watching over?

The white-clothed worshippers and the naked, ghostly bodies part for me as my body beelines for the inner circle.

I walk barefoot over the candles and feel no pain. Even as I take the machete from Sammy's outstretched hand, I feel no fear.

Only the howling of nothingness, vacant and icy as the corridors of his eyes when I slit Sammy's throat.

"This is your time," says the Egúngún.

Its voice is the music of the spheres, the harmony of twirling atoms.

When I look toward the ground, where the body would have fallen, there is no body.

Deane!

Deane is fading. As if she were ectoplasm only manifested for this one performance, she begins to dematerialize. Her image, eyes fixed on me, wavers.

Pet, she seems to say. *My sister.*

Her hand, increasingly transparent, is holding out a small mud figure.

With one last gaze—pity? remorse?—she vanishes into the ether.

No Sammy. No Deane. No circle of worshippers. As I stoop to pick up the mud figure, the Egúngún, with a *whoosh* of its tremendous wings, flies away.

The figure is me, biceps flexed.

Here, you tell yourself, is a woman who could pull a lot of weight.

EPILOGUE

We travel back through the night, passing from wherever we have been to wherever we are going.

Barnett puts his arm around my shoulder and the heat from his body is one kind of cure.

And so is the sun, soon to rise.

Encouraged, you keep traveling on.

ABOUT THE AUTHOR

PATRICIA GEARY is a native of Southern California. She is presently serving as Writer in Residence at the University of California at Irvine. STRANGE TOYS is her second novel.

Spectra Special Editions